To Martin

Enjoy!

Bob Coyle

17/4/12

Bob Coyle was born in Cambuslang, Scotland. He was eight years old when the family moved to Coventry. He sat his O-Level GCEs at Bishop Ullathorne Grammar School and went on to study advertising design and graphics at Coventry College of Art, which also involved a brief spell at college of art in Germany.

After graduating, he entered the world of advertising and spent many years as a freelance, designer, visualiser, illustrator and art director. In December 2000 he moved to Grand Cayman where he was co-founder of an advertising and public relations agency of which he was creative director. He returned to England in 2008, to write books.

FALLEN

Bob Coyle

FALLEN

Vanguard Press

VANGUARD PAPERBACK

© Copyright 2012
Bob Coyle

The right of Bob Coyle to be identified as author of
this work has been asserted by him in accordance with the
Copyright, Designs and Patents Act 1988.

A CIP catalogue record for this title is
available from the British Library.

ISBN 978 1 84386 835 4

*Vanguard Press is an imprint of
Pegasus Elliot MacKenzie Publishers Ltd.*
www.pegasuspublishers.com

First Published in 2012

**Vanguard Press
Sheraton House Castle Park
Cambridge England**

Printed & Bound in Great Britain

1

Anton Munro crawled out of bed nursing the mother of all hangovers, reached for the whisky bottle on the bedside cabinet and held it up to the light. There was just about a single measure left, he smiled, downed it in one gulp, let the bottle drop to the floor and shuffled along the hallway to the bathroom. By the time he'd washed and dressed a strange feeling had swept over him, Munro was feeling lucky and he hadn't felt like that in years. He walked into the kitchen, kissed his mother on the cheek, borrowed ten pounds from her and gulped down a large mug of strong black coffee.

'I worry about you, Anton. You will not see old bones my son, if you keep drinking so much. You are still a young man and have so much to offer. Why do you waste your talent and your life this way?' she said, rosary beads in hand.

'Please, mum, I know what I'm doing. Don't keep worrying about me. You're an angel and I love you.' Munro picked her up in his arms and kissed her. 'Hey, I've a feeling my luck's about to change.'

'I hope so, Anton. Perhaps the Lord has answered my prayers.' She raised the rosary beads to her lips and kissed the silver crucifix.

'I'll know the answer to that by 3.45 this afternoon. Don't wait up for me,' he mumbled, as he dashed from the kitchen with a doorstep of toast clenched between his teeth.

She called after him. '3.45? What's so important about 3.45?' But it was too late, he was gone. 'Be careful, Anton. Don't do anything silly,' she whispered.

The frail old woman smiled warmly, it felt good to see her only son, so buoyant. She walked over to the statue of the Virgin Mary that stood in a kitchen recess, lit a candle and bowed her head in prayer.

Tall, unshaven, strikingly handsome with black shoulder length hair, Munro caught the bus into the city centre, strode confidently into the bookies and placed a fiver on Trouble and Strife, a 100-1 outsider in the 3.30 at Kempton Park. The fact that his designer label clothes had seen better days did little to deter the admiring glances of the brassy blonde behind the counter.

'See anything else you fancy?' she said, fluttering her eyelashes.

Her brazen invitation went unnoticed, Munro's eyes were glued to the television screen, the horses were under starter's orders and his heart was pounding. When the unfancied filly romped home by three clear lengths for her first win of the season, it was time to celebrate and Munro did it in the only way he knew how, he put on a happy face and got hammered. After being ejected from every pub in town, he poured himself into a taxi, disembarked at Belle Vale and staggered into the Ring O Bells, a seedy pub that was affectionately referred to by the locals as The Viper's Nest. It was 9pm when Munro ordered his first double whisky and 10.30pm when he drank his last, before crashing out in a drunken stupor. By 11.15pm the pub was heaving with lowlifes, all of them baying for blood, as they watched a burly, foul-mouthed blonde punch a gangly redhead senseless, just for looking at her. In the centre of the room, a floorshow of a far more artistic nature was taking place. A scruffy old man wearing a toothless grin, battered bowler and ragged overcoat, played

Mule Train on his harmonica, while his Jack Russell bitch, resplendent in a pink tutu and diamante headband, danced in circles on her hind legs. Lost in the gloom of a far corner, Munro sprawled face down across a table and if appearances were anything to go by, he'd drank himself to death. And if that were truly the case, not one person in the bar would have cared a jot. This was Belle Vale, a bleak man-made concrete wilderness where brutality was king and death through violence and substance abuse were commonplace.

At 1.30am, the last of the raucous lowlifes spilled out of the pub. The battling blonde and her bloodied opponent, now locked in an alcohol induced embrace, gazed lovingly into each other's eyes like long lost friends. Their bloody encounter was nothing but a distant memory, as they staggered off, laughing and joking, into the murk of the desolate Belle Vale shopping precinct. His shirt, like a wet chamois leather clinging to his flesh, the circus-fat landlord wheezed and gasped as he struggled to bolt the reinforced doors, once the job was done, he shuffled into the bar, helped himself to a large whisky then dumped his bloated frame onto a stool. One of the lowlifes had left a cigarette smouldering on the edge of the bar and despite the red lipstick that coated the filter he placed it between his flabby lips and inhaled long and hard. Something for nothing in Belle Vale was always satisfying and the fat man smiled appreciatively.

In the gloom of the far corner, Munro erupted violently into life, arms flailing he knocked a glass to the floor. The landlord froze, too scared to breathe. He felt unnaturally cold. 'Take whatever you want. Just don't hurt me!' he croaked, whisky dribbling from the corners of his mouth as he scanned the shadows for his would be assailant.

Munro rose unsteadily to his feet and stumbled against a table, knocking more glasses to the floor. 'Bollocks! Sorry! Sorry!' he muttered, feigning an apology and emerged from the shadows into view. 'I'm sorry about the breakages, gaffer. It wasn't intentional, I assure you.' Munro's face lit up with a false smile. 'It's moments like this, fatso, that remind me of what John Lennon said… *Overy clown has a silver lifeboat.*'

The fat man stared back at Munro, mouth hanging open, breathing heavily, clearly perplexed.

'It's a play on words,' said Munro, smiling, eyebrows raised. 'That went over the top of your greasy head, didn't it?' Munro shook his head. 'I can see that schooldays passed you by in a bit of a blur. I was referring, in a light hearted vein, to the fact that fewer glasses mean less washing up for the cleaner. Get it? It was a joke! You're supposed to smile.' Munro surveyed the seedy room. 'On second thoughts, if you cleaned this cesspool, it would probably fall down!'

'I'm a chronic asthmatic. Please don't hit me!' wheezed the fat man. 'Do anything you want. Take anything you want. But please, don't hit me!' he pleaded, his bulbous, bloodshot chameleon-like eyes swivelling nervously in their sockets.

'Relax, fatso! Don't shit yourself. All I want is a drink,' said Munro, with a wry smile as he pulled up a stool and sat down at the bar. 'And you shouldn't be smoking if you're an asthmatic. Christ, man! Your chest sounds like a clapped-out accordion! Haven't you got one of those inhaler contraptions?'

When he realized the stranger was nothing but a harmless drunk, the fat man grabbed a baseball bat from underneath the counter. 'This is all you're going to get from me you drunken bastard! And if you don't get your arse out of here, I'll spread your fucking brains all over this pub!' he wheezed, sweat dripping from the tip of his bulbous chin like fat from a pig roast.

Munro threw both hands above his head in mock amazement.

'Hallelujah! It's a miracle! Fatso's developed a backbone!'

'Start moving towards the door. Now!' the fat man snarled, as he advanced menacingly towards Munro, waving the bat from side to side.

Munro shrugged his shoulders in resignation. 'I guess that means a stay-back's out of the question then.'

'Move it!' barked the fat man. 'And unbolt those fucking doors!'

With the fat man holding all the trump cards, Munro did exactly as he was told. There was no point in pushing his luck.

'Now get your smelly arse out of here!'

'Something's been puzzling me, fatso. Perhaps you can fill me in. How long has the beautiful Belle Vale estate been twinned with the Gaza Strip?'

'I'll fill you in, alright, you piss taking bastard!'

The fat man bludgeoned him across the back of the head. Munro keeled over, unconscious before he hit the floor. He dragged Munro outside and left him lying face down on the slabs.

'Don't show your scabby arse in here again!' he yelled. 'If you do, you'll be leaving in a body bag! You'll rue the day you tangled with Degsy Chandler!'

He cleared the phlegm from the back of his throat and spat on Munro's back.

The fat man was long tucked up in bed when Munro finally came to and the full moon shining overhead was so bright it hurt his eyes. If ever he needed a large whisky it was now. His wallet lay open at his feet and the three hundred pounds he had put aside for his mother was gone. In the gloom of a nearby doorway, a pack of mongrel dogs fought savagely over a discarded Chinese take-away, probably left there by the same lowlife who had robbed him. Munro wasn't taking any chances and gave them a wide berth. Images of his mother pacing the kitchen, rosary beads in hand, worried out of her mind, swirled inside his head as he took a short cut through the derelict children's playground.

Unaware that his every move was being watched from the window of a parked car. It was the same burly blonde who'd been fighting in the pub that night and she wasn't alone, a man was sitting next to her. She wound down the window and called out to Munro.

'Can you spare a few quid for a girl what's down on her luck, mate?' Her tone was like that of a little girl asking her dad for more pocket money.

'I'm skint,' mumbled Munro, still grieving over the money that was stolen from his wallet.

'Tight bastard!' she rasped menacingly, kicking the little girl approach swiftly into touch.

Munro ignored her and walked on. They got out of the car and tailed him. Munro quickened the pace and for the first time in three years, he regretted being so drunk. The situation demanded a cool clear head, not one that was befuddled by alcohol and racked with pain.

'Hey! Don't be daft? I was only pulling your leg back there.' yelled the girl, trying her best to sound sincere. 'We don't mean you any harm.'

Munro knew different and quickened the pace even more.

'Hey! I'm fucking talking to you! Don't walk away from me when I'm talking to you!'

Even in his drunken state he could see that running was futile, so he turned to confront his pursuers. A powerfully built youth in his mid-teens, grabbed a fistful of Munro's jacket, pressed a knife against his throat and pushed him backwards against a wall.

'Gimme your money!' he snarled.

For all his aggression, his hands were trembling and his breathing was heavy. He was clearly anxious, his eyes danced about in their sockets and he kept glancing at the girl, as if seeking her approval. The fat bitch from hell with the electric pink

16

hair and nasal studs was much older than him and she was the one egging him on. It was obvious to Munro that the youth was trying to impress her.

'I haven't any money. If you don't believe me, search my wallet!' Munro motioned with his eyes towards his inside jacket pocket.

She removed the wallet and thumbed through it. Apart from a photograph of Munro's mother and the stub of a winning betting slip, it was empty. A grotesque sneer on her face, she tossed the wallet away and hunted through his pockets. The cupboard was bare and Mother Hubbard wasn't pleased. She rounded on the youth, arms flailing wildly, screaming like a madwoman.

'The bastard's loaded, Danny. He's got bread on him somewhere!' she ranted. 'He's been tossing whisky down his neck in the pub all day. I saw him!' She moved closer to the youth and growled in his face. 'Chiv him and be done with it.'

The youth looked confused and more uncertain than ever.

'You gutless little shit!' she screamed. 'Give me the blade, I'll do it! I'll slit the bastard's throat!'

Cold blooded murder was clearly one step too far for a small-time thief like him, panic set in and he relaxed his hold. Munro seized his opportunity, grabbed the youth's wrists and wrestled him to the ground. Screaming abuse, the bitch jumped on Munro's back, punching and clawing at his face. The youth emitted a startled squeal and his body went limp. The knife was buried in his stomach, up to the hilt and blood spurted from the wound. In seconds his face had taken on a corpse-like ashen hue and his young eyes begged Munro for help. The youth looked scared... a pathetic, helpless, terrified of dying scared.

'Bastard!' screamed the bitch, more in frustration over the aborted robbery than for the plight of her young friend. She stabbed wildly at Munro's arms and shoulders with her nail file while he cradled the dying youth in his arms. Munro lashed out with his free hand and punched her mouth, knocking out one of her teeth and splitting her lip.

Snarling and spitting blood, she drew back her leg and kicked Munro in the face.

'Ashley! Help me! Please!' groaned the youth. His voice was barely audible.

'Serves you right, Danny!' she growled. 'You should have done him when you had the chance!'

The bitch turned on her heels and fled into the night.

Munro cradled him in his arms until there was no sign of life. The flow of blood was nothing more than a trickle now and even though he was dead...he still looked scared. His clothing drenched in blood, Munro struggled to his feet. He looked around, to see if anyone was watching. The mongrel dogs seen earlier darted from the shadows to lap greedily at the pool of blood around the body. They were the only witnesses. Munro staggered off down an alleyway, leaving his wallet where the bitch had thrown it.

The following day, a Black Maria screeched to a halt outside a run-down block of high-rise flats on the Belle Vale housing estate. Three officers in riot gear cordoned the vehicle while four others ran towards the stairwell. They followed the trail of blood until they reached their destination on the sixth floor, smashed the door off its hinges and rushed inside. Dumbstruck, Munro's mother watched from the kitchen as they raced down the hall and kicked open the bedroom door. Empty whisky bottles littered the room and Munro sprawled face-down across a bloodstained bed. Unconscious from drink, he offered no resistance as they placed the handcuffs around his wrists. A short, pot-bellied arresting officer notified him of his rights before having him bundled out the door.

'Why you take my son? What has he done?' said the old lady. There were tears in her eyes and her hands were trembling.

DS Percy Rudge wasn't listening to her, his mind was elsewhere. He'd made the pinch and that's all that really mattered to him. He motioned to a constable. 'Have a WPC come over here pronto to keep an eye on the old dear.' He pulled the constable to one side and whispered. 'I don't want her doing anything silly and fucking things up for me!'

The old lady tugged at his coat sleeve. 'Please, sir. For love of God! Why you take my son?' Her pleas fell on deaf ears.

Rudge wandered around the flat opening cupboard drawers, poking around inside and looking at family photographs. He stopped at a dresser, wiped his finger across the top and examined it for dust. 'Spotless! That's what I like to see. I can see you're house-proud, just like my old mum was, Mrs. Munro.' Rudge placed his hand on his heart and raised his eyes to the heavens. 'When she was alive that is. God bless her!'

Rudge pointed at a crucifix hanging on the lounge wall. 'I thought all you Indian people worshipped gods that have elephant heads and lots of arms and legs sticking out all over the place! Are you one of them converts or something?'

'No, I come from Goa. There are many Catholics in Goa.'

'You don't say! I'd never have thought that. A pal of mine went to Goa, last year. He had a great time. He said the weather was brilliant, the food was smashing and there were some great bargains to be had in the markets.' He pinched the end of his nose. 'Mind you, he did say the toilets were filthy. Now, that would have put me right off. I'd have caught the next flight home. Still, you can't have everything I suppose.' Rudge opened the bathroom door and looked inside. 'There's no excuse for filth. My mum kept our toilet spotless. And by the look of things, so do you, Mrs. Munro. Oh, dear. I spoke too soon. What have we here then?' Rudge emerged holding an empty whisky bottle at arm's length,

19

like someone carrying a dead rat by the tail. He shook his head disapprovingly. 'I'd put that in the bin, if I were you. We don't want you tripping up and splitting your head open, Mrs. Munro. There's already one member of your family down the nick covered in blood, we don't want any more.'

'Please, sir. Please, answer my question?'

'I bet you knock up a great Ruby Murray!' Rudge smacked his lips. 'I'll have to pop round one night with a couple of the lads. We'll bring our own beer. What do you say to that, eh?'

'Please sir. Why you take my son away?'

'How come your last name's Munro, then?' he said, avoiding eye contact as well as the question.

'My husband is Scottish. He died ten years ago,' she sighed, unable to hide her frustration.

'Married a Jock did you?' He sniggered and nudged the constable standing next to him. 'No accounting for taste, eh!'

Rudge made his way along the hallway and stopped at the battered door. He glanced over his shoulder at the old lady. 'You've nothing to worry about darling. Our carpenters will have this door back on its hinges in no time!'

His comb-over wisps of ginger hair flapping in the breeze, Rudge skipped down the stairs, a jubilant, self-satisfied smirk stretched across his podgy, pock-marked face. He was confident that he'd got his man bang to rights. Munro's wallet had been found at the scene of the crime, the victim's blood was on Munro's clothing and a female eye-witness with pink hair, a fat lip and missing tooth, was waiting patiently at the nick to point the finger. He sensed his gaffer would be more than just pleased with him. An ambitious copper's life didn't get much better than this.

When Munro finally opened his eyes, he was stretched out on a bed in a holding-cell. It was dark outside and as his eyes drifted aimlessly over the graffiti strewn walls, the ceiling-light flickered suddenly and died leaving him alone in the musty darkness. He pulled the shabby blanket over his head, curled into a ball and closed his eyes. He'd never known fear such as this. The grisly events of the previous night still screaming hysterically inside his head, he wrestled with thoughts of suicide.

Rudge's optimism about a guilty verdict being a formality was fully justified. The forensic evidence proved conclusive. Ashley Madonna Roper was virtue personified when she took the stand and testified how she and her boyfriend Danny Gordon were subject to an unprovoked and vicious attack by the psychopathic drunkard, Anton Munro. The fat man, Degsy Chandler was only too happy to testify how Munro had put him through the most terrifying ordeal of his life. The atmosphere in court was bitterly hostile. Members of Danny Gordon's family had to be ejected from the public gallery for constantly howling abuse and threats of vengeance. Munro's notoriety merely fanned the flames. The jury's decision was unanimous, Munro was found guilty and at precisely 3pm on October 6, 1995 the judge ordered that Munro should serve a fifteen year mandatory life sentence in Kingswood Prison.

Kingswood was the oldest maximum security prison in the country and despite being top of a government hit-list for demolition it was still very much in use. It had been extended and modernized over the years and five days prior to Munro's arrival had received a fresh coat of pale yellow paint. Thirty-five years of age, his life was effectively over, a lost soul being ushered to a cell in B-Wing and his ill-fated appointment with the unknown.

'My missus is still a big fan of yours,' said the gawky screw, as he unlocked the cell door. 'It didn't matter to her that you stabbed that young boy! Not one little bit.' He shook his head in disbelief. 'Can you believe that? Never try and figure out what's going on in a woman's mind, because they don't know themselves! That's what my old dad used to say.'

Munro said nothing. The screw pulled a notebook from his jacket pocket. 'Hope you don't mind, Munro. The missus asked me to get your autograph. She reckons it'll fetch a few quid on eBay. What with you being a convicted killer and all that,' he guffawed, snorting through his nose like a camel.

Munro took the notebook. 'What do you want me to write?'

'Just put *To Dierdre, with love, Anton Munro*. Oh, and don't forget to put the date. Thanks big man. By the way, my name's George Challis and if there's ever anything you need. Don't waste your time asking me!' Challis heehawed, to reveal a row of yellow twisted teeth. It occurred to Munro that a stunned slug displayed a higher degree of intelligence than this buffoon.

Munro entered the cell. There were two beds, one was occupied by an older man of medium height and build, his thick grey hair was swept back and quite long at the back.

'I'll leave you two lovebirds to get acquainted,' said Challis, raising his eyebrows and hunching his shoulders like a naughty schoolboy.

'This will take some getting used to,' said the older man, closing his book. His tone was friendly without being over-welcoming. Munro said nothing and set about organizing the few personal possessions and toiletries he had brought with him, placing them on the shelf above his bed.

'I'm Cedric Quigley.'

Munro remained silent and lay on top of the bed with his back to him. Quigley said nothing and returned to reading his book. An hour later, Quigley glanced at his watch, closed his book and pulled the covers over him. Seconds later, the lights went out with a dull click and the cell was plunged into darkness. Munro listened to the sound of Quigley's breathing as he dropped into a deep sleep and elsewhere on B-Wing a lifer called out to another inmate and hurled abuse at one of the screws. The first day of the rest of his life had come to a close, his heart sank as he closed his eyes and a single warm tear rolled down his cheek onto the pillow.

By the morning of the ninth day, Munro had yet to exchange a single word with Quigley. He joined the line of inmates and headed for the canteen, collected his breakfast and looked for a table. Quigley was already seated with four other lifers. The only unoccupied spot Munro could see was in the far corner. He weaved his way through the sea of tables and sat opposite a puny little man with black wavy hair and the kind of face that even the most doting mother wouldn't kiss.

'You that celebrity fellah what stabbed the boy!' he gasped, eyes wide with excitement.

There was no response from Munro.

'Luigi Stallone.' The little Italian reached across to shake his hand. 'Everybody here, they call me Rocky.'

Munro ignored him.

'My nickname Rocky, it usually make people smile. But not you eh! What's the matter? You don't want to talk to a small time fellah like me, because you used to be a big shot on television?'

Munro continued to ignore him and pushed the food around the plate with a spoon, as if he was searching for something. After taking a spoonful he gagged, spitting it back on the plate.

'Pretty bad, eh? What I give for a big plate of mama's pasta!' Rocky raised his eyes to the heavens clasping his hands in prayer.

Munro grimaced, tossed the plate to one side, rose from his seat and headed for the exit.

A burly screw, with eyes like a Pit Bull and a face flushed red by years of alcohol abuse, barred his path to the exit. 'What's up Munro? Prison food not to your liking?'

'I'm not hungry! Do you have a problem with that?' said Munro, stretching to his full height, he wasn't backing down.

'Dead right I've got a problem with that, pretty boy! And you're it! A jumped-up Paki has-been who enjoys stabbing young boys!' he growled, exposing a jagged row of badly stained teeth.

Both men inched forward until their noses were almost touching. The rancid stench from the Pit Bull's breath turned Munro's stomach. A senior officer stepped between them and pushed them apart. 'That'll be enough of that, O'Farrell! I don't want a bloody riot on my hands!'

'The prisoner was being abusive sir and moaning about the grub!' snarled O'Farrell.

'Just get back on your rounds, O'Farrell. Come on. Move it!' he barked, nodding in the direction he wanted the Pit Bull to take.

O'Farrell sneered at Munro, and stormed off.

'Don't do anything stupid, Munro. If Officer O'Farrell tries that again, just ignore him.'

'That's all I have to do eh,' said Munro, over his shoulder as he headed back to his cell.

He'd only been back five minutes when Challis popped his head around the door. 'Come with me, Munro. There's someone who wants to meet you,' he grinned, wiggling his eyebrows up and down. 'You're going to enjoy this. I'd be happy to swap places with you.'

Munro followed Challis to the administration wing where he was shown into an office. Sitting behind a large desk was an attractive girl with shoulder length blonde hair. By Munro's reckoning she was in her mid to late twenties. She was soberly dressed and wore her spectacles perched precariously on the end of her nose. 'Please. Take a seat Munro. I'll be with you in a moment.' Her voice was gentle and had a subtle, huskiness to it. Most men would find it sexy, but not Munro. In his gospel, the absence of a wedding band or an engagement ring could only mean one thing. She was either wrestling with her lesbianism or just plain frigid. She finished what she was doing and grabbed a file from the in-tray.

'My name is Charlotte Blake. I'll be your liaison officer for the duration of your term in Kingswood.'

'What do you mean by liaison officer?' snapped Munro, eyes blazing.

'Forgive me. Allow me to explain. As your liaison officer I shall be working with you on a regular basis to help you adjust to life in prison. I'll also be helping you to utilize any skills you may have in a positive and constructive way and introduce you to new areas of development...'

Munro cut her off. 'You mean like a probation officer, a fucking social worker! Listen lady! I'm in here for a crime I didn't commit. The last thing I need is some dried-up, goody-goody dyke showing me how to weave baskets and knit woolly jumpers! You want to help me? Get me the fuck out of this nut house!'

'Please, try and remain calm Munro. Adopting an aggressive attitude will only make life more difficult for you and ....'

Munro interrupted once again. 'Tell me one thing lady! Do I have to sit here and listen to all this Good Samaritan crap?'

Blake leaned back in her chair. 'On the contrary, Munro, you may walk out of here whenever you choose. Just bear in mind, that my evaluation of your progress or regress, whichever the case may be, will have a direct bearing on your chances of parole.'

'Fucking parole!' barked Munro, jumping to his feet. He leaned across her desk until their faces were just inches apart. 'Despite your poker face darling, you clearly have a wicked sense of humour. They gave me fifteen years, sweetheart! Why not drop by and see me in ten years' time!' Munro stormed out of the office and Challis escorted him back to B-Wing.

'She's a right little cracker our Miss Blake. Gorgeous little arse that you could sink your teeth into. Nice firm tits! You wait till the summer, when she's not wearing a bra. Fairly gets the old heart a thumping when she walks by I can tell you. It's got to be worth your while being banged-up in here, if you're seeing a little beauty like her on a regular basis. Wouldn't you say so, Munro?'

Munro glared at him. Challis got the message and said nothing until they reached the cell.

'Here we are then, home sweet home. Oh, by the way, my missus decided to hang on to your autograph, rather than bung it on eBay. I was telling her the other day what a bad tempered sod you were and that there was a good chance you might lose the plot before long and chiv one of the screws. Her eyes lit up when I told her that. She reckons an incident like that would make it even more valuable as a collector's item. That's my Dierdre for you, shrewd little bugger. Never misses a trick where money's concerned. You have to get up early in the morning to put one over on her.'

Munro wasn't listening. He threw himself on top of the bed and closed his eyes.

'Didn't go well eh?' said Quigley.

Munro didn't answer, rolled over and faced the wall.

Quigley leaned forward and prodded Munro firmly in the back.

'I'd turn and face me if I were you?'

Enraged by the confrontational tone of Quigley's voice, Munro squared-up to him.

Quigley tapped the side of his head with an index finger. 'Me and the little man inside my head have shared this cell for four years now and we've never had a cross word. It would be fair to say that in the passage of time we've become bosom pals. Some would say we are kindred spirits. And that's just the way we like it. So don't go getting it into your head that you can stroll in here

26

with all your emotional baggage and upset us. We're not going to let that happen. Do you get my drift?' said Quigley. His tone was calm and alarmingly assertive.

Munro shrugged his shoulders indifferently. 'Why don't you stick your nose back in your book, and stay the fuck out of my face, *old man*!'

Quigley lunged and clamped both hands around his neck. Almost instantly, Munro could feel the strength leave his body as he struggled to break free. The harder he tried the more paralysed he became, his eyes bulged and the veins on his face and neck stood proud like cords. Whether by a sheer fluke or simple know-how, Quigley had rendered him helpless and he was clearly no stranger to violence.

'Get this into your head. I don't really care about you and whatever it is that has got you so bent out of shape. All I want is a pleasant atmosphere in this cell,' said Quigley, with a false smile. 'I believe they refer to it as ambience in the restaurant business? A famous celebrity like you must know all about ambience.' Quigley tilted his head to one side and grinned like a game show presenter. 'So what is it to be?'

Munro's face had turned an unhealthy shade of reddish blue and he was gasping for breath, Quigley released his hold. Munro coughed and spluttered, massaging his neck with both hands. Quigley allowed him sufficient time to recover, reached behind a cabinet, pulled out a thermos flask and poured what looked like cold tea into some plastic cups. 'Here,' he said, handing one to Munro. 'Or are drinking alcohol and being civil, something you *never* indulge in?'

Munro's hands were trembling as he raised the cup to smell the content. It was malt whisky. Up until now, he'd never taken much notice of Quigley but he was obviously a man who was used to calling the shots. Still shaken by the ordeal, he sipped at the whisky before speaking. 'You must learn to be more direct when you're trying to get your point across,' croaked Munro, still massaging his neck. 'Where did you learn to do that pressure point thing? Christ! When you grabbed my neck I couldn't move?'

'An old friend of mine, a Japanese bloke,' said Quigley, smiling. 'We met at a wedding ceremony in Osaka many years ago. They're very clever people the Japanese, they know far more about the workings of the human mind and body than we do.' Quigley tapped the side of his head with his index finger. 'What they can't do with herbs and potions isn't worth knowing.'

Munro's mind was elsewhere and clearly troubled, he nodded politely and sipped the whisky. 'Being thrown in here for something I didn't do is killing me! I can't think straight. My brain's scrambled. My mother being alone in Belle Vale, while I'm locked up in here, is driving me crazy! Have you ever been to Belle Vale?' said Munro.

'No, but I've heard about it,' said Quigley, nodding his head disapprovingly.

'You'll know what I mean then. As far as the police are concerned, it's a no-go area. They only go into the place when they're arresting somebody. So, if anything happens to her, it's not as if she can call out for help and a copper will come running!'

'Aren't there any relatives who can keep an eye on her?'

'I'm all she's got.' Munro got to his feet. 'I tried to persuade her to go into a nursing home when this shit happened, but she wouldn't hear of it. She's always been so proud and fiercely independent. Fucking great isn't it! I'm all she's got and I'm locked away in this fucking shit hole!'

'That's another thing. Don't swear in my company,' said Quigley, firmly. 'I don't like it.'

A long silence followed. The kind you experience in the waiting room at the dental surgery. Quigley was first to break the ice. 'What should I call you?' he asked, topping up the cups.

'Munro will do fine.'

'In that case, just call me, Quigley,' he said, reaching out to shake his hand. 'I saw your run-in with Declan O'Farrell in the canteen this morning. Watch your back where he's concerned. He's uglier on the inside than he is on the outside, believe me. A cruel, sadistic bully, who gets his kicks from watching illegal dog fights and making people suffer. Why he hasn't been fired is a mystery to me. The screw that broke it up is Jack Dobson. Jack's alright, he's the senior officer and a decent bloke. You can trust him, and he's good at his job.' Quigley paused to sip some whisky before continuing. 'Nice looking girl, Miss Blake. What did she have to say?'

'She looked pretty average to me,' said Munro, indifferently. 'How did *you* know I went to see her?'

'It's standard practice for new lifers. Besides, there isn't much that goes on that I *don't* know about.' Quigley tapped the side of his nose with his index finger.

'She didn't get the chance to say much, Quigley. I lost my rag and ended up bawling her out. I called her a dried-up, goody-goody dyke.'

'Used all your natural charm, eh?' said Quigley, slowly shaking his head from side to side. 'As for her being a dyke, I wouldn't have thought so. You're way off the mark there, Munro.'

Munro smiled dismissively. 'Whatever. What good can she do? She's only a glorified social worker.'

'You won't know that till you try, Munro. Look on the bright side. When you're with her, you won't have to stare at me.' Quigley smiled. 'I know what I'd rather do.'

Munro was eager to change the subject. 'What are you in for?'

'I killed a Rumanian named Bela Petrescu. He came into the country in the back of a lorry and described himself as an asylum seeker. In reality, he was one of Nicolae Ceausescu's most ruthless hit men and he'd been on the run for eighteen months. Despite being wanted for countless murders, armed robbery and rape on his home turf, our authorities did nothing to deport him.'

'You killed him for crimes he'd committed in Rumania?'

'No! I killed him because he raped my granddaughter. She was only thirteen. Messed her up real bad he did. She'll never be right in the head. The specialists reckon she'll be on medication for the rest of her life.' Quigley shook his head. 'She won't even let her own father touch her. That animal walked out of court on a technicality because someone *allegedly* hadn't followed the correct procedure when taking DNA samples. Well, that was the official line. Personally, I believe there was a lot of political manoeuvring that went on behind the scenes.' Quigley raised his eyebrows and smiled. 'All politicians have this innate ability to overlook the most heinous crimes if it benefits their political agenda. Petrescu was smiling from ear to ear, when he left the court. Well, he isn't smiling now. Relatives of mine picked him up one night and threw him in the back of a van. They delivered him to me at an abandoned warehouse in the docks.' Quigley paused for a moment to reflect. 'I took my time killing him. And do you know what? I enjoyed every minute. I enjoyed it so much, I got careless. That's how the police caught me. Daft really, because I didn't need to do it myself, people were queuing up to nail this bloke for me. But that would have been nowhere near as satisfying. There are some things you must do yourself. Besides, this was about family, not business, and family is everything to me. I wanted him to know what it felt like to be helpless, alone and scared out of your mind, like my little girl must have been. I needed to smell his fear and see the despairing look in his eyes when the lights went out for the last time.' Quigley smiled wryly. 'It's funny. I didn't even notice what he looked like when he died. All I kept seeing was my little girl, lying in that hospital bed.' Quigley got to his feet. 'By the time I'd finished with Petrescu he was crying like a baby. I did things to him I never knew I was capable of. Perhaps we're all capable of barbarism if the right buttons are pushed.' Quigley shook his head from side to side. 'His last words were "mama". Can you believe that, a pig like him, calling for his mama? I'm glad I did it, Munro. Lowlifes like him deserve to be put down. We shouldn't be wasting our time, money and energy keeping scum like that alive. It's the victims we should be caring for, not the lowlifes. There's a big difference Munro, between what is *just* and what is *right*. *Justice* allowed Petrescu to walk out of court a free man and I did the *right* thing when I killed him.' Quigley looked Munro in the eye. 'I'd argue the toss with God himself on that one.'

Quigley placed his hand on Munro's shoulder. 'Never put all your eggs in the one law-basket Munro, you'll end up *very* disappointed!

'Have you always felt that way?'

'Not always, Munro. When I was a boy with my backside hanging out of my trousers, my dad told me the law was there to protect us and I believed him. He didn't tell me that those laws were laid down by the rich and powerful and when it came to the crunch, there was one interpretation of the law for them and one for us. I was in my teens when it happened. I had, what people in religious circles would call, an epiphany. I decided that I would live by *my* laws.'

Munro nodded, reflecting on his own situation while Quigley poured another drink.

'The judge described me as an evil and twisted killer. He'd have seen things differently if his daughter had been beaten up and then brutally raped!' Quigley smiled at Munro.

'I bet you never thought you'd end up sharing a cell with an evil and twisted killer, Munro. I should watch my back if I were you,' he quipped.

'Somehow, I don't think that will be necessary, Quigley. From what you've told me, the judge was talking through his arse!' Munro drained the cup. 'Sorry! I mean he was talking through his *backside*.'

'That's it Munro. See, you *can* get by without swearing, if you make the effort.' Quigley smiled.

'You'll just have to be patient as far as swearing is concerned, Quigley. It's not going to happen overnight. I've been swearing professionally for ten years.'

'Swearing for a living?' Quigley looked bemused.

'Yes, on my TV show. The viewers loved it when I swore at the guests on the show, browbeating them until they burst into tears.'

'And somebody paid you a lot of money to do that, I suppose.' Quigley rolled his eyes. 'The entertainment business has changed since I was a kid.'

'They paid me an obscene amount of money, Quigley. And if I told you how much they were paying me, you'd think I was being delusional.'

'No thanks, Munro I'd rather you didn't go there. I'm confused enough as it is.'

'Doesn't it bother you at all that you took a man's life, Quigley?'

'Look, Munro, we're all sinners to some degree, and because of that, each of us must decide how much sin we're prepared to live with. I killed Bela Petrescu four years ago and I still get a good night's sleep. What's more, I never have nightmares. I live in harmony with *my sin*, Munro. My conscience is very clear. Why do you ask?'

'No particular reason, Quigley. You're the first person I've ever met who deliberately killed someone, that's all.'

'There's a first time for everything. What about you, Munro? You're hardly the personification of sweetness and light. You took a life when you stabbed that young boy. How's your conscience bearing up?'

The smile faded from Munro's face. 'I didn't stab that boy, Quigley. *He* was the one who came at me with a knife. I was defending myself. His death was an accident.'

'I've only your word for that, Munro. Give me one good reason why I should believe you.'

Munro jumped to his feet. 'I can't!' He paced the cell becoming more agitated by the second. 'If I'd been able to do that I wouldn't be here.' He turned to Quigley. 'You'll just have to trust me. Surely that's not a lot to ask of you?'

'That's quite a *big* ask, Munro. After all, I've only known you for fifteen minutes. I'd like to know if I need to watch, my back. That's all.' Quigley rolled over onto his back and stared at the ceiling. 'We'll be banged up in this cell for a long time and I don't want any nasty surprises.'

'I believe *you*, Quigley. Why can't you believe me?'

'There's one big difference between you and me, Munro. I've confessed to my sin. I've owned up to my evil deed. You, on the other hand, appear to be in denial and I've yet to meet the lifer who doesn't feel hard done by, Munro. They've all got a hard luck story to tell. And you can take it from me that every nick in the country's full of them. They start off by feeding a pack of lies to their lawyers about what took place, hoping they'll swallow it and get them off. By the time the trial comes around, they actually believe their own lies and swear blind that they're innocent. A bit like the slick tongued advertising men believing the bull they write about their clients' products.'

'Listen, Quigley. I swear to you on my mother's life. I was the one who was attacked!' He raised his voice defensively. 'I may be a lot of things but I'm not a killer!'

Munro described everything that had taken place on that fateful day in February.

'Who defended you?' said Quigley.

'I can't even remember his name. I was on legal aid, so it was never going to be *Kavanagh QC*.' Munro ran his fingers through his hair. 'Even if it had been Kavanagh, it wouldn't have made the slightest difference. By the time the prosecution and the witnesses had done their worst it was Charles Manson who was on trial, not Anton Munro. I didn't have a prayer. Jesus! If my mother had been on the jury, even she would have found me guilty!'

Quigley stretched out on the bed, placed his hands behind his head and closed his eyes.

'I've done four years, Munro, with eleven to go. And just like everyone else, I'd love to be on the outside. But it's pointless me thinking about parole.'

'Don't be daft, Quigley? Everyone is entitled to apply for parole.'

Quigley gave him a wry smile. 'I applied six weeks ago. But when they asked if I've learned the error of my ways, I told them, no.' Quigley chuckled. 'The bit that really made them nervous was when I told them I'd do it again, without hesitation.' Quigley heaved a long sigh. 'To the best of my knowledge, no one's ever escaped from here and I've never known anyone receive a pardon. So, it looks like the only way you're going to get out, is by doing the time, keeping your nose clean and obtaining parole. There is no quick fix, Munro.' Quigley rolled over on his side. 'So, unless you have something special up your sleeve, like a magic wand or a flying carpet …I bid you welcome. Welcome to the Kingswood Lifers' Social Club!'

2

A smug smile on his fat face, Herb Cohen sprawled across the leather sofa sipping his favourite brand of Costa Rican coffee. His eyes fixed on Yvette Munro's firm breasts as she lay asleep on their king-size bed. Herb was feeling more relaxed than usual, especially now that Munro was behind bars. For the first time in years he could finally sleep with Yvette Munro without fear of reprisal. All those nerve-racking trysts in back street hotel rooms had been far too stressful for a weasel like Herb. Yvette on the other hand craved excitement, and secretly preferred things the way they used to be. If anything she found their legitimate lifestyle a touch on the dull side. She stirred, shielding her eyes from the shafts of sunlight that streamed through the chinks in the blinds.

'How's my beautiful baby this morning?' whispered Herb, abandoning the sofa to sit by her side.

'Tired and hung over!' she sighed, massaging her temples.

'Would you like a coffee, baby?' he fawned, like a puppy craving attention.

'No! I'd like a bag of ready-mix cement! Of course I want a coffee, you fat clown!' Herb scampered off to fetch her coffee and placed it within easy reach on the bedside cabinet. He sat on the bed and massaged her shoulders gently with his fingertips. 'Is that how baby likes it?'

'You'd shit yourself if I said no!' She pulled the covers over her head. 'Just leave me alone, Herb! Fucking leave me alone! My

35

head is pounding and I can't stand you pawing and poking me when I feel like this.'

Herb backed off with his tail between his legs, retreated to the sofa and lit a cigar. Yvette fell asleep. An hour later she stirred, opened her eyes and yawned like an old lioness. Herb was still there, watching over her, a doting smile stretched across his face.

'Christ! Sometimes Herb, you give me the fucking creeps. Make yourself useful and bring me some fresh coffee. This is stone cold!'

'Sure, baby!' he said, jumping to his feet, like a devoted and faithful dog, always at the ready to please his kindly master, or in Herb's case, a self-centred and ever demanding mistress. The desire to make love to her at that moment was overwhelming. No other woman aroused him like Yvette and short of slitting his own throat he would do anything to keep her happy. She could treat him like dirt and he'd still come back and beg for more. Yes, he despised himself for being so weak, because when it came to business affairs, no one could treat him that way. And if anyone tried, he'd bury them in a heartbeat. Herb got rich by being ruthless, not by being soft. He was always ready to remind his clients that soft was for his Aunt Miriam's sponge cake, not for running a profitable business.

Yvette took the coffee cup from Herb's outstretched hand and drained the contents while he retreated to the sofa. Moments later, she slipped out of bed and slinked towards him like a wild animal stalking its prey, her luxurious mane of hair, black as a raven's plumage, cascading over her shoulders. Thin bands of sunlight streamed through the blinds, undulating across her magnificent body and her hazel eyes were laden with the promise of pleasures to come. She sidled between Herb's legs and gently pulled his face into her breasts. He flicked his tongue delicately over her nipples and moaned with pleasure.

'I'm going for a shower,' she said, shoving him away.

Crestfallen, Herb sat alone in the room and finished his cigar. By the time Yvette emerged from the bathroom he'd forgotten his earlier disappointment. She smiled at him coyly. Herb knew that inviting look so well.

'Oh baby, how does a big lump like me, hang on to a beautiful creature like you?' he sighed, diving on his knees to bury his face in her crotch.

Yvette smiled at her reflection in the dressing table mirror and fondled the diamond pendant that hung around her neck. Just one of many expensive trinkets he'd bestowed on her as a token of his undying love. 'You hang on to me baby because of all the little things you do for me. And if you keep on doing that, then everything will fine. Yvette will always be here for you.' She stooped and kissed the top of his head. 'I'll never leave you, baby,' she whispered, still admiring the pendant.

Yvette let her silk dressing gown fall to the floor, took him by the hand and led him to the bed. 'You're such a naughty boy, Herb Cohen. Now I'll have to take a shower again when we've finished making love,' she purred.

Herb's smug smile had risen from the grave. These were the moments that he lived for. Every nerve in his body tingled. Herb couldn't run up a flight of stairs but he was no slouch under the sheets. Which was fortunate for Herb, because Yvette craved sexual pleasure more than she cared to admit and would have ditched him long ago if he hadn't been up to scratch. Being the manipulative bitch that she was, Yvette delighted in keeping Herb on the back foot. She constantly reminded him how only Munro had taken her to extreme heights of sexual pleasure and that sex with Munro was the only thing she really missed about him.

When their lustful intimacy had subsided, Herb lay back on his pillow, smiling up at the ceiling as if it was a long lost friend. Then, in keeping with their post-sex ritual, Yvette reached for the humidor by the bedside table, withdrew a large Havana cigar and moistened the end, rolling it between her lips, in a manner that made Herb's eyes glaze over with desire.

'You ever think about him, baby?' Herb whispered, like a man on borrowed time. Herb always felt insecure after sex and wouldn't feel confident until they made love again. Munro was a tough act to follow and that bothered him greatly.

'Who are you talking about?' barked Yvette, being deliberately evasive.

'Munro,' he said, gulping as if the name was stuck in his throat.

'Yeah, I think about him. When I see his money sitting in my bank account,' she said, gleefully.

'It must be hell doing life. Fifteen years locked away behind bars. Crap food. No freedom. No booze. No sex,' said Herb.

'Surely you're not feeling sorry for him. Fuck him, Herb! And don't be so bloody naïve. Munro would never go without sex, there's bound to be some lucky boy waiting for him when he takes a shower.' She nudged him with her elbow. 'And thanks to you, Herb. Munro won't have a pot to piss in when he gets out. You bad, bad boy!' she said, deliberately reminding him of his complicity in stripping Munro of all his assets.

Herb stared at her like a puppy that had been scolded for peeing on the floor. She reached across and lightly stroked his nipples with her fingertips.

'So! Are you going to lie there talking about Munro all day or fuck me? Which is it to be, *big boy*?'

Herb smiled. He was starting to feel secure again.

'Let's go to Stefano's this evening. I always feel hungry after sex,' purred Yvette as Herb slid between her legs.

'I know you do baby. Whatever you say baby, whatever you say.'

Ten months had passed and Munro was still wallowing in self-pity. He was fortunate that Quigley had proven to be an able and understanding listener.

'I was never one for watching television, Munro. Being bombarded constantly with commercials isn't my idea of entertainment. I preferred to go to the cinema and watch a good film. That's what I call a night out. And that being the case, I never saw any of your shows. Mind you, from what I've heard about them, I can't say I'm sorry I missed them. I was talking to Tommy the Tout yesterday and he told me you were big. So, how come the wheels fell off the dinner-trolley?' Quigley smiled. 'No pun intended.'

'It's hard to know where to begin. Yeah, I was big, Quigley. My Christmas Special in 1990 still holds the record for viewing figures and my weekly show regularly pulled in something like twenty five million viewers, most of them women. I had everything going for me.' Munro sighed, screwing up his face. 'Then I made my big mistake. The billionaire who owned the network, Chesney Latchford, threw an A-list party at his country mansion. I was in my element, surrounded by fawning sycophants and brown nosing hangers-on, all telling me how much they loved the show and how wonderful I was.' Munro paused and looked at Quigley. 'Don't look at me like that, Quigley. That type of adulation can go to your head very easily. Even when you know it's nothing but bull. It becomes like a drug, you start to depend on it. And next thing you know, you're hooked. I'd become a bullshit junkie. Sorry about my language.' Munro rolled over and stared at the ceiling. 'Being drunk most of the time didn't help. But it was when I was drunk that I was at my insulting best. People used to queue up to be insulted by the one and only Anton Munro! Can you believe it?' Munro shook his head. 'So there I am, having a ball at Chesney's party, when this young, extremely attractive and promiscuous young thing starts giving me the big come on. She's flirting with me, brushing her breasts against my arm at every opportunity, making with her big baby blues like she wants me to f...' Munro stopped himself in time. 'Making like she wants me to have sex with her. It was no secret that my wife Yvette and I had what people call, an open relationship. Yvette didn't go to the party. So, in accordance with the gospel of Munro, I was a free agent and opportunity was knocking at my door with a battering ram. Baby blues takes me by the hand, and leads me into the garden. Next thing I know, we're in the gazebo and I'm banging her brains out. This girl's orgasm was so intense that she was speaking in tongues and using language that would make a hardened dockworker blush. Suddenly, I could sense a pair of eyes burning into my naked buttocks, a sensation that was rapidly followed by the most ear-piercing, wailing and screaming that I'd ever heard in my life. I turned around to find Chesney's wife, Daisy and she's staring at me, her eyes hanging out of their sockets. You'd have thought she'd just found me having sex with her mother's corpse. But it was far worse than that, the girl I was having sex with was her darling daughter, Celeste. Daisy runs into the house howling like a Dervish and the proverbial crap hits the fan. To say that Chesney was furious with me for having sex with his daughter, who happened to be under the age of consent, would be a vast understatement. His minders gave me a kicking and threw me out. Now I know it's common to hear the accused in sex trials, pleading that he didn't know how old the girl was, but that was honestly true in my case. For a so-called thirteen year old innocent, Celeste had been around the block more than once, believe me!' Munro nodded his head. 'And no one knows more than I do, about women who've been around the block. As soon as I got home I told Yvette what happened and she responded by dragging me into the sack. She insisted that I tell her everything that had happened, right down to the smallest detail. What Celeste sounded like when she had an orgasm, the things she said, the look in her baby blue eyes, her private parts, everything about her, over and over again.' Munro raised his eyebrows and pursed his lips. 'Ironically, my transgression with Celeste resulted in the best sex that Yvette and I ever had.' Munro paused for a moment. 'It would also be the last time we'd have sex together. The following day, I phoned Chesney to apologize. He was having none of it and I could hear Daisy in the background, still howling like a Dervish and still mourning the defilement of her precious and innocent little darling. Chesney told me that Daisy's nerves were shot to pieces and that she was going to need urgent psychotherapy. The fact that his wife was having problems didn't bother me in the least. And even when he told me that he's pulling the plug on me *and* the show, I wasn't too concerned. Chesney needed me, the network needed me and I was their cash-cow. At least, that's what I was foolish enough to believe. As soon as Yvette gets wind of Chesney pulling the plug on me, she walks out the door and moves into my accountant Herb Cohen's penthouse, making him the happiest man in the world. I knew they'd been banging each other for ages, so it wasn't a surprise.'

Quigley shook his head in disbelief, a wry smile on his face. 'What did you do?'

'I got stinking drunk. Not tipsy drunk or a little bit merry drunk, I mean flat on my back, unconscious wino on the park bench drunk. I couldn't care less about Yvette and Herb. He was welcome to her. I was confident another network would take me on. But I hadn't reckoned on the newshounds. This was the juicy bone that the gutter press had been praying for. They ripped me to pieces like a pack of hungry wolves. The papers were awash with it. None of the networks would talk to me let alone consider employing me. Chesney cast a long shadow in the entertainment world. Before I could say, the next round of drinks is on me, I was rendered unemployable.' Munro gave Quigley a wry smile. 'Don't ever believe that any publicity is good publicity. I was dead and buried within two weeks… without a headstone.' Munro sighed as he ran his hands through his thick mane. 'Even the food company that produced my own range of curry sauces quickly followed suit and pulled the plug. *Anton Munro's Unique Curry Sauce "It tastes as good as I look!"* That's what it said on the jar. Christ! I must have been on a real bender of an ego trip when I wrote that tag-line!' Munro shook his head in disbelief. 'All my assets were in Yvette's name. You know, for tax avoidance reasons. Herb had seen to that and I trusted him implicitly.' Munro paused to reflect. 'Sorry, I take that back. I didn't really trust him implicitly. I was drunk most of the time and too busy having a good time to pay heed to my business affairs. But never for one minute, did I think they'd screw me out of every penny I had. Next thing I know, I'm out on the street along with my mother and Yvette was now a wealthy woman. She'd certainly come a long way since I found her wrapping herself around a chrome plated pole at the Femme Fatale.'

Quigley interjected, eyebrows lowered. 'Femme fatale?'

'Yes, Quigley, a femme fatale is a dangerous and attractive woman...'

Quigley interrupted. 'I know what it means, Munro. Just get to the point.'

'Sorry about that, Quigley. The Femme Fatale I'm talking about is a seedy inner-city strip club that I frequented from time to time. You know the kind of place, lots of naked women running around, fondling men and peddling their wares at extortionate prices.'

'So it's not only in the Houses of Parliament where that sort of thing goes on?' said Quigley. His wisecrack bringing a flicker of a smile to Munro's face.

Munro continued. 'It was lust at first sight for me when I saw her magnificent body and love at first sight for Yvette when she saw the size of my bankroll. We got married three weeks later and for the first time in her life, Yvette had money to burn. She was as happy as a chronic shopaholic in Oxford Street for the Boxing Day sales.' Munro got to his feet and paced the cell. 'To cut a long story short, it was farewell to the good life for me and my mother and welcome to the seedy world of the Belle Vale sink-estate.' Munro shook his head. 'I'll never forget the look on my mother's face when she saw where we would be living. I was ashamed of what had become of us and hit the bottle so hard I put seasoned winos to shame.'

'So, who's to blame?' said Quigley.

Munro stared at Quigley, unable to answer.

'From where I'm standing, you brought this on yourself,' said Quigley.

'Hold on there, Quigley. It's not *all* my fault. You don't know what life in show business is like,' said Munro, looking very aggrieved.

'If only you could hear yourself, Munro. I've known chronic alcoholics who were less in denial than you. I think you know that you loused up but can't admit it because you feel guilty about what it's done to your mother.' Quigley sat on the bed. 'There's very little difference between allowing something bad to happen and making it happen, both carry the same burden of guilt.'

Munro didn't reply, rolled over onto his side and faced the wall. Quigley buried his nose in a book. A long, sulky silence ensued. It was Quigley who decided to break the ice an hour or so later.

'Am I right in thinking it's your mum who is Asian?' said Quigley.

Munro was still sulking and took his time before answering.

'Yes, she's from Panaji in Goa.'

'And your dad is Scottish?'

'Yes, he's from Lochgilphead. They met in Lisbon and were married there. Lochgilphead is where I was born and raised. I only moved to Glasgow with my mum after my father died. He was captain of his own trawler, but he perished twelve years ago, he drowned in a violent storm off the Orkney Islands. The bodies of the crew were never found. If he hadn't drowned I would probably have been a fisherman just like him. It's funny how things work out.' A shadow fell over Munro's face. 'Or don't work out as in my case.'

'You haven't got a Scottish accent.'

'It comes and goes. Depends on whom I'm speaking to,' said Munro, flatly. Talking about his parents was clearly making him depressed. So Quigley tried to inject some levity into the conversation by changing the subject.

'Two new Scoobys started this morning, Munro' he said, peeking over the top of his reading glasses.

'Scoobys?' Munro's tone was frosty.

'Scooby-doo's. Screws,' said Quigley. 'You know, Scooby-doo, as in the big stupid cartoon dog.'

'What do you want *me* to do? Jump up and down?' Munro was still peeved with Quigley for being so frank with him earlier.

'Come on, Munro! Lighten up man! Admittedly, it's not exactly a personal visit from Clint Eastwood, but it's something. A little something, that may well disrupt the monotony of our humdrum existence. You never know.'

Munro closed his eyes, threw his head back on the pillow and sighed. 'Christ! I can't take fifteen years of this!'

Quigley put down the book and rose to his feet. 'So you can't take it, eh? Then why don't you kill yourself?' Quigley was calm and very matter of fact. 'I'll help you if you like! Come on, Munro. You can do it, no one should be afraid to die. Dying is simply the final stage of living. People in Asia and the Far East are into the reincarnation thing in a big way. It's one of many complex strands that make up Hinduism, Sikhism and Buddhism. Even some of the ancient Greek philosophers were into it. So why not give it a whirl Munro? Pull the plug, just for the hell of it and see where it takes you. You might even discover that you were Alexander the Great in a former life.' Quigley rubbed his chin and stared questioningly at Munro. 'No, you could never have been Alexander. Not with a track record like yours. He had a penchant for young men, and you've bedded more women than Warren Beatty.'

Quigley began to pace the cell, his eyes glued to the floor. 'Many years back, I knew a bloke who had everything going for him. A lovely wife, four kids, nice home, the works, and for fifteen years he envied no one. Then one day his wife told him she didn't love him anymore. She packed her bags and walked out on him and the kids. He felt like someone had sawn the top off his head and tossed a hand grenade down the hole. Everything he treasured most in the world had been wiped out, in one brief moment. Three failed suicide attempts followed. He was driving everyone nuts that he came in contact with and it had got to the point where his friends would hide if they saw him coming. And that included me. Two years later I bumped into him. He had a lovely girl on his arm and a smile on his face,' Quigley sat down on his bed. 'We went for a coffee and had a long chat. He told me the road to recovery began, while contemplating slashing his wrists. He began thinking how devastated his mother and kids would be when they discovered his blanched corpse. So he decided not to go through with it. He said it was the first time in two years he had been able to stop thinking about his own feelings and consider someone else's.' Quigley clapped his hands together. 'That was the *real* turning point! The moment he decided to stop feeling sorry for himself!' Sensing Munro was about to start whining, Quigley continued. 'Something tells me you don't have many friends, Munro.'

Munro thought about it for a moment before replying. 'When you're surrounded by hangers-on it's difficult to make *real* friends. Show business is crawling with people like that. You know, acquaintances and the like, but no one I would call a friend. The only real friend I have is my mother,' said Munro, a sardonic smile on his face. 'She's the most loving, selfless person I've ever known and she has never stopped loving me.' He shook his head slowly from side to side. 'Sad isn't it?'

'It's not sad, Munro. You're a lucky man and it seems to me that your mother is a lovely lady. There are a lot of people out there who've never known what it's like to have a *real* mother.' Quigley placed his hand on Munro's shoulder. 'Acquaintances will come and go Munro. As for true friends, now that's a different matter. You'll be a lucky man indeed, if on your deathbed, you can count on one hand the number of true friends you've acquired in your lifetime.' Quigley poured a whisky and handed it to Munro. 'Listen, Munro, if you can't move forward for yourself, why not try for your mother's sake? Give her some hope. It's the least she deserves. Give it your best shot.'

Munro's eyes were shining, swimming with tears.

A strange voice interrupted the conversation. 'Which one of you is Munro?'

Peering through the doorway was the blackest face and the widest smile they had ever seen. 'I've been sent to pick up Anton Munro.'

'That's me,' said Munro, getting to his feet.

'The governor wants to see you.'

'And who are you?' said Quigley, walking towards him.

'Prison Officer Winston Greene,' he said, still grinning from ear to ear.

'You're kidding!' Quigley's mouth hung open. 'Winston Greene! You're working in the wrong nick with a name like that. They've got a prison named after you just up the road in Birmingham.'

'I know, but it's not the same spelling. My granny lives just around the corner from it. She wanted me to work there when I transferred from Saint Catherine Prison in Jamaica. But I came here instead. I thought that by coming here to Kingswood, I wouldn't get any stick from the inmates. But so far, it ain't working out the way I hoped it would.'

Wearing a smile to rival Winston's, Quigley turned to Munro. 'What did I tell you, Munro? A little something that breaks the monotony of our humdrum existence!' Quigley shook his head from side to side. 'Winston Greene. That certainly takes the biscuit!'

On the way to the governor's office, Munro chewed over everything Quigley had said and Winston never stopped smiling. The governor, a tall slim man with thinning white hair and a ruddy complexion was wearing a grey pin-striped suit. He had ex-army stamped all over him. Charlotte Blake was also there, seated by the window, but it was the governor who was first to speak. 'Sit down, Munro. I'm Major Bernard Morris and I believe you've already met, Miss Blake.'

Munro glanced in her direction. 'Briefly sir,' he replied with veiled sarcasm.

The Major looked stern, sitting in his high-back leather chair, with his arms folded. He looked uncannily like Munro's old headmaster, who had the same expression when he was about to administer the cane to unruly pupils. 'I'll get straight to the point, Munro. I'm very concerned that you have decided not to partake in Miss Blake's evaluation sessions. You should realize that these sessions are the only accurate means we have of determining at a later date, whether you are suitable or not suitable to rejoin society. It's my duty to advise you that if you continue down this obstinate path, you'll never be recommended for parole and shall serve the full term of your sentence…'

Munro interrupted. 'When would you like me to start?' he said, with a smile.

The Major and Blake looked equally stunned.

'Why the sudden change of heart, Munro?' Blake eyed him somewhat warily.

'You're the one with the degree in psychology, Miss Blake. You tell me,' said Munro.

'Excellent!' The Major clapped his hands together in triumph. 'I must say that after reading your report, Miss Blake, I expected this meeting to be a complete waste of everyone's time.' He stared at her accusingly.

'It wasn't Miss Blake's fault, sir. It was mine. I've had a lot of time to give the matter some serious thought and have come to realize how negative I was. I'm sure that with my full cooperation, Miss Blake will be able to help me no end.'

Munro gave her the famous celebrity smile. Blake was unimpressed and remained po-faced. She withdrew a large diary from her briefcase and made an entry.

'I'll send for you a week on Friday then, Munro.' Her tone was very officious and matter of fact.

'Damn it! I have an appointment on that particular Friday. She's a very important client of mine. We're doing lunch at The Savoy in London. May we re-schedule? ' Munro pretended to look concerned.

Blake stopped writing, clearly unimpressed by his sarcasm. She nodded in the direction of the Major. 'Perhaps Major Morris can make arrangements for your client to dine here in the canteen.'

The Major was lost for words and twiddled with his moustache looking confused. 'Well, that seems to conclude our business for now, Munro,' he said, shuffling the papers on his desk.

Munro rose from the chair and started to leave.

'Just hold on a moment, Munro. That television show of yours, was all that bad language and insulting behaviour, the real *you* or was it just an act?'

'Good heavens, no sir. I can assure you it wasn't anything like the real me. The real me, behaved far worse than that. What you and millions of other viewers saw was the expurgated version.'

'But, surely it was you, who personally prepared all those wonderfully exotic dishes?' said the Major, looking more disillusioned by the second.

'Don't be daft, sir! We had a team of chefs slaving away backstage. I can't boil an egg. It was all a con.'

'What about all those amazing recipes? You created those, didn't you?' The Major stammered, looking like a bridegroom on his honeymoon, who has just discovered that his bride is a transsexual.

'They were my mother's recipes. The entire show was one big lie! But that's show business for you!'

'Oh, bugger! And I was thinking of having you prepare something for the wife and I!' He shook his head. 'She was a big fan of yours, you know. She'll be bitterly disappointed.'

'Don't worry, sir. I'll rustle up some beans on toast for you whenever you wish. You only have to ask. Which would you prefer?'

'Prefer?' said the Major, his mouth hanging open.

'Yes sir, the baked beans. Do you prefer Heinz or Branston? Personally, I prefer Branston, the sauce has much more flavour and not quite so salty.'

'We *never* eat beans on toast. The bloody army put us off them for life!' he barked. 'Just thinking about beans gives me chronic flatulence!'

Munro winked at Blake and opened the door.

'In that case sir, I can always make cheese on toast. Which bread would you prefer to have, thick sliced, thin sliced, brown or white? Cheddar, Red Leicester, Wensleydale or…?'

Blake cut him off. 'That'll be enough, Munro. Close the door on the way out!' she said, with an air of finality.

Munro left the office to find Winston Greene waiting in the hallway, smiling as ever.

'Don't you ever get pissed-off, Winston?'

'Nah, man. What's the point of that? Getting pissed-off only makes me unhappy. Life is just like the song, man… *Don't Worry, Be Happy.*'

Munro nodded. 'Ok Winston, I get the point… laugh and the world laughs with you and all that shit.'

'Yeah, man. Laugh and the world laughs with you. Me granny used to say that to me all the time. Who was it sang that one?' he said.

'I'm not aware that it was made into a song. I know it only as the first line of a poem entitled Solitude that was written by a woman called Ella Wheeler Wilcox.'

'She never made it into the music charts then?'

'No Winston, she died in 1919 and they didn't have music charts then. At least not as we know them.'

'How they know if it was a smash hit then?'

'By how much money they had in their bank account, Winston. That's something that has never changed.'

The Major was visibly shaken by Munro's startling revelations.

'My wife will go berserk when I tell her what Munro just said. She thought Anton Munro was marvellous. Good lord, she even planned our holidays around his bloody shows! I must say, it's given me a bit of a turn as well.'

'Things aren't always what they may seem, sir,' said Blake, not that she gave a damn.

'At least the meeting went well, don't you think?' said the Major, a look of relief on his face as he adjusted his regimental tie. 'No wild remonstrations. No tantrums. No need to send for the guards.' The Major's nine year tenure at Kingswood had been trouble free and a fat retirement pension was looming. That's all he was really interested in.

'That's what concerns me, sir. It all went too well. Munro's sudden change of heart surprises me. He could be up to something,' said Blake with a frown.

'Well, just watch the bugger. We've never had a serious incident in Kingswood on my watch and I don't intend to start now! I'm due for retirement in a few months and nothing must jeopardize my unblemished reputation.' He cocked a proud snoot in the air.

'You don't understand, sir. I don't believe Munro would harm me in any way. He's not the type. I just think he's up to something. But I can't put my finger on it.'

'Not the type! Not the bloody type! The man is doing time for murder, so don't you forget it. He was also extremely hostile towards you not so long ago. What on earth makes you think the man's incapable of harming you?'

'That was only a verbal assault, sir. It had more to do with his insecure frame of mind than anything else. I never once felt physically threatened by him.'

'Nevertheless, you'd best have an officer with you, when you see him. It's pointless taking unnecessary risks.'

'Please, sir! He'll never open up with someone else in the room. None of the detainees would under such circumstances. If delicate counselling such as this is to be successful, we must have privacy. There has to be a high degree of mutual confidentiality and trust. Please, bow to my experience. I do know what I'm talking about.'

Eyes narrowed, the Major pondered for a moment, sucking on the end of his pen. 'Ok. But if anything goes wrong you'll be held responsible. Just be damn careful. And don't be fooled by his dashing good looks. The man's a known scoundrel with the ladies and not to be trusted.'

'Have no fear, sir. Munro may be reasonably handsome in a rugged sort of way, but he is also one of the most arrogant, wanton and obnoxious men I've ever met. That being the case he's *definitely not* my cup of tea! Besides, he's in here for life, so his *prospects* aren't exactly the most promising, are they?'

Briefcase in hand, Blake left the office only to return moments later.

'Can you get hold of the case files from Munro's trial? I'd like to study them before our next meeting.'

'Don't see why not. I'll get on to it straight away.' He picked up the phone immediately.

Blake left the room then pressed her ear to the door.

'Hello darling. It's Bernard. You'll *never* believe this! I've just been speaking with that Anton Munro chap. Yes! The television chef fellow and guess what…'

Greene ushered Munro to the canteen. Quigley was nowhere to be seen.

'Where's Quigley?' said Munro, looking bemused.

'We haven't seen him since breakfast, Munro,' said one of the lags. 'There's a good chance he's got the shits! There's a lot of it going around. You'll probably get them next.'

3

Quigley was alone when O'Farrell opened the cell door. 'You've got a visitor, Quigley,' he muttered, totally uninterested.

'It's Wednesday. There's no visiting on a Wednesday,' said Quigley, looking surprised.

'I'm just the messenger, Quigley. The man upstairs told me you've got a visitor. So get your arse off that bed and get moving! Come on, move it! I'm not standing here for my fucking health!'

'Do you know who it is?' said Quigley, adjusting his clothing.

'A woman, that's all I know,' grunted O'Farrell

Quigley had a feeling that something was terribly wrong. The short trip to the visitor's room seemed to take forever and he felt like he was walking against the flow of a conveyor belt. The visitor's room was deserted when they arrived. O'Farrell directed Quigley to a cubicle. Moments later his daughter Connie entered the room, she approached the glass partition, tearful and distraught.

'Connie! What's wrong sweetheart?' He placed the palms of his hands against the glass.

'It's Linda, dad...!' She broke down, unable to continue, her body, trembling with emotion.

'In your own time sweetheart, in your own time,' he said, softly.

Quigley turned to O'Farrell.

'Ask someone to bring her a cup of coffee!'

'It's against prison regulations, Quigley. She's had plenty of time for refreshments in the waiting room. Christ! You've been in prison long enough, to know that, so don't go looking at me like I've just kicked your dog.'

'Sod the regulations, man! Can't you see how upset she is?'

'That's her problem, Quigley. Regulations is regulations.' O'Farrell sneered dispassionately and turned the other way.

'I won't forget this, O'Farrell!'

'I don't give a shit, Quigley!'

'It's alright dad,' Connie tapped on the glass. 'Don't create a fuss! I'll be OK in a sec.'

'Sweetheart, what's upset you so much?'

'It's Linda, dad. She's...' Connie paused, tears flowing freely.

'Easy, Connie, just take your time sweetheart,' said Quigley, clearly distressed by his daughter's emotional state.

'She topped herself, dad! My Linda slashed her wrists! I found her in the bath last night...' Connie broke down yet again, struggling to breathe.

Quigley stood up and banged his head repeatedly against the glass partition.

'Sit your lousy convict's arse down, Quigley! And stay away from the glass!' screamed O'Farrell.

Quigley couldn't hear him. His mind was elsewhere, a myriad of memories swirling around inside his head.

'Sit down, Quigley! I won't tell you again!' growled O'Farrell, as he seized hold of Quigley's arm.

Quigley broke free and drove him against the wall. O'Farrell hit the wall with a thud and they fell to the ground, exchanging blows, their legs flailing wildly, scuffing crazy black patterns on the floor tiles with their shoes. O'Farrell's height and bulk proved too much for Quigley to handle, he pinned him to the ground with ease, grabbed him by the hair and pounded his forehead against the tiled floor until Quigley lay unconscious. Connie screamed hysterically when she saw the blood spurting from her father's head. Two officers rushed in and dragged her from the room. O'Farrell struggled to his feet, close to exhaustion, his chest rising and falling rapidly. In stark contrast, Quigley lay face down, motionless and barely breathing.

Two hours later, O'Farrell was summoned to the office of Senior Officer, Jack Dobson. 'Jesus Christ, O'Farrell! I can't believe you couldn't restrain a man twice your bloody age, without putting him in hospital!' bellowed, Dobson.

'He got what was coming to him! The crazy old bastard was trying to kill me! And he would've done if I hadn't whacked him first!'

'Whacked him? You nearly bloody killed him! You're suspended from duty until further notice, O'Farrell. Now get your useless arse out of here!'

O'Farrell got as far as the door.

'How long have you been working here, O'Farrell?' said Dobson, leaning against the back of the chair.

'Seven months!' barked O'Farrell.

'Only seven months.' Dobson shook his head. 'It seems like ten years. And I bet you don't know anything about the man you've just beaten half to death,' he said, drumming his fingers on the desk.

'What's there to know? O'Farrell snarled. 'He's just another lifer as far as I'm concerned.'

'I thought so. You don't have a bloody clue what Cedric Quigley did on the outside. Do you?'

'So! Is that a crime? And what's that got to do with me giving him a good spanking?' said O'Farrell.

'You'll find out soon enough,' said Dobson, with a nod of his head.

'What's that supposed to mean?' said O'Farrell, screwing up his face.

'It means exactly what I said, O'Farrell. You'll find out soon enough.'

'Have you finished?'

'I haven't quite finished with you yet, O'Farrell. You are truly the most vile excuse for a human being that I've ever encountered. It's hard to believe that you had a mother. You're detested by your fellow officers and even the most violent inmates despise you. There's no place here for a contemptible thug like you. Not this side of the bars. I've changed my mind about placing you under suspension. You're fired. Now get your loathsome arse out of here!'

'Don't expect me to lose any fucking sleep over it, Dobson. Those are pretty brave words coming from a man who knows there are three guards on the other side of that door.' O'Farrell approached Dobson's desk and lowered his voice to a whisper. 'Just pray to God that you're not alone when you bump into me on the outside, one dark foggy night. You'll be sorry you ever spoke to me like that. I'll be seeing you, Dobson.' He paused, the corners of his mouth curling into a smile. 'And that's a promise.'

O'Farrell slammed the door behind him.

Quigley came off the critical list two weeks later. Munro begged Blake to seek the governor's permission for him to visit Quigley in hospital. When permission was granted, Munro was handcuffed and taken to the hospital by George Challis and two armed guards. Challis for once had nothing to say. They arrived at Quigley's ward just as the Major was leaving.

'He's one tough bugger,' said the Major, with admiration. 'We could have done with a few more chaps like him in my old regiment.' He paused to look at Munro. 'I hope you appreciate my granting you permission to make this visit, Munro. I stuck my bloody neck out for you!'

'I do, sir. Thank you very much,' said Munro, his mind elsewhere, walking past the Major as if he wasn't there.

Munro sat by Quigley's bed. 'Hey, how are you feeling?' he chirped, trying to appear upbeat.

Quigley didn't reply. His eyes darted about and his lips were moving as if he was having a private conversation with himself. Munro sat waiting for him to respond. Ten minutes passed before he spoke.

'I expect you heard about my Linda, topping herself? She would've been twenty one on her next birthday,' he said, emitting a long sigh.

'Yes. I did hear, Quigley. I'm sorry. I know how much she meant to you,' said Munro, lowering his head and gazing awkwardly at the floor.

'My Connie was in to see me yesterday. And do you know what she said? She said, in some ways it's a blessing dad, because Linda won't be suffering anymore.' Quigley looked at Munro, his eyes filled with pain. 'I can't get my head around that thought yet. I know what Connie's trying to say. But I just can't get my head around that thought. How can it be a blessing when I won't ever see her face again or hear her call my name?' he said, choking back the tears.

Munro clasped his hand. 'Don't go upsetting yourself, Quigley. Take it easy.'

Munro remained silent for a while, allowing Quigley time to regain his composure.

'O'Farrell was kicked into touch,' said Munro, moving away from the topic of Linda.

'Yes, I heard. Doris from the sick bay was in to see me a couple of days ago. She told me Jack Dobson wanted to prosecute O'Farrell but the governor wouldn't hear of it. I told Doris there was no way the governor would sully his unblemished record for an unrepentant lifer like me,' said Quigley, resignedly. His eyes were strangely cold and unfeeling, which wasn't like him at all. He fell silent once more. It was almost as if part of him had died with his granddaughter. Munro had never seen him look so vulnerable and just as he was struggling for something to say, Challis came to the rescue, albeit inadvertently.

'Time's up, I'm afraid, Quigley. The Sister's giving me the nod. Munro will have to get on his bike and head back to the nick,' he said, with a stupid apologetic grin on his face. Challis never called anyone by their first name. It was nothing personal, just one of his little quirks. He didn't like to get over friendly with the inmates unless there was something in it for him.

'It won't be easy. But I'll do my best to come and see you again,' said Munro, squeezing Quigley's hand. 'It all depends on what mood the Major's in.'

'You try and do that,' whispered Quigley, before closing his eyes.

Back in the cell, Munro lay on his bed staring at the ceiling, unable to get Quigley out of his mind. Apart from his concern, there was precious little he knew about the man and it bothered him. Next morning, he was collected from the cell by one of the new officers, the one that arrived on the same day as Winston Greene. He was six inches shorter than Munro, a bit on the chubby side and had a red birthmark on his forehead, just below the hairline.

'Morning, Mr. Munro, you're scheduled for a meeting with Miss Blake,' he said, with a cheery smile. 'By the way, I was sorry to hear about what happened to your friend, Mr. Quigley.'

'Thanks. He should be fine in a few weeks,' said Munro. 'You're one of the new screws, aren't you?'

'Yes. Henry Jessop's the name,' He reached out and shook Munro's hand.

Munro stared at Jessop, looking slightly puzzled.

'Why the funny look, Mr. Munro?'

'Sorry, Jessop, take no notice of me. I thought I knew you from somewhere, that's all. Being locked up in this place plays strange tricks with your mind.'

'I wish we had met before, Mr. Munro. My wife and I never missed your television show. Sarah was a huge fan of yours.'

'That's nice of you to say so, Jessop.' Munro shrugged his shoulders. 'Those days are dead and buried now. The show doesn't even get re-run slots anymore.'

'You never know, Mr. Munro. They'll probably turn up on the repeats of *All Our Yesterdays*, one of these days. Just think of the royalties.' Jessop stood waiting for a smile that never arrived.

Munro didn't respond.

'Have you met Winston Greene yet?' said Jessop, changing the subject. 'What a character he is! If smiling was an Olympic event that lad would win the gold medal every time.' Jessop was a refreshing change to the other screws. He was laid-back, polite and genuinely sincere. Munro found him easy to talk to and by the time they'd reached Charlotte Blake's office, they were getting on like old school chums.

'How's Quigley?' said Blake, without looking up.

'He'll live,' said Munro, somewhat churlishly.

'Sorry I asked, Munro.' Blake was clearly disappointed with his tone.

'Forgive me, it's me who should be sorry!' said Munro. 'Seeing Quigley in that state has made me more cynical than usual, I guess. Thanks for swinging it for me to visit him in hospital, by the way. I really appreciate your help.'

'Don't mention it, Munro,' said Blake, who had yet to look up from her desk. 'I was just doing my job. I'd have done the same for any prisoner in a similar situation.'

'I see! You didn't go out of your way, then?'

Blake looked up from her desk. 'Heavens no, why should I?' She removed her spectacles. 'I treat every prisoner the same as the next. There are no exceptions.'

Munro's eyes blazed.

'What makes you think I should treat you any differently, Munro?'

'I don't!' barked Munro, shuffling about restlessly on the chair.

'Now you're angry with me. Why do you *always* end up getting angry with me, Munro?' She leaned back in the chair.

'Hah! You really want to know? Then listen up. That ice-cold psychologist's mantle and your frosty veneer get right up my nose! Try ditching them for a just a moment and perhaps relations between us might improve. Christ! Don't you ever show your feelings, Charlotte? Why does everything in your life have to be so black and white?' Munro's face contorted with rage.

'We're not bosom buddies, Munro, so please do not address me as, *Charlotte*. In answer to your question, of course I get emotional, but I choose to control it. It's non-productive and a waste of energy.'

'Well here's a little non-productive something that might make you, just a tad emotional, *Miss Blake*!' he barked, emphasizing the Miss. 'Did you know that most of the bottom-feeding, lowlife fucks who attend your sessions, only come here to ogle? And if I were you, I shouldn't take that as a compliment, *Miss Blake*. Because apart from old Doris in sick bay, you're the only woman most of them have seen in years!'

She peered at him over the top of her spectacles, totally unruffled.

'Tell me something new, Munro. Yes, I am well aware of that. I'm afraid, it goes with the territory. But what about you, why are you here, Munro? Apart from the need to feed your insatiable appetite for rage and self-pity, are you here to ogle also?'

Munro was lost for words. He never expected her to remain so unflappable.

'No insolent riposte, Munro? That really is most out of character. You usually have an answer for everything. Perhaps it would help if I rephrased the question. Are *you* one of the bottom-feeding, lowlife fucks that come here, just to ogle?' She stared into his eyes, calmly waiting for an answer.

Munro couldn't answer. She had him hopelessly on the back foot.

'I don't find you sexually attractive, if that's what you mean,' he mumbled, bitterly disappointed that his response had been so feeble.

'That's such a relief, Munro. I think I'll sleep much better at night, knowing that.' She manufactured a smile, stood up, walked away from her desk and gazed out of the window. The sunlight shone through her dress revealing every superb curve of her long legs. 'Besides, what could a macho hunk like you possibly want with a dried-up, goody-goody dyke like me?'

Munro threw his arms above his head in a mock display of surrender. 'Ok! For God's sake stop! You win. For Christ's sake, you win!'

Blake sat down at her desk, replaced her spectacles and assumed her business as usual posture. 'Now where were we? Oh, yes. I've a feeling you may not like what I have to say, Munro. And should that be the case, you're free to walk out at any time and not return.' She pointed at the doorway with her pen.

'I promise not to rip the head off my teddy,' he said, struggling to veil the tension and anger in his voice.

She looked at him for several moments before speaking.

'Why are you wasting my time and more importantly *yours*? You've been coming to these sessions for months now and it's obvious that your heart's not in it. All that flannel you gave the Major and I about wanting to make a constructive contribution was nothing more than bullshit, Munro. You've just been playing at it. For heaven's sake, what's the point? It's not going to get you anywhere! Take up reading, oil painting, build ships out of matchsticks, do something useful and stop taking up my valuable time that could be spent with prisoners who are appreciative and genuinely seeking help.'

Munro sat motionless, a stunned look on his face.

'Would you like me to continue?' She leaned forward, her hands clasped together, inviting a response.

Munro nodded.

She rose from her chair and paced the room.

'Be warned, Munro. That little rant was only the preliminary to the main event. When the bell rings I'm coming out fighting with the gloves off, so make sure you have a gum-shield in, because I fight dirty.'

'That's fine by me, *Miss Blake*, as long as you don't hit me below the belt.'

'It's my belief that you found success without ever having to try for it, Munro. Everything fell into your lap. Yes, you were extremely fortunate to be blessed with a great talent and that's not a crime. However, because you've been a taker all your life you went to pieces the moment your luck ran out. You were incapable of handling it. And look where you've ended up, you're swimming around in a stagnant pond with the bottom-feeding lowlifes you despise so much. It's time for you to take a long hard look in the mirror, Munro. It's time that you scraped away the pond-slime and saw the frightened rabbit that you really are. You're addicted to self-pity and sadly you can't see that it's getting you nowhere. If you really want to overturn what *you alone* see as a gross miscarriage of justice, it's going to require the heart of a lion for that fight and not that of Bugs Bunny. The sooner you realize this, the better. Then and only then, can you hope to move forward!'

Munro sat in silence, reflecting that Quigley had more or less said the same thing, though not in so many harsh words. Blake moved tactfully on. 'I've been reading your case file, Munro. Legally, you don't have grounds for appeal. But I'm sure you already know that. However, you can shorten your sentence quite considerably, but that will depend on how you apply and conduct yourself while in prison. If you're successful, it's possible they might reduce your sentence by six years or maybe more. Attaining parole *must* become your chief objective. To achieve that, you must first convince the governor and then the parole board that you are worthy of rejoining society. In the meantime something might turn up that may prove your alleged innocence, you can never discount that happening. Everything revolves around Ashley Roper, the dead boy's lady friend. She alone appears to hold the key to your freedom. But that would mean her coming clean and admitting not only to perjury but also aiding and abetting Danny Gordon in attempted armed robbery. Personally, I can't see that happening.'

'You don't believe I'm innocent?' Munro leaned forward, a look of disappointment on his face.

'I *want* to believe that you're innocent, Munro,' she sighed, shaking her head slowly from side to side. 'But having studied the case files, there's nothing in there to convince me that you are.'

'I guess it was too much to expect.' Munro lowered his head, looking like a castaway who'd just seen the rescue plane crash into the sea in a ball of flames.

'My work brings me in contact with all manner of villains, Munro. I also know a liar when I meet one. You're a belligerent, selfish degenerate, but you're not a liar.' She shrugged her shoulders. 'Unfortunately, the case against you is watertight.'

Munro stared at her, despair etched in his face, a man resigned to his fate.

'That's all I have to say, Munro. I hope you'll respond to my criticism in a positive way. I sincerely hope, that our next session will be a positive and productive one.'

Munro nodded pensively and rose from his chair to leave, when he reached the door he stopped.

'Cedric Quigley. Who is he?'

'I'm not sure what you mean, Munro?' She looked somewhat bemused.

'Quigley has never told me what he did on the outside. Only on the rare occasion has he ever spoken about his immediate family. He doesn't even have any family photographs in the cell. I've been cooped up with a man for over two years and I still don't know anything about him!'

Blake gave her head an incredulous shake and smiled.

'My word, you really do have a knack for surprising people, Munro. I have to take my hat off to you in that respect. I thought every man and his dog knew about Cedric Quigley.'

'Don't forget, Miss Blake, for quite a few years now, I haven't really been on the same planet as most people.'

Blake folded her arms across her chest and lay back in her chair.

'Cedric Quigley is a major player in London's underworld. For want of a better word you could call him a godfather. If there can be such a thing as a gangster with high moral principles, then Cedric Quigley is the poster boy. His organization has always steered clear of drugs, pornography and prostitution, so in that respect they've kept themselves squeaky clean. Quigley has always been Mister Untouchable. At least he was, until that terrible business when the Rumanian hit man, Bela Petrescu brutally raped Quigley's granddaughter. When Quigley murdered Petrescu the vast majority of people in this country not only condoned his retributive actions but also the brutal manner in which he did it. Quigley owns a dozen or so successful and strictly legitimate bookmaking shops in London but the shops are just a smoke screen for their real cash-cow. Crime is where they make the real money. Don't let the fact that he's locked up in here fool you. Quigley is still very active, believe me! It's strictly a family business and no outsiders have *ever* worked for him. Nepotism has been the key to Quigley's success.'

Munro was speechless.

'Quigley's definitely a one off as far as the criminal class is concerned. You think highly of him, don't you?' she said, with a knowing smile.

'Yes I do. He's the most honest man I've ever met.' Munro paused to smile at the irony of his statement before continuing. 'It's hard to believe that he is the same man who killed that rapist so brutally. Quigley has helped me to keep it together when he didn't have to. And at the risk of sounding clichéd, he's been like a father to me from day one. I also admire and respect the way he puts his family first, before all else. But since he lost his granddaughter, there's a shadow hanging over him, a vital spark's gone out of him and that upsets me. I hate to see him like that and as God is my judge I'll do everything in my power to help him.'

This was a side to Munro she'd never seen, until now. Part of her wished she hadn't been so brutally frank with him earlier. He nodded, thanked her and left.

Much to his disappointment, Munro was denied permission to visit his cell-mate in hospital again and by the time Quigley was released, he'd spent a total of twenty days in care and missed his granddaughter Linda's funeral. It was Jessop who escorted him back to the cell.

'I hope you've left some malt whisky for me, Munro,' said Quigley, with a nod in the direction of his cabinet.

'Quigley! How are you doing?' Munro jumped off the bed to embrace his cell-mate.

Quigley rubbed his index finger across the huge diagonal scar on his forehead. 'I'm fine, Munro, the blinding headaches apart. Mind you, during the last few weeks I've swallowed more pills than Keith Richards ever did. Didn't you hear me rattling when I walked in?' He flopped on the bed and stretched out. 'Well then, what's new, Munro?'

'Not a lot really,' said Munro, pulling a blank face. 'Oh, there's Henry Jessop.'

'Henry Jessop?' Quigley looked puzzled.

'Yeah, he's the screw who escorted you back to the cell. He's a really nice bloke. It was him who kept me updated on your progress at the hospital.'

'A decent and helpful screw, eh. Now there's a first.' Quigley smiled cynically. 'It sounds to me like he's in the wrong job. I heard that the parson will be leaving here soon. He's off to sunnier climes, some mission or other in Africa. Perhaps your mate, Jessop, should put his name down to replace him at Kingswood.'

'Don't be like that, Quigley. God, you're a tough man to please.'

Quigley gave him a wink. 'But that's just how I like it and that's the way I'll always be.'

Munro changed the subject.

'I've been doing just like you told me and kept all my appointments with Charlotte Blake.'

'That's good to hear, Munro. How did they go?'

Munro lowered his head.

'Only a few of the sessions have gone OK, I'm afraid. You know what I'm like, for losing my rag.' Munro shrugged his shoulders apologetically. 'I lost the plot a couple of times. I can't explain it, Quigley, but she seems to have a knack for winding me up.'

Quigley rolled his eyes towards the heavens and sighed.

'It's not her, Munro. It's you!'

'How can you say that, Quigley? You've never been party to our heated exchanges.'

'Now, that's what I'd call a Freudian slip, Munro! You see your sessions with Miss Blake as heated exchanges! I don't know what she's done to make you so belligerent but you've got to sort yourself out. The sooner you start treating her like a trusted ally and confidant the better.'

'By the way, she doesn't believe I'm innocent,' said Munro, tactfully manoeuvring away from the way he treated Blake.

'What made you think she would?'

Munro scratched his chin. 'I don't know. I was just hoping she'd believe me, that's all.' He was visibly deflated by Quigley's pragmatic response.

'Even if she did believe you Munro, it wouldn't change a thing as far are you're concerned. So why get depressed about it?' Quigley suspected there was more to Munro's feelings for Blake than he wanted to declare.

'I'm *not* depressed!' snapped Munro, like a foolish schoolboy who'd been ridiculed by the teacher in front of his classmates.

'Look Munro, the main person you must convince of your innocence, is the judge. He's the only man who can unlock that thing there.' Quigley pointed at the cell door. 'And to do that, you're going to need the biggest slice of luck you've ever had. What else did she say?'

'She's studied the case file from my trial and reckons the only chance I've got is for Ashley Roper to confess!'

'You don't say! I bet she was awake all night working that one out. So, just what does she intend to do? Write her a letter? Dear Ashley, I'd be extremely grateful if you were to hand yourself in to the police and confess that your entire testimony was nothing more than a pack of lies!'

Munro slumped on the bed crestfallen, head cradled in his hands.

'Look Munro, if it's any consolation, *I do believe you're innocent*. However, that alone isn't going to get you out of here! It'll probably make you feel a bit better about yourself, but come lights-out, you'll still be here in the dark, serving a mandatory life sentence for murder.'

A fog of silence fell over the cell.

Quigley and Munro were slightly late getting to the canteen. There were welcoming smiles from one or two inmates, but no more than that. The majority of the lifers were interested in no one but themselves and it wouldn't have mattered to them if O'Farrell had splattered Quigley's brains all over the ceiling. After collecting their food they sat at the usual table, the regulars had finished eating and were on their way out. Both men remained taciturn while they ate. Munro was first to break the silence, speaking in a whisper.

'Why did you tell me that story about your pal turning despair into joy? Did you make that up just to stop me feeling sorry for myself? And why are you giving me such a hard time?'

'No! It was all true. I wouldn't lie to you, Munro.' Quigley frowned. 'And what's this rubbish about me giving you a hard time? You'd know all about it if I gave you a hard time, Munro.'

'You've done nothing but put me down since you got back,' said Munro.

'I can't believe how negative you've been, Munro. Let's take the meetings with Miss Blake. You don't seem to realize how important they are. Having someone like her in your corner is a bonus. It looks to me that she's trying her best to help you. Meanwhile, all you want to do is squabble. It's madness, Munro. Pure undiluted madness of the highest order!'

Munro lowered his gaze.

'You must get a grip, Munro. No more poking fun at the Major and taking pot-shots at Miss Blake. That's such a dumb thing to do! These people take themselves seriously and hate being ridiculed, especially when they're trying to help you. Never alienate anyone in a senior position of authority that may be useful to you. You're not in a position to turn down help. The next time you see Miss Blake, apologize and tell her you want to make amends by cooking dinner for the governor and his wife.' Quigley paused. 'I presume you *can* cook?'

Munro remained silent and nodded his head.

'The governor's arranged for me to visit my granddaughter Linda's grave next week,' whispered Quigley, putting an end to the conversation.

Munro took Quigley's advice and at the first opportunity he told Blake that he wanted to cook for the Major and his wife.

'Why, Munro?' she said, looking wary.

'I've done nothing really constructive since I've been here. I think it's time I put Bugs Bunny to the sword. That's all.' He looked at her. 'You remember Bugs Bunny don't you?'

'Do you mean the Looney Tunes version or the Munro swimming around with the lowlifes at the bottom of a stagnant pond version?'

'The Munro version. I mean it this time, Miss Blake. I realize that I have to change my attitude.'

'Why is it, Munro, that whenever you speak to me of change, I see a gigantic, flashing neon sign hovering over your head that spells out the word, Bullshit? I'm afraid it'll take far more than words to convince me of your desire to change.' She peered over the top of her spectacles. 'As far as preparing a dinner for the governor and his wife is concerned, I'll ask him. But don't bank on him saying yes. He was pretty disillusioned with you after the last meeting. In fact, it's safe to say that any monetary value he and his wife once placed on you is no longer legal tender in their house.' She smiled reassuringly. 'But, I'll do my best.'

'Thanks. You'll not regret it.'

'Just make sure it's not *you* who lives to regret it, Munro!'

As he reached the door she called out to him. 'I hope you *can* cook!'

Munro winked. 'Better than that degenerate, foul-mouthed clown who used to be on television.'

'Just remember not to insult them like you did the guests on your television show!' said Blake, quietly pleased that Munro appeared to be on an upward spiral at long last.

Three days later, Challis escorted Munro to the Major's office.

'So, Munro, all that stuff you fed me was a pack of lies, eh. Poor show, old man. That's all I can say. Bloody poor show! It's just not cricket, bowling a chap an underarm googly like that.'

'I agree, sir. And I want to make amends by cooking a wonderful meal for you and your good lady.'

The Major rose from his chair and stared out the window with his hands clasped behind his back.

'What did you have in mind, Munro?'

'I thought we'd start with…' Munro ran through his proposed menu. By the time he had finished the Major's eyes had glazed over and he was salivating.

'Before you leave, give the menu to Shenstone, my secretary. She'll run off a copy for my wife to browse over.' The Major wagged his finger at Munro. 'I'm not promising anything Munro. You're not exactly flavour of the month at Chez Morris and

Felicity will have the final say. However, if she does give it the thumbs-up, what will you need from me?'

'I'll supply you with a list of the ingredients and perhaps your secretary or your wife would pick them up for me. If not, then perhaps I could get a taxi into town…'

The Major's eyes bulged.

'Only joking, sir,' said Munro, smiling apologetically before continuing.

'I've been told there's a reasonable sized kitchen next to the meeting room. That should be adequate for my purposes. You'll have to supply the wine though, as our stocks are depleted since we threw a Going over the Wall party for Bogie Reznik a couple of weeks ago…'

The Major's eyes bulged once more.

'Please accept my apologies, sir. I just couldn't resist that one either. It's my Scottish upbringing, you see. We folk from Lochgilphead are noted for having a wicked sense of humour. Especially, the trawlermen. It's how they fend off the harsh weather.'

Unsmiling, the Major led him into Shenstone's office.

The following day Winston Greene handed Munro a note, it was from the Major. Munro's eyes lit up when he read it. The Major had given him the nod. All he needed now was an assistant chef!'

At precisely 1.30am, a man wearing a black jacket with the hood pulled over his head, darted across the car park towards a dilapidated block of high-rise flats. He clutched a bag at his side and kept to the shadows, carefully avoiding any street lighting that still remained operational. Cautiously, he climbed the staircase, until he reached the head of the stairs on the sixth floor. Sprawled across the walkway fast asleep, an elderly drunk and his mongrel dog blocked his path. As he stepped over them, the dog stirred, whined softly then shoved its muzzle inside the drunk's overcoat. The hooded man scurried along the walkway, checking the numbers on the doors as he went, finally coming to a halt outside number 127. Unlike the other flats, 127 appeared to be well maintained, the front door had recently been painted and the brass letterbox had been polished. After checking the coast was clear he placed the bag on the ground, withdrew a large metal can and unscrewed the top. He propped open the letterbox flap with a rag and slowly poured the contents through the gap. He lit a match, dropped it through the letterbox and the hallway burst into flames. There was no time for caution as the arsonist fled, waking up the drunk and the mongrel dog as he clambered over them. The dog was up in a flash to give chase, snapping and growling at his heels. When he reached the car park, the arsonist turned, catching the animal off-guard then delivered a vicious kick to its ribcage. There followed a loud crack and the wretched animal was left squealing and writhing in agony on the ground. As the arsonist disappeared into the shadows at the far side of the car park, the flat went up like a bomb had hit it.

Challis woke Munro at 5.30am. 'The governor wants you right away, Munro!'

'What's it about, Challis?' said Munro, hurriedly throwing on some clothes.

'I haven't a clue, Munro,' he said, yawning and stretching his spindly spider-like arms.

An ominous silence greeted Munro when he entered the office. The Major was sitting at his desk, visibly troubled and ill at ease. He cleared his throat repeatedly before addressing Munro.

'Please, Munro. I think you should sit down,' he muttered nervously, pointing at the chair facing his desk. The Major blinked anxiously for several moments, struggling to find the words he wanted to say. He placed his hands behind his head, looked up at the ceiling and sighed heavily. 'There's simply, no easy way to say this Munro. It's the worst possible news, I'm afraid. Last night, someone set fire to your mother's flat. She couldn't get out in time. Your mother was burned to death.' The Major lowered his gaze. 'She wasn't the arsonist's only victim, a mother and three young children in the flat above were also burned to death.' His voice was but a whisper, as if trying to lessen the impact.

The sound of heavy rain driving against the window panes filled the room as Munro sat in silence, his face expressionless. The only good thing in his wretched life had been cruelly taken from him. A terrible sense of loss swept over him and much as he felt like crying, the tears simply wouldn't come, his emotions suppressed by his own profound sense of guilt. 'Do they know who did it?' he said, his voice devoid of any emotion.

'They don't. The only witness to come forward, a seventy two year old drunk, was very vague. He saw a hooded man run from the building and into the car park just before the explosion but he couldn't give a description. Most people on that estate are far too scared to open their mouths for fear of reprisals, so it's highly unlikely that anyone who did get a clear view of what happened will come forward. You used to live there, Munro. So I don't have to tell you what it's like. The forensics people said that petrol was poured through the letter box and set alight. So it was definitely deliberate.' The Major paused, gathering his thoughts. 'I'll be brutally frank with you, Munro. They don't believe they'll ever find this person.'

'This is my fault. It would never have happened if I wasn't locked up in here,' said Munro.

The Major was genuinely upset. He rose from the chair and gave Munro's shoulder a consolatory squeeze.

'I'm truly sorry for your loss, Munro,' he sighed. 'Don't be too hard on yourself lad. Chin up, chest out, eyes front and all that. Under the circumstances, there was nothing you could do. It wasn't your fault.'

Munro didn't speak, rose from his chair and walked out of the room.

Eleven days later, Munro travelled to the cemetery under armed guard, his wrists in shackles. There were no familiar faces among the four guards, not that it would have made much difference to his solemn mood. It was a miserable day and despite the driving rain and biting wind that penetrated his outer garment, he felt nothing. His heart skipped when he saw Charlotte Blake standing alongside the priest at the graveside. When the service was over, she handed Munro a single rose to place on his mother's coffin as it was lowered into the grave. No words were exchanged and it was only when he was being escorted back to the van that he thought about the marble headstone. He turned back and spoke to her.

'Thanks for coming, Miss Blake. It means a lot to me. There's something bothering me, perhaps you can throw some light on it. All I could afford was a floral tribute. Who paid for my mother's headstone?'

'I honestly don't know, Munro. I presumed it was you who'd organized that,' she said, looking equally bemused. 'Perhaps a relative arranged it?'

Munro looked at her blankly and shook his head. 'There are none. Well none that matter. My mother's family severed all contact when she married my father and that was fifty-odd years ago.' Munro shrugged his shoulders. 'There are no surviving members of my father's family. I'm all that's left.'

Munro stared into her eyes through the pouring rain as she sheltered underneath the umbrella. The bitter weather had brought a rosy blush to her complexion and her blonde hair hung in delightful rain-drenched ringlets. He'd never seen a woman look so natural and so exquisitely beautiful. He wanted to take her in his arms and feel the warmth of her lips. He stepped towards her.

'Let's be having you, Munro. It's time we headed back!' said the guard, tugging on his arm. He ushered Munro, into the Black Maria.

4

Jack Dobson kept his promise and saw to it that O'Farrell would never work in the Prison Service, ever again. O'Farrell was now drawing dole and spent most of the time locked inside his grubby high-rise council flat watching hard core porn and drinking cheap lager straight from the can. Apart from the occasional trip to the bookies, O'Farrell's life was excruciatingly dull and monotonous. One night, after a rare outing to the local pub, O'Farrell stood on the landing outside his flat, hunting through his coat pockets for the door key. The drunken Irish trollop standing next to him, with a roll-up dangling from her mouth, swayed back and forth, clutching a carrier bag of Kentucky Fried Chicken.

'Sufferin' shite Paddy, hurry up! Me grub'll be feckin' freezin' by the time you get the feckin' door open!' she slurred. 'I'll be going home, if you've lost the feckin' key.'

'If you don't shut it, you dozy Irish cow, I'm going to shove that key up your arse when I find it!' he barked.

When he discovered that the key had slipped through a hole in his pocket and into the lining of his coat, O'Farrell was furious. He tore at the lining like a man possessed until the key fell to the floor. The instant he opened the door, four men pounced from behind and bundled the pair of them into the hallway. Their leader was a tall, Oriental with shoulder length blond hair and only scar tissue remained where his left eye had once been. Before she could utter a sound, he caught the trollop on the tip of her chin with a short left hook, dislodging her dentures and what remained of her roll-up. She was out like a light by the time her head cracked against the wall. Like a felled pine tree she toppled slowly sideways onto the floor with a dull thud, still clutching her precious KFC carrier. After stuffing a rag into O'Farrell's mouth, they dragged him into the lounge and pinned him to the floor. The Oriental crouched over him.

'Someone told me that you're not a nice man, Mr. O'Farrell,' he said with a smile, revealing a gold incisor on either side of his mouth. 'This person, who wishes to remain nameless, said you like to hurt people. But I don't believe everything that people tell me, so I've come to your home to find out for myself. I'm going to ask you some questions, Mr. O'Farrell and because you have that rag in your mouth and can't speak, I want you to blink for yes and close your eyes for no. Is it true that you like to hurt people, Mr. O'Farrell?

Panic stricken, O'Farrell closed his eyes.

'Now you're lying to me, Mr. O'Farrell. I'll ask you once again. Do you like to hurt people?'

O'Farrell didn't respond.

'Does it make you feel important when you hurt people?'

Beads of sweat bubbled to the surface of his raddled face, O'Farrell closed his eyes. The Oriental leaned forward and whispered in his ear.

'I can see you're not going to answer my questions truthfully, Mr. O'Farrell. That being the case, I advise you to listen very carefully. The terrible pain you are about to experience will seem like a full body massage in a luxury health spa, compared to the pain I shall inflict should you attempt to tell the police about me once I've gone. Please take my word for it, if you do try to expose me, I shall find out. And that will leave me no other choice but to call on you again,' He smiled, his gold incisors gleaming in the half-light. 'And you wouldn't like it if I came back to see you, Mr. O'Farrell.'

The Oriental removed O'Farrell's shoes and socks and placed them underneath the kitchen table. O'Farrell's muffled pleas for mercy filled the room, as he struggled frantically.

'I hate untidiness,' said the Oriental, glancing around the room. 'Shame on you, Mr. O'Farrell, I can see that you're a very untidy man. Didn't your mother ever tell you that cleanliness is next to godliness? How can you live like this? Where is your self-respect?'

The faint glow from a solitary streetlight barely lit up the room, but it was bright enough for the gruesome task in hand. The Oriental pulled a blacksmith's hammer from a holster inside his overcoat. O'Farrell closed his eyes, steeling himself for the ordeal to come. The Oriental's face was expressionless as he began hammering O'Farrell's toes. Seconds later, the man in the flat below banged on the ceiling with a broom handle.

'Stop that banging, you crazy Irish bastard! You're knocking the plaster off my fucking ceiling!' he bellowed.

O'Farrell couldn't hear him. He'd already passed out, the pain was too much for him to bear. By the time the Oriental had finished, O'Farrell's toes had been reduced to piles of mincemeat. The trollop was still lying unconscious in the hallway when they left the flat. One of the men plucked the carrier from her grasp, while another retrieved her dentures from the hallway and shoved them partially into her mouth. She looked like a grotesque gargoyle taking a nap.

'Hey lads, the KFC's still warm,' he said, holding the carrier aloft. 'There's no point in letting it go to waste. I'm bloody starving and I can't see those two being up for a KFC when they come to.'

As the four men descended the stairs, the irate neighbour charged past them clutching a claw-hammer. He threw himself at O'Farrell's door, took it clean off the hinges and dashed inside.

'It won't do you any fucking good hiding in the dark, you Irish bastard!' he bellowed.

O'Farrell was still unconscious when the ambulance took him away. The following day it was big news on national television and awarded front page status in the national press. One London tabloid ran with the headline *'Screw gets hammered!'* while another took an ethnic approach *'Here toe-day and gone, begorrah!'* The surgeon who operated on O'Farrell was quoted as saying *'Mr. O'Farrell will be confined to a wheelchair for a long time.'* And a spokesperson for the police said *'Mr. O'Farrell and a neighbour, who wish to remain anonymous, have been unable to shed any light on the identity of the four men who are responsible for this heinous crime. However, the public can rest assured that we shall continue with our investigation until these evil men are apprehended and put behind bars.'*

Munro mentioned it to Quigley. 'Please don't take this the wrong way, Quigley. Did you have anything to do with that O'Farrell business?'

Quigley closed the book he was reading and put it to one side. 'Where do you get these crazy ideas from, Munro? A thug like O'Farrell has spent most of his life making enemies. I would lay odds that even his mother detested him. I had nothing to do with it. Yes! I'm delighted that it happened, because he's worthless scum and he came close to killing me.' Quigley reached for his whisky flask. 'It was because of him that I missed my Linda's funeral.' Quigley took a swig. 'And for that, I hope he rots in hell. As far as I'm concerned, he's history, nothing more.' Quigley picked up his book. 'Don't mention O'Farrell to me again, Munro! Do you get my drift?'

Munro nodded.

The Major considered that six weeks should be more than sufficient time for Munro to have finished grieving over his mother, so he asked him if he would like to do a dinner party. The Major also convinced himself that he'd be doing Munro a great service, by giving him something else to focus on besides his mother. Munro said he'd be more than happy to and asked Quigley to assist but he declined.

'No offence, Munro. I just don't like the smell of spicy food. Pie and mash with green liquor or a pot of jellied eels from time to time are the limit of my tastes exotica.'

None of the other lifers were remotely interested in doing anything that would benefit the governor and his wife. Apart from Adam Reznik, who jumped at the chance. Reznik acquired the nickname 'Bogie' because of his obsession with Humphrey Bogart, his alleged alter ego. And Munro wasn't exactly overjoyed at the prospect of being cooped up for several hours in a confined space listening to someone with a strong Polish accent who looked remarkably like Albert Einstein, giving his crazy take on dialogue from Bogart movies. When Reznik volunteered for duty it was in true Bogart style.

'There's no need to do a thing, Munro? Nothing at all. You could whistle, if you want. You can whistle, can't you, Munro? You just pucker up your lips and make a wheeeee noise.'

Come the big day, George Challis and Henry Jessop were the officers assigned to watch over the proceedings. After four hours of intense activity in the kitchen, Kingswood prison smelled like a curry-house in Bradford. Curry worshipping lifers and screws alike, drooled in blissful torment as the exotic aroma of Indian food drifted through the prison. Everything was going according to plan until Reznik served the first course. His lips began twitching Bogie-style, as he approached the Major's wife. *'Of all the pubs, in all the towns, in all the world. Why the bloody hell has she come into mine?'*

The Major's wife stared at him dumbstruck.

Reznik smiled politely, placed the dish in front of her and left the room.

'That foreign chap, he isn't right in the head, Bernard. I hope he's not going to do anything violent,' she whispered, staring wide-eyed at her husband.

'Have no fear, Felicity. Officers Challis and Jessop are outside keeping a watchful eye on things. Reznik talks in Humphrey Bogart movie dialogue all the time. He drives everyone insane. No one will share a cell with him.'

'Whom did he kill to end up in here?'

The Major couldn't answer. His mouth was full of food.

'Whom did Reznik kill, Bernard?' she demanded, impatiently.

'He killed his wife, my dear. He throttled her with his bare hands.'

The Major greedily shovelled a large spoonful of food into his mouth. 'This is wonderful Felicity! Simply wonderful!' he enthused, smacking his lips.

'He throttled her with his bare hands! Oh, my God!' she gasped, placing her hand over her mouth. 'Why, for heaven's sake?'

'Reznik was watching a Humphrey Bogart movie on television. I believe it was Treasure of the Sierra Madre. Well that's what he told the police. She arrived home from the bingo hall and switched channels without consulting him. She wanted to watch the final of one of those dreadful talent shows! Reznik jumped out of his chair, seized her by the throat and throttled her. It said in the report that he didn't call the police until he'd finished watching the movie. Interesting, what?'

'Good Lord! How on earth can a man throttle his wife over something so trivial? He's definitely not right in the head, Bernard.' she exclaimed, looking terribly concerned for her own safety. 'Just keep the crazy little bugger away from me.'

Her concerns evaporated the moment she tasted her starter. 'Hmmm. I agree darling, this is simply wonderful! Simply divine! It just melts in the mouth!'

Challis and Jessop were wolfing down food when Reznik re-entered the kitchen.

'Reznik! Cut out the bloody Bogart lingo when you're serving them! Especially Mrs. Morris,' said Munro, wagging a cautionary finger.

Reznik stared at him and smiled, his lips twitching like his screen idol. *'Anton, I think this is the start of us becoming really great mates.'*

Jessop handed Reznik an empty plate. 'That was truly amazing, Munro! The best curry I've ever had! Don't you think so, Challis?'

'It's OK, I suppose. But it's not as good as the curry sauce I get from the local chippy. My mate Giorgos has got it down to a fine art and his don't pong like this does. Mark my words, what the Greeks don't know about making a proper curry sauce, ain't worth knowing.' He guffawed, propelling fragments of food from his mouth. 'You also have to take into account that Munro's a bit rusty. This is the first batch of grub he's had to rustle up in ages.'

Munro ignored him and spoke to Jessop. 'You're more than welcome, Jessop. I'm grateful for what you did when Quigley was in hospital.' Munro glanced at Challis's mouth. 'Scrape the coriander off your teeth, Challis. I wouldn't like Dierdre to think I'd been feeding you grass.'

When the dinner was over, the Major and his wife rose from the table. A warm, sated glow etched on their faces.

'That was excellent, Munro. Truly excellent! We must do this again in the not too distant future,' he said, turning to his wife. 'You'd like that very much, wouldn't you, my dear?'

'Yes indeed, Bernard. What do you say to that, Mr. Munro?'

'I'd be more than happy to, Mrs. Morris.'

She looked up into Munro's eyes, her expression like that of a caring mother. 'It's such a pity that your life fell apart, Mr. Munro. You have a very unique talent.'

Munro smiled and shrugged his shoulders. 'I didn't kill that boy, Mrs. Morris' he said calmly. 'I want you to know that I'm not a killer.'

Clearly embarrassed by Munro's comment, she glanced at her husband, lowered her head and said nothing.

'Come on now, Munro. This isn't the time or place for that sort of thing, there's a good chap,' said the Major, frowning disapprovingly.

'I'm sorry, sir. I'll make sure it doesn't happen again. I promise.'

As the Major and his wife were leaving, Reznik waved and called after her. '*Here's me looking at you, kiddo!*'

She looked up at her husband and tugged at his arm. 'No, Bernard. That creepy little bugger's definitely not right in the head!'

Despite Jessop and Challis lending a hand to clear everything away, it was long past lights-out by the time they'd finished. Challis escorted Munro back to his cell. Once inside, Munro undressed as quietly as possible so as not to wake up his cellmate. Munro had been in bed for some time when Quigley spoke. 'My God, you reek, Munro,' he groaned.

'Sorry about that, Quigley. Occupational hazard I'm afraid. The dinner went well, by the way. They really enjoyed it.' Munro chuckled. 'Old Reznik scared the crap out of Mrs. Morris. You should have seen her face.'

'I'm glad it all went well for you, Munro. In fact, I'm so delighted I won't be able to sleep,' grunted Quigley, his voice laced with sarcasm. 'Do me a favour. Next time, have a wash before you come back to the cell. My son took me to a Balti house in Birmingham once and you smell just the same.' Quigley sighed as he wrestled with his pillow. 'Why does everything that you lot cook have to pong so much? Give me pie and mash with green liquor any day. That's real food.'

Heads turned and passing cars slowed down as Yvette Munro sashayed from the department store wearing a bright red and very revealing two-piece outfit that looked as though it had been airbrushed onto her body. Turning heads was something that she loved doing, it turned her on, and it didn't matter if the voyeur was male or female. On this occasion she was far too busy admiring her reflection in the shop windows to notice the man shadowing her. He tracked her along the high street and into the multi-storey car park, where together with an elderly woman and her Yorkshire terrier they entered lift. The elderly woman got out on Level 3, leaving Yvette alone with the man. In his mid-thirties, smartly attired, he was quite handsome in a boring, clean-cut kind of way and looked like a Jehovah's Witness. So there was no reason whatsoever for her to feel threatened. When the doors opened with a judder at Level 5, Yvette and the man went their separate ways. Yvette was standing next to her red Mercedes hunting feverishly through her handbag for the car keys, when the same man appeared at her side. He snatched the handbag from her grasp and pushed her to the floor. Her screams echoed through the car park. A man appeared from nowhere, and brought down the thief with a rugby tackle. Yvette's handbag flew into the air, its contents flying everywhere. Heavy blows were exchanged as the two men rolled on the ground, locked in combat. At the first opportunity, the thief jumped to his feet and ran off. Bloodied and out of breath, the rescuer got to his feet. His expensive, but badly torn, Armani suit and the gold Rolex wristwatch told Yvette he had money... lots of it.

'Are you OK? I hope he didn't hurt you!'

'Just a bit shaken,' she said, her voice wavering from shock. 'Just look at the state of your clothes, they're torn to shreds!'

'It doesn't matter, I was taking them to the charity shop tomorrow anyway,' he joked, clearly unconcerned that his Armani suit and shirt were beyond repair.

'Oh dear, you're bleeding too,' gasped Yvette, feigning concern as she mopped his wounded chin with a tissue, just to be near him. Other than Herb, this was the closest contact she'd had with another man in months. Tall, blond and ruggedly handsome, the warm sweet smell of his breath and the body odour emanating from his sweat stained shirt turned her on. Her expectations rose when she saw that he wasn't wearing a wedding ring. Not that it would have made any difference, married or single, male or female, they were all fair game as far as she was concerned and when Yvette Munro wanted something badly enough, she just went out and took it.

'Let me take you for a drink. It'll help to settle your nerves,' he said, picking up the contents of her handbag from the floor of the car park. 'You'd be crazy to drive while you're so badly shaken up.'

'That would be nice,' she said, without hesitation. Yvette had the bit between her teeth and she was determined to fuck him before the day was out.

'I'm staying at The Plaza Hotel. It's only a couple of blocks away. Let's go there. Besides, I need to change my clothes.'

Formal introductions were made on the short walk to the hotel and while he showered and changed, she waited patiently in the lounge bar, fantasizing about what he would be like in bed. Not since Munro had she felt so sexually aroused and she grew quite moist, just thinking about him.

'Sorry to keep you waiting,' he said, with a smile that had her reeling like a star-struck schoolgirl.

'That's OK, Bryan. The good things in life are worth waiting for. That's what my mother used to say.'

'I'm deeply flattered,' he said, with a courteous nod of his head. 'What would you like to drink?'

'A dry Martini would be nice.'

Bryan summoned the waiter and ordered two.

'Are you here on business, Bryan?' she asked, deliberately crossing her legs in the most revealing manner.

'Yes,' he said, running his fingers through his mane of blond hair.

'And what kind of business would that be?'

'I use other people's money to make them lots of money. And I make lots of money in the process,' he said, self-confidence oozing from every pore.

She giggled. 'You're not a counterfeiter are you?'

'I wish,' he joked. 'I'm an independent financial advisor. I make astute investments in the stock market and that kind of thing. It's all pretty boring really.'

Yvette could hear the cash register pinging as she toyed with the emerald pendant hanging around her neck. 'And what advice would you give me?' She dipped forward to adjust the ankle straps on her shoes, revealing a little more cleavage in the process.

'Don't chat with strange men in hotels,' he said, clearly enjoying the view.

'Not even with a chivalrous knight in shining armour, who's just risked all to save a damsel in distress?'

He placed his hand on her knee. 'Especially knights in shining armour.'

Four Martinis later, she could suppress her desire no longer, Yvette's eyes were glazed over and it wasn't from alcohol. She took him by the hand and led him into the lift. 'Which floor?' she purred, confident that he wanted her as much as she wanted him.

'Seventh.'

As he reached over her shoulder to press the button, their lips met. Two hours later, her body glistening with sweat, she rose from the bed, to shower. Bryan joined her and they made love once more. She'd already lost count of the number of times they'd made love that afternoon. It was 7.30pm when she finally got dressed.

'Will I see you again?' she said, as she was about to leave the room.

'That's entirely up to you.' His smile suggested that he wanted to see her again.

'Yes, I'd like that very much. Do you know when that's likely to be?' she said, concerned that it might be weeks away, because of business commitments.

'I'll be back here next week. You have my number, just call me.'

She blew him a kiss and then planted a kiss on the mirror by the door.

'Something to remember me by,' she chirped, pointing at the lipstick imprint.

'Let me walk with you to the car, Yvette.'

'No Bryan. I'll be fine. Besides, you need to rest after all the exercise you've had today,' she said, giggling like a naughty schoolgirl. There was a lively spring in her step when she left. Bryan had proven to be more than the average fuck on the side. She was smitten, big time.

Yvette walked into the penthouse to find Herb with a hang-dog expression etched on his face and nursing a large scotch.

'You'll never believe what happened today!' she squealed, throwing her bag on the sofa.

Herb didn't bother to reply. The look on her face, told him exactly what had happened. He knew that well-fucked look only too well.

'I was mugged in broad daylight! Can you believe it?'

Herb's mood lifted and he felt somewhat guilty for jumping to the conclusion that she'd been fucking someone else. His expression changed to one of concern for her well-being. 'Are you OK baby?' he said, leaping from the chair. 'When did all this happen, baby?'

'Oh, around 1.30 I guess. I'd just left Madame La Salle's and was standing by my car in the multi-storey car park when the mugger pounced on me. Lucky for me, a stranger came to my rescue,' she said, disappearing into the bedroom to change her clothes.

Herb's face assumed the hang-dog look once more. 'So where have you been for the last seven hours?' he said, somewhat peeved.

'Well, I was so shaken up, the man offered to take me for a drink to settle my nerves. He said it would be a bad idea to drive in such a state. And he was right, Herb. I felt so much better afterwards.'

'You were drinking with a complete stranger for *seven* hours?'

'No you fool!' she yelled. 'We talked for a time and then he had to leave for a business appointment. I decided to take a walk around the stores for a while. I thought it would be better if I worked off the alcohol before getting back behind the wheel of my car.'

Yvette emerged from the bedroom and placed her arms around him. 'You've got that jealous teeny-bopper look in your eyes, Herb.'

'No baby. I was just worried. You should have called me.' He raised his voice. 'Why the hell didn't you call me?'

'Fuck this Herb!' she rasped. 'What are you, my probation officer? Do I have to check-in every hour?' Yvette pushed him away and stormed off.

'Sorry baby! Please forgive me!' he begged, running after her. 'If you knew how worried I was you'd understand. I thought you'd been involved in a car crash. I was just about to call the police!' he said, lying through his teeth.

She stopped in her tracks.

'Ok! But don't ever question my movements again! If you do Herb, I'm out of here! Is that understood? What I do when I'm not in this apartment is my business. Not yours. Don't ever come this irritating, third degree shit with me again! If you do, you're fucking history!'

Herb took her in his arms. His eyes were fearful and his hands trembled.

'Sure baby, sure. Anything you say. It won't happen again. I promise,' he whispered meekly. 'I was worried out of my mind, that's all.'

Yvette smiled triumphantly.

'Let's go out and eat. I could eat a horse!'

A shadow fell over him. She was always hungry after sex and she'd just confirmed his original assumption that she'd been fucking someone else. For a split second, he thought about confronting her then decided not to go there. A wise move, it was safer not to argue the toss with Yvette when she was in such a belligerent frame of mind.

'Ok, baby. Whatever you want, I want.' He kissed her forehead.

She gave him a quick peck on the cheek and dashed into the bedroom.

'I've changed my mind about these jeans. They're the wrong colour. It'll only take a moment to change them!' she yelled. 'We've missed the last sitting at Stefano's. So let's go to the Golden Pagoda, their food is always good and they never close till the last customer leaves.'

Herb poured himself a consolatory triple scotch. Once again she'd beaten him up emotionally and shoved his self-esteem through the meat grinder. He stared in the mirror and drank a toast to his sorry reflection. What the hell! Yvette was worth the humiliation. Minutes later, she emerged from the bedroom wearing a short red leather jacket, black t-shirt, black skin-tight jeans and ultra-high red stilettos. No doubt about it, she'd be turning heads in the restaurant.

'The man who chased off the mugger, I've a feeling he could be financially beneficial,' she chirped.

5

At precisely 9.15pm, a taxi pulled up at the entrance of the Belle Vale estate. Charlotte Blake stepped out, popped her head through the window and spoke to the Asian driver. 'Don't forget. Pick me up here, at 11.30pm. Please don't be late.'

'No problem. I'm sorry I can't take you all the way in there. The buses only come out this way in the daytime. It's not worth me taking the risk.' The driver shrugged his shoulders apologetically. 'They've got ten-year-old kids in there that will steal the hub caps from your car while it's moving.'

'I understand. Don't look so worried, I'm not carrying anything valuable.'

'It's not your valuables you should be worrying about,' said the driver, as the taxi pulled away in a cloud of exhaust fumes.

Before her sprawled the derelict wasteland of the sink-estate, obscene and racist graffiti adorned the walls and most of the accommodation was either boarded up or burned-out. Blake was venturing into uncharted territory and felt extremely nervous. Only one thing was certain, her upper-middle class upbringing had not prepared her for this. She had however, gone to great lengths to dress for the occasion. She hadn't washed her hair for three days and with a few strategically placed transfer tattoos on her neck and the back of her hands, heavy make-up, cheap jewellery, a shabby hooded jacket, torn jeans and battered trainers she looked like one of the locals. She kept to the middle of the road, hoping to avoid the packs of stray dogs that scavenged for scraps amid the countless mounds of rotting household waste that littered the entrance of every tenement block. By the time she reached the Belle Vale shopping precinct she hadn't encountered a soul. At the far end of the precinct, looking more like a concrete pillbox than a public house, stood the Ring O Bells, every window was covered with sheets of corrugated tin and only three letters glowed on the flickering neon sign, ...*ell*. Blake hoped this wasn't a portent of what lay ahead. Thick blue clouds of cigarette smoke rushed passed her as she heaved open the heavy reinforced doors and shards of broken glass snapped and crunched under her feet as she made her way inside. The handful of lowlifes loitering at the far end of the bar paid little heed as Blake waited to be served. They were all listening intently to a burly foul-mouthed girl with pink hair. She was reeling off a crude joke, about a fat man who had a tiny cock and gigantic testicles. The moment she delivered the punchline, the lowlifes howled like hyenas and pointed at the circus-fat landlord who was slouching behind the bar. He wasn't amused. Fortunately for him, he spotted Blake and seized his chance to escape further ridicule. He waddled towards her smirking like a monitor lizard on heat, reached across the bar and took hold of her hand. The touch of his scaly, reptilian skin made her flesh crawl.

'I hope you're not just here for a drink, darling?' he slurred, looking her up and down with his rheumy, bulbous eyes.

The fetid stench of cheap whisky and tobacco on his breath turned her stomach and one glance at the glasses on the shelf persuaded her it would be much safer to drink from the bottle.

'A Bacardi Breezer mate and don't bother with a glass,' she said, in the best sink-estate brogue she could muster. The fat man didn't notice anything strange about her manner of speaking, so she relaxed a little.

She took her drink and sat in the corner next to the jukebox, her eyes fixed on a girl with pink hair as she reeled off one crude joke after another. Blake had a gut feeling she was looking at Ashley Roper. Everything about her fitted the description Munro had given her.

'I'll be back in a minute, lads. Got to go and squeeze me lemon!' the joke teller cackled before heading for the toilet.

'I'll come with you and you can squeeze mine!' howled one of the lowlifes.

The joke teller stopped in her tracks and walked slowly towards him. His fellow lowlifes watched in petrified silence.

'What did you just say?'

'Sorry Ashley.' The colour drained from his face as he backed away. 'It was only a joke. I didn't mean anything by it. Honest, I'm really sorry.'

'Don't be here, when I get back from the bog!' She clamped her hand around his face and squeezed. 'If you are still here, I'm gonna dance all over your stupid mug.'

Blake followed her into the toilet and immediately wished she hadn't, the place was like an open sewer, discarded syringes and scraps of aluminium foil littered the floor along with other unpleasant lowlife by-products. A skinny teenage girl hunched over a filthy wash basin was throwing her guts up. The stench of vomit took Blake's breath away. The joke teller was already inside one of the cubicles. She was peeing like a racehorse.

'You'd better clean the puke out of that basin when you're finished, Mandy. If you don't, I'll shove your scrawny anorexic face in it, you dirty little cow!' she roared. Moments later, she emerged without flushing the toilet, wiping her hands on the sleeve of her jacket. 'There's never any bog paper in this place when you need it!'

Blake took a handful of tissue paper from her bag and tossed it to her.

'Hey, ain't you Ashley Roper, the girlfriend of that lad what was stabbed by that cook what used to be on the telly?' she said, trying her best to appear impressed.

'Who wants to know!' she lisped, vigorously mopping her hands. Blake's attention was drawn to the gap in her teeth, a souvenir from her confrontation with Munro.

'Gemma McCardle's my name,' said Blake. 'When I saw you at the bar, I thought I recognized you from the photo what was in the paper a while back. You look just like her. Sorry for bothering you. I didn't mean any harm.' Blake turned to leave.

She grabbed hold of Blake's arm and pulled her back. 'You're from one of those scummy, shit-stirring newspapers, ain't ya? You've probably got a tape recorder whirring away under that jacket!' She began to frisk her.

'Christ! I only asked for your name! There's no need for all this shit. I'm out of here!' Blake wrenched her arm free and headed for the exit, much relieved that her last minute decision not to wear a recording device had proven to be an inspired one.

'What if it was me in the paper and I am Ashley Roper? What the fuck's it got to do with you?'

'Ha! I knew it was you,' said Blake, clapping her hands together. 'I never forget a face!'

Roper pulled a gun from inside her jacket. 'Ok, it *was* me in the paper! What of it?'

'Jesus! There's no need for the gun! I was just curious, that's all,' croaked Blake.

They stood facing each other. It was like a one-sided shoot-out from a western, Roper the hired gun and Blake the helpless, unarmed storekeeper. Suddenly, the door burst open and a girl rushed in.

'Fuck off!' screamed Roper, waving the gun at her. The girl fled. Roper pointed the gun at Blake's face and inched towards her, a cigarette dangling from her lips. If there was one place on earth where Blake would have chosen not to die, it was here in this vile cesspool, she wanted to close her eyes but couldn't. Roper's eyes were cold and unfeeling as she squeezed the trigger. There followed, a loud click.

'Haaa! Haaa! I had you going there!' she roared, lighting her cigarette from the flame coming out of the barrel. 'You nearly shit yourself there, girl. These lighters are magic! They look just like the real thing.'

Blake stood paralysed, she could see Roper's lips moving but the sound had been switched off. Still laughing, Roper left the toilet and returned to the bar. The girl that burst in earlier reappeared and dashed towards the sink, spewing violently over the floor before she could reach it. Blake was now seriously questioning her decision to come to this godforsaken place, she pictured herself running through the empty streets of Belle Vale to meet the awaiting taxi. Then she thought of Munro and the reason she had come here. She glanced at her watch, time was running out. You can do this Charlotte, she told herself. Just one final roll of the dice is all you need. Blake walked up to the bar. 'Put one in for Ashley,' she said to the circus-fat landlord.

'If you hang around till all the punters have gone. I'll be happy to put one in for you, sweetheart,' he slurred, wiping the sweat from his brow with the back of his hand.

His grubby innuendo made her flesh crawl. Blake took her drink, sat by the jukebox and waited. It didn't take long for Roper to join her, complimentary drink in hand and a smug grin on her face.

'Cheers, girl,' she said, raising the glass. 'I thought you'd have gone by now. Know what I mean.' She nudged Blake with her elbow and winked. 'I got the feeling you didn't much like the friendly little get-together we had in the bog,' she chuckled.

'No, it was my fault. I should mind my own bloody business,' said Blake, pulling a face. 'I've always been too nosey for me own good!'

'That's it, girl! Ain't no point in getting your knickers in a twist over something like that.' Roper shook her hand. 'No hard feelings, huh?'

'No hard feelings,' said Blake, making a mental note to soak her hand in disinfectant at the first opportunity. 'Would you like another drink?'

'Is Idi Amin a darkie?' cackled Roper. 'Bring it on, girl. Bring it on!'

Blake continued to ply Roper with drinks until she was well on the way to being pie-eyed. 'It must have been terrible for you. I mean, seeing your boyfriend attacked and stabbed like that. Right in front of your eyes! Jesus! You must have been in a right state!' said Blake, feigning concern.

'Sort of,' said Roper, with an indifferent shrug of her shoulders. 'That bastard, Munro, got what he deserved and that's all that matters!' She drained her glass and stared at Blake. 'How come I ain't seen you in here, until now?

'I live in Broughton. Me boyfriend sells hard core porn movies and all that shit. He asked me to pick up some money from a geezer in Belle Vale.' Blake crossed her fingers, hoping that Roper wouldn't ask where he lived.

Roper smiled. 'I'm partial to a bit of hard core, myself.' She nudged Blake's arm. 'Mind you, I'd rather be doing it, than watching it.' She nudged Blake again. 'But I wouldn't say no, if you dropped a couple off, when you're round this way again.'

'Sure. No problem,' said Blake, breathing a sigh of relief.

'Toss that drink down your neck, girl.' Roper pointed at the half empty bottle.

'I can't drink much,' said Blake, thinking on her feet. 'I shouldn't really be having this. I've got a liver condition... hepatitis. It runs in me family.'

'That's a shame, girl. One crying shame, if ever there was one.' Roper placed a consolatory arm around Blake's shoulder. 'Listen, girl. We're all going back to my place later, for a few laughs and a bit of the old legs at a quarter to three. Why don't you come? I mean, like there ain't nothing stopping you from having a fuck, is there? Like, you ain't got the clap as well as that hepawotsits thing you just told me about?'

'No! I've got to see me boyfriend later. That's all. He's picking me up at the front entrance.' Blake smiled apologetically.

'That's a pity, because one of the lads has been giving you the eye, girl. That's him there, the tall, gangly one with the swastika tattoo on his neck. He looks like one of them fucking stick insects what David Attenborough shows you on the telly.' Roper leaned across to whisper in Blake's ear. 'He ain't no film star, but he's got a massive cock!' she howled, loose phlegm rattling in the back of her throat.

Blake tried her best to look anxious. 'Sorry Ashley, if I'm late tonight, he'll hammer me. He can be a right nasty bastard when the mood takes him.'

'Send him to see me. I'll sort the porn dealing fucker out!' slurred Roper. 'Ooops! Got to go for a piss! Come and keep me company, girl. What with all them drinks you been pouring down me neck, I could be in there for hours!' she squealed, struggling to stand upright.

'Can I get you a drink, Ashley?' yelled one of the lowlifes, currying favour.

'Get your tongue out of my arse! ' she barked, giving him the finger.

Once inside the toilet she staggered into a cubicle, and slammed the door shut.

'Aaah! I nearly didn't make it girl!' she gasped, chuckling with relief. 'This place stinks of puke. I'll batter that little junkie's face in, when I see her!'

It was nearing Blake's 11.30pm rendezvous with the taxi, so she decided to go for broke.

'Listen Ashley, I'll have to leave and meet me boyfriend and if I don't go now, I'll have a couple of black-eyes and a fat lip next time you see me. Something's been bothering me and I hope you won't take it the wrong way. It's just me being a nosey cow again, I guess. Somebody told me a while back that you and Danny Gordon tried to rob that cook what was on the telly. Just tell me one thing. Is there any truth in that or is it just a load of bollocks?'

Roper didn't reply.

'Come on, you can tell me, Ashley. I wouldn't breathe a word to anyone,'

A long silence ensued.

'You really *are* a nosey cow, ain't ya! And what's it to you if we did try to rob him?' hiccupped Roper, as she lit a cigarette.

'Nothing, I just like the idea that you stitched him up, that's all!' said Blake, injecting venom into her voice. 'Six Pakis attacked my dad one night and robbed him. They worked him over so bad, he ended up in a wheelchair!'

'That's typical of those bastards!' snarled Roper.

Another long silence followed interrupted only by Roper's hiccups.

'Yeah, I reckon it can't do any 'arm telling you, girl. You're all right you are. Yeah, me and that useless twat, Danny tried to rob him,' she confided. 'But Danny let him get the better of him and he fell on his own knife! Next thing I know, Danny's lying on the floor, dead.' Roper cleared her throat. 'So I made sure that Munro got his comeuppance!'

Blake was seized by an overwhelming sense of outrage, tears welled in her eyes. Munro's pleas of innocence had finally been confirmed.

'I got that fucker sent down for fifteen years, girl!' Roper crowed, from behind the cubicle door. 'Who's a clever girl then?'

There was no answer. Blake was long gone.

Roper emerged from the toilet and walked into the bar. Blake was nowhere to be seen. 'Where's Gemma?' she said to the lowlifes.

The gangly one with the swastika tattoo on his neck shrugged his shoulders.

'She left about five minutes ago,' said the circus-fat landlord. 'She didn't even bother to kiss me goodbye.'

Roper let out a scream, picked up a chair and threw it against the wall.

'Get her! Get that cow and bring her back here!'

The lowlifes' response was immediate, they poured outside, split themselves into groups of three and set off in different directions.

'Nicked something of yours, did she?' said the landlord, with a smirk.

'Mind your own fucking business, Degsy. And if you don't wipe that stupid smirk off your ugly fat face I'll burn you and this smelly shit hole to the ground.'

Tears streaming, heart pounding, gasping for breath, Blake ran through the deserted streets until she reached the gateway to the estate. The taxi wasn't there and her heart sank. Behind her in the distance she could hear a group of youths calling to each other from different parts of the estate, the agitated tone of their voices suggested that they were searching for something. As the minutes passed by the voices drew closer. Blake's heart leapt into her mouth when she realized they were searching for her, so she hid in the shadows of the gateway wall. Moments later they were in hearing distance, she recognized three of the lowlifes from the bar, their conversation was heated and they were throwing their arms about in the way people do when they're making excuses.

'Psycho will kill us if we don't find that bitch. Keep looking. You two split up and I'll wait here, just in case she hasn't got this far.'

Muttering angrily under his breath, the remaining lowlife sauntered towards the gateway entrance and lit a cigarette. He was so close, Blake could hear him blow the cigarette smoke from his mouth and her heart was pounding so hard she feared it would betray her presence. She'd never experienced fear like this and her stomach was churning so much, she wanted to throw up. She clasped her hand over her mouth and waited, holding her breath. Moments later, the lowlife flicked his cigarette butt into the air and she watched it bounce off the tarmac in an explosion of tiny sparks. Her hopes rose when she heard the faint sound of a diesel powered car engine chugging in the distance. The lowlife stepped into the road and peered at approaching headlights. Arms spread-eagled, Blake pressed against the wall hoping he wouldn't see her. The lowlife turned and walked back into the estate. As the taxi pulled up, Blake dashed from the shadows, climbed in the back and slammed the door.

'For God's sake, drive!'

The lowlife spotted her, turned and gave chase.

The driver jammed his foot on the accelerator and the taxi screeched away in a cloud of burning rubber. The lowlife's futile pursuit lasted for sixty metres or so, then exhaustion kicked in and he collapsed at the side of the road.

The driver looked at her through the rear-view mirror. 'Sorry I'm a few minutes late, Miss.'

Blake gagged, clasped a hand over her mouth, wound down the window and was violently sick. She retched until there was nothing left then wiped her mouth with the sleeve of the jacket.

'Please, lady. Don't be sick in my taxi.'

'It's alright, driver. I haven't been sick *inside* the taxi. But I'm afraid you'll have to jet-spray the bodywork. I'll give you some money to cover that.' She sat back in the seat. 'I'll be fine, now. Thanks for coming back for me. God knows what would have become of me if you'd left it any later. You've just saved me from making what could have been the biggest mistake of my life.'

'Your boyfriend is very angry.'

'Good heavens, no! He's not my boyfriend. I wouldn't be seen dead with an animal like that.'

'Are you sure you're OK, lady?' He was struggling to make sense of what she was saying.

'Thanks for your concern, driver. There's nothing wrong with me that a long hot shower won't cure and as soon as I've burned these dreadful clothes, everything will be just fine.'

When the lowlifes returned to the Ring O Bells, Roper was sat at the bar, her face like thunder. She leapt from the stool and grabbed one of them by the throat.

'Don't tell me you couldn't find her?' She grabbed a handful of his shirt and drew him closer. 'You're a waste of space. Every last fucking one of you! That's what happens when you send a piddling little boy to do a man's job!'

She grabbed his balls with her free hand, squeezing so hard he whined in pain, gasping for breath. When she released her hold he fell to his knees. The others stood like statues, too terrified to move. A girl on the far side of the room burst out laughing. It was Mandy, the girl who had been sick in the toilet. Roper stormed across the room and punched her in the face so hard, the sound of her nose breaking could be heard on the far side of the room.

'That's for stinking out the shithouse, you scabby little junkie!'

Mandy picked herself up off the floor, blood streaming from her nose. Her boyfriend sat motionless, too scared to help. Roper, walked across the room towards the exit, when she reached the door she stopped and turned, eyeing everyone in turn.

'Boo!' she yelled, and was gone.

The following morning, Blake went straight to the Major's office.

'You did what?' he roared, rolling his eyes to the heavens. 'Have you taken leave of your senses, Miss Blake? You might have been killed or even *worse*!' The expression on his face indicated that by *worse* he meant a brutal sexual assault. 'You're employed by the prison services as a liaison officer, not as a bloody assistant to Miss Jane Marple! If things had gone seriously wrong, I'd have been left with a lot of sticky egg on my face and my chances of retiring with a full pension would have been well and truly scuppered!'

'I've had verification of Munro's innocence sir! Surely that must mean something to you!'

'You haven't got a thing, Miss Blake. It's your word against hers. This doesn't change anything! Not one damn thing! Why can't you get that into your head?'

'How in God's name do you expect me to forget that an innocent man is rotting away in jail for a crime he didn't commit?' she said, raising her voice. 'We must do something! No! *You* must do something! It's *your* responsibility.'

'Don't take that tone with me, Miss Blake. I don't need you to remind me of my responsibilities. I'm simply trying to impress upon you that unless that dreadful Roper woman volunteers to tell the truth, we've got nothing in the eyes of the law. Not a damn thing!' He picked up a case file from the top of his desk. 'So if

102

you'll excuse me, Miss Blake, I have a lot of work to do. Even if, *you* don't,' he barked. '*Do not* raise this business again unless you have concrete proof.'

Blake said nothing and left the room, this was not what she had hoped for and she dreaded giving Munro the bad news. Her phone was ringing as she opened the door to her office, it was Jack Dobson, a prisoner called Nathaniel Kent had attempted suicide yet again and Dobson thought it would be a good idea if Blake were to spend some time with him, just to settle him down. When she arrived at the sick bay, Challis was sitting outside.

'Are you here because of Nathaniel Kent?' she asked, looking surprised.

'Kamikaze Kent? Not me, Miss. I'm here because of Quigley,' said Challis. 'Quigley collapsed a couple of hours ago!'

'Is he going to be OK?' she asked, genuinely concerned.

'Who? Kamikaze Kent?' Challis had an obtuse look etched on his face.

'No Challis, Cedric Quigley. Is he going to be OK?'

'Don't know, Miss. They're doing what they can for him now. According to Munro, he's been suffering with really bad headaches for some time now. Not sleeping and tossing painkillers down his neck, like they were Smarties.'

Doris the nurse stepped into the corridor and spoke to Challis.

'Tell Munro, that thanks to his speedy initiative, Quigley's going to be alright. We've sent him to the city hospital for a more thorough examination.'

Challis nodded and got to his feet. Blake seized the opportunity.

'Officer Challis, I'd like a word in private with Munro. Please escort him to my office and wait for me there. I'll be along as soon as I've attended to Nathaniel Kent.'

'Sure, Miss. Anything you say, Miss,' said Challis, grinning lecherously. 'Oh, by the way Miss, perhaps you could explain to me why a bloke like Kamikaze always chooses to drown himself in the toilet bowl?' Challis chuckled. 'That's how he got his nickname, Miss. He sticks his head down the Khazi. Get it?'

'Yes, Challis. I do get it. I'm glad you find Kent's mental disorder so entertaining.'

After attending to the needs of Kamikaze Kent, she returned to her office. Munro and Challis were waiting outside. She ushered Munro into the office and after closing the blinds, she told him about her encounter with Ashley Roper in The Ring O Bells pub and the governor's negative response.

'I had to get to the truth, Munro,' she whispered, apologetically. 'Please, don't think badly of me.'

Munro smiled and shook his head.

'How could I think badly of you? You risked your life.' He took a deep breath and sighed. 'I'm glad you found out the truth. That means a lot to me, but if anything bad had happened to you I couldn't have lived with myself,' he said, lowering his voice to a whisper. 'But I'm afraid all your efforts have been in vain. It's hopeless. I'll never get out of this place without doing the time. I'm a mandatory lifer and the sooner I accept that the better. Isn't that what everybody keeps telling me to do?'

'Don't talk like that Munro!' snapped Blake, leaping out of the chair. She approached him and took hold of his hands.

'You mustn't give up hope, Munro.'

Their faces were so close they could feel the warmth from each other's breath. Blake's hands started to tremble.

'For someone, who told me she treats every prisoner the same as the next. You certainly went out of your way, for me,' said Munro, a mischievous twinkle in his eyes.

'I suppose I had that coming,' she said, shaking her head. 'And there was I thinking that you never listened to a single word I said.'

'The sound of your voice is with me every minute of the day. Just promise me you won't take any more unnecessary risks.'

'I promise,' she whispered, gazing into his eyes. 'And I'll do everything I can to help you, Munro.'

Munro lowered his head until their lips met. No longer trembling, she melted in his arms. They were as one, and the feelings they'd suppressed from the moment they first met, finally erupted in one glorious moment. This was a new experience for Munro. He'd never kissed a woman in such a way before and never with so much feeling. Yes, he wanted to make love to her, but this was much more than a physical attraction. This was something special, something very special.

'This is madness,' he whispered, looking into her eyes.

'I know. Oh, dear God, I know,' she sighed.

Yvette was now seeing Bryan on a regular basis at The Plaza Hotel and although she was still living with Herb their sex life was non-existent. Herb lived in the hope that her new sex toy would soon be consigned to the scrapheap.

'No chance, Yvette. I can't let you.' said Bryan, firmly.

'I know it's a lot of money baby. But I want to.' Yvette slid her hand down his muscled torso and took hold of his erect penis. 'Let's go for number four darling. Four is my lucky number.'

Yvette wrapped her legs around him, digging her nails into his back. She moaned with wanton abandon as he entered her, lunging again and again until their bodies were moist with sweat. They climaxed together, she crying out and gasping for breath. 'Again,' she giggled, half joking.

'Just give me two minutes,' said Bryan, with a self-satisfied smile.

'I don't want this to end,' she said, throwing her arms around his neck. 'I want to stay here, with you, forever!'

They lay in silence, eyes closed, wrapped in each other's arms. It was some time before Bryan spoke. 'Remind me how much you made on that little deal I put through for you?'

'Thirty five thousand pounds, baby.' She tweaked his nipple. 'And I adore you for being so clever.'

'Just imagine what you would have made, if you'd invested more than five thousand pounds.'

He kissed the tip of her chin working his way down to her navel.

'Hmmm. I know baby, that's exactly why I want to be in on your next deal.'

'Well that's not going to happen, Yvette. I don't want you to risk your money.' Bryan's tone was adamant.

'But you told me there wasn't a risk.' She pulled a face like a little girl who can't get her own way. 'I'm beginning to think you don't want me to make a lot of money.'

'Don't be like that, Yvette,' he said kissing the nape of her neck. 'Of course I want you to make lots of money.' He rose from the bed and took a bottle of water from the fridge. 'There isn't a risk. I don't take risks. I leave the risk taking to the mugs who toss their wages away at the bookies every Saturday. I just don't feel comfortable seeing you invest such a huge sum of money.' He stooped to kiss her tenderly on the lips. 'Is that so wrong of me?'

Yvette wasn't interested in how Bryan felt, and being told that she couldn't have something only made her want it more.

'Please, let me in on it!'

'No honey. I'd feel better if you didn't. But one thing's for sure, this is the *big one* and it will be my last. I'm putting every penny I have into it. I'm going to retire. I'm getting out while I'm young, healthy and active enough to enjoy the millions I'm going to make. I've been doing this shit for too long, and I'm bored with it.' He rolled onto his back, placed his hands behind his head, stared at the ceiling and smiled the smile of a man in control of his destiny.

'I've already lined up a villa in Monaco and an apartment at The Dakota Building in New York.'

'Isn't that where John Lennon lived?' she said, eyes wide.

'That's the one,' said Bryan, nodding proudly.

'What about me? Do I not feature in any of this?' Yvette sat upright, looking somewhat angry and shell-shocked.

'What about you, honey? I thought all this was just a bit of fun on the side for you. I thought you were happy with the loose arrangement you had going with Herb.'

'Fuck Herb! I haven't let that fat pig touch me since I met you!' She threw her head back on the pillow, a look of dismay etched on her face. 'Jesus! This can't be happening to me! Can't you see I want to be with *you* Bryan… only *you*.'

'Honey, I'm sorry. I never realized you felt that way. Hey. As soon as I get set up, you can come and spend a few weeks with me. What do you say?'

'I don't want to be your occasional fuck!' she screamed. 'I just want to be with you! What part of that do you not understand?' Yvette's world was crumbling before her eyes, she lit a cheroot. Bryan removed the cheroot from her hand, stubbed it out and took her in his arms.

'Marriage is a trip I don't intend to take, honey. It's not on the list of places I plan to visit.'

'Me neither, Bryan,' she said softly, shaking her head. 'I don't want your hand in marriage,' she sighed, kissing his neck. 'I just want you, baby. *You*, that's all.'

'From the first moment I saw you screaming your head off in that multi-storey car park, I could see you were different, Yvette.' He kissed her nose. 'I was scared that if I came on too strong, you'd pack your bags and walk away.'

'Then, let's just see how it works out. Just you and me, having a great time, living together with no strings attached.' She snuggled up to him. 'The minute it turns sour we'll go our separate ways.'

'Sounds good to me, honey,' he whispered, kissing her breasts. 'Let's celebrate and go for number five. That's *my* lucky number.'

A mischievous smile on her face, Yvette bit his shoulder, pushed him onto his back and straddled him. As she deftly lowered herself onto his erect penis, she emitted a tiny squeal of pleasure. She leaned forward, allowing her breasts to gently brush his chest and rode him slowly and expertly, pulling out every trick she knew, until she sensed he was nearing a climax. Then she stopped.

'Promise I can invest my money before I continue,' she teased, holding him to ransom.

'God, you're one determined bitch of a woman,' he moaned. 'OK! OK! You can come in on the deal. Now can we finish making love?' He seized her by the arms and rolled her onto her back.

'That's all I wanted to hear, baby,' she whispered, a self-satisfied twinkle in her eyes. 'Now take me, baby! I'm all yours for the taking!'

6

When Quigley was released from hospital, he was a shadow of his former self. 'I'm falling to pieces, Munro,' he joked, putting on a brave face.

'Nonsense, Quigley. You'll be back to your old self, in no time.' Munro tried hard not to look shocked.

'No, Munro. I don't think so.' He tapped the side of his head. 'There's something not right in here.'

'You're imagining things, Quigley. Surely they'd have told you if something was seriously wrong?'

Quigley shrugged and gave him a cynical look. 'Thanks, Munro. Thanks for giving me the kiss of life. Mind you, it's all very embarrassing to discover that my cell-mate took advantage of my unconscious state and kissed me for minutes on end,' he said, with a cheeky smile and for a fleeting moment he looked like his old self.

'No problem, Quigley. I'd have done it sooner, if I'd known you were such a great kisser.' Munro winked and blew him a kiss.

Quigley threw a book at him.

'When you get a minute, I need to talk to you, Quigley. Something's been driving me crazy.' Munro's expression was deadly serious.

'Fire away, Munro. I'm all ears as the elephant said to the giraffe.' Quigley sat on the edge of his bed.

'Do you believe in love at first sight, Quigley?'

Quigley face broke into a smile. 'Yes, I do. I knew I wanted to marry my Elsie the minute I laid eyes on her. Sixteen she was, selling fruit and vegetables from her old man's stall. I walked past that stall so many times, her old man thought I was planning to rob him.' Quigley chuckled at the memory. 'It took me weeks to pluck up the courage to ask her out and I was terrified she'd say no. We went to the Empire cinema on our first date. I was so nervous I can't even remember the film that was on. We were married six weeks later and spent our honeymoon in Brighton.' Quigley smiled. 'Three days in a tiny bed and breakfast tucked away up a side street. It was all we could afford. The best three days I've ever had in my life.' He looked at Munro. 'Why do you ask?'

'Well it's happened to me. I've fallen in love.'

'I presume we're talking about Miss Blake,' said Quigley, smiling. 'It couldn't be anyone else really, because Doris in sick bay's old enough to be your mum.' Quigley held up his hand in apology. 'Sorry, I didn't mean to be disrespectful about your late mum, you know what I mean.'

'That's ok. No offence taken. Yes, it is Charlotte that I want to talk to you about. We've fallen in love, Quigley. It just happened.'

'*It* just happened!' Quigley looked shocked. 'When did *it* just happen?'

'After you'd been dispatched to hospital, she called me to her office. She told me how she had gone undercover to try and get the truth out of Ashley Roper.

'What truth, Munro?'

'That it was Roper and Danny Gordon who attacked me with a knife and that she had lied in court.'

'And did she succeed?'

'Yes, she did.' Munro rolled his eyes. 'Not that it will do me any good.'

'How come?'

'There were no witnesses.' Munro sighed and shook his head in frustration. 'That's not what I want to talk about, Quigley. I want to talk about Charlotte.'

'Forgive me, Munro. This is all a tad confusing. Please carry on. You were saying... *it just happened.*'

'Yes. We talked for a time, about a number of things and then it happened.'

'Surely you didn't make love to that girl in her office?'

'Christ, Quigley!' Munro furrowed his brow. 'What do you take me for? We kissed, that's all.'

Quigley held up his hands and smiled apologetically.

'I fell for Charlotte the first time I saw her and I realize now, why I was so hostile to her. The most beautiful creature I'd ever laid eyes on was sitting in front of me and I knew she was out of my reach. I felt like the poor orphan kid on Christmas Eve, gazing longingly through the shop window at all the toys I could never have. And no matter how hard I tried, I couldn't stop the bitterness welling up inside me.' Munro took a sharp intake of breath. 'I just couldn't stop myself, Quigley. I wanted to hurt her. I wanted her to feel as miserable as I did.' He paused for a moment before continuing. 'Believe me, Quigley, this is different. I've never felt like this about any woman. This isn't a here today, gone tomorrow sexual attraction thing. I love her, Quigley. She's in my thoughts every minute of the day.' Tears welled in Munro's eyes. 'I'm scared, Quigley. I don't know what to do.'

'Look, please don't take this the wrong way, son.' Quigley hesitated, thinking carefully about what he was about to say. 'Let's face it. You've haven't exactly got a great track record when it comes to women, Munro. Are you absolutely sure it's not just because you're banged up in here and she's the only woman in the place that's easy on the eye?'

'I'm sure Quigley and so is she. I've never been so sure about anything in my life.'

'In that case, there's only one thing you can do. You run with it and see where it takes you. I'll say this for that girl, Munro. If she went alone to Belle Vale and wangled the truth out of that Roper girl, she's got some bottle. That took a lot of nerve and it also says a lot about what she thinks of you.' Quigley shook his head, a wry smile stretched across his face. 'So, Ashley Roper came clean, well I never. I'd love to have been a fly on the wall when that happened.' Quigley looked at Munro and smiled. 'You remind me of a Jack Russell terrier my cousin Reggie used to have. Catastrophe was his name. Reggie called him that because he was always getting into scrapes. That little so and so never took the easy route, he'd dive headfirst down a hole and minutes later he'd limp out yelping and covered in blood.'

'This isn't funny, Quigley. I'm asking for your help.'

'I know you are, son.' Quigley patted Munro's shoulder. 'But much as I'd like to wave a magic wand and put everything right, I can't. Just run with the Charlotte situation for now and see where it takes you. That's the best advice I can offer.'

'This feels worse than being banged up for something I didn't do, Quigley.'

'I believe you, son.' Quigley nodded. 'I can see it in your eyes. Just hang in there. You never know what's around the corner.'

The cell door clunked open. It was Challis, grinning like a loony. 'You've got a visitor, Quigley. I think it's your daughter.'

Still weak from his term in hospital, Quigley took his time getting to the visitor's room.

'How are you feeling, dad?' Connie beamed, through the glass partition, her eyes brimming with affection.

'I've never felt better, sweetheart.' Quigley gave her his Sunday-best smile.

'You could have fooled me. I don't see any improvement from when I last saw you in hospital. Are you sure you're ok?'

'Blimey! You'd look peaky if you'd been stuck in a hospital bed for three weeks. The next time you see me, I'll be good as new, just wait and see.'

Quigley stole a glance at Challis who had his nose buried in the Sporting Life. He leaned forward and beckoned Connie to inch closer to the glass.

'Listen sweetheart, before I forget, there's a couple of things I'd like you to do for me ...'

Herb was in his office when Yvette rang. 'You've done what, Yvette?' he squealed in disbelief.

'I've left you Herb, and I won't be coming back. It's over, so please don't try and talk me out of it. My mind's made up,' she trilled down the phone, unable to contain her joy. 'I'm moving on to bigger and better things, baby. It was great fun while it lasted Herb and I'll miss you in lots of ways, but it's time you found someone who'll appreciate you, for who you are. Find someone less demanding. And take a little word of helpful advice from someone who knows, Herb. If you don't want to lose the next lady in your life, stop picking lumps of wax from your ears with a matchstick while watching television and don't leave nasal hair clippings in the washbasin. God, it used to turn my fucking stomach! I guess that's just about it, Herb. I've arranged for a removal firm to collect my belongings, and they'll send them on to me in New York. I've left my forwarding address under your Gordon Gecko *Lunch is for Wimps* fridge magnet. Please make sure they don't fuck it up, Herb. I know I can rely on you, baby, because that's the kind of sweet considerate guy you are. Oh, by the way Herb. This isn't about sex, baby. You were better than average under the sheets, baby. But you weren't in the same league as Munro and my new guy. But there again, who is? If I had to give them marks out of 10, it would be 12 out of 10 apiece. I'm not joking, Herb. This new guy is mind-blowingly good. Christ, I get moist just thinking about him.' Yvette blew him a kiss before hanging up.

The receiver still pressed against his ear, Herb sat motionless, staring blankly at the ornate framed photograph of Yvette that stood on the corner of his office desk. The receiver still pressed against his ear. Tears welled in his eyes and rolled down his puffy cheeks. He put down the phone and turned to look out of the window. A mass of black storm clouds gathered on the horizon. Lightning flashed spasmodically and some tiny drops of rain spattered against the cracked window pane. Like an old man falling asleep in his chair at the nursing home, his head dropped slowly onto his chest. Herb bawled like a child in pain, his large shoulders shaking with every sharp intake of breath.

Six weeks had passed since Yvette first moved into the hotel with Bryan. As he emerged from the shower and approached the bed, her eyes devoured every inch of his athletic frame.

'In two days' time we'll be in New York, with nothing to do but count our millions,' he crowed, snapping the air with his towel.

'I'll always find *something* for you to do baby,' she cooed, throwing back the silk sheet to reveal her magnificent body. She spread her legs invitingly and Bryan duly obliged.

'Where are we eating tonight baby?' she whispered, when they'd finished making love.

'I don't really care. I'll leave it up to you. Where would you like to eat?'

Bryan's phone rang before she could answer him. He kissed her before placing it to his ear.

'That's brilliant, Gerald!' he said, unable to contain his excitement. 'No! Don't do that, Gerald. Don't mail it. I'll pick it up myself. I'll be there in thirty minutes!' He checked his watch. 'No, better make that forty-five minutes! The traffic's bad at this hour.'

'Was that the call you've been waiting for?' she asked, her eyes glowing with eager anticipation.

Bryan stared up at the ceiling, grinning like the man whose numbers had just come up on the lottery. 'Twenty one million, four hundred thousand, eight hundred pounds and fifty pence!' he roared, punching the air triumphantly. 'We're rich, honey! Filthy rich! Stinking rich! Shitting gold bricks, rich! We'll be farting through silk, for the rest of our lives!' He kissed her breasts. 'We're going to be hard pressed to spend the interest alone. New York and Monaco here we come!'

Yvette threw her arms around him. 'I can't believe it!' she squealed.

'I've got to pick up the money draft before he leaves for the airport and if I'm to get to the hotel on time, I'll have to fly.' He sprang from the bed and headed for the bathroom. 'I want you looking like a million dollars, when I return. Tonight, you and I are going to tear this town apart!'

The Major summoned Munro to his office. He was sitting behind his desk fidgeting nervously with his tie. 'I'll get straight to the point Munro. It's Felicity's birthday next Saturday.'

'And you'd like me to prepare a meal,' said Munro, laughing. 'Sometimes, sir. Your face is like an open book.'

'Er, yes, Munro, that's precisely what I want.' The Major was struggling to conceal his embarrassment. 'What do you say?'

'Consider it done. I'll prepare a menu and let you have a list of ingredients for Shenstone to pick up.'

The Major rubbed his hands together. 'Thank God, Munro! My wife would have filed for divorce if you'd declined!'

'Will that be all, sir?'

'Er, yes Munro. Thank you. You're a damn good sport,' said the Major, clearing his throat, as if choking on the compliment.

Munro got as far as the door. 'Why not invite Miss Blake, sir? She's tried so hard to help me over the last year or so and it would be nice to be able to repay her in some small way.'

'That's not a bad idea, Munro. A bit of additional conversation should make it a far more enjoyable evening. I'll run it up the old flagpole and see if Felicity salutes it.'

The Major gave Munro a knowing look.

'Are you sure, that's the only reason you want Miss Blake to be there?'

Munro shook his head from side to side, pursing his lips.

'I'm afraid I don't know what you mean, sir. What other reason could there be for suggesting that Miss Blake be there?' said Munro, looking every inch the paragon of virtue as he closed the door behind him.

The following afternoon, Jessop handed Munro a sealed envelope. He read the note to Quigley.

*Munro, it gives me great pleasure to inform you that Miss Blake has graciously accepted Felicity's invitation. Further to this, Felicity thinks it would be a splendid idea if you were to join our happy gathering. But **only** if you can guarantee, that your presence at the dinner table will not undermine the quality of the cuisine. Bernard Herbert Morris, Governor.*

Munro smiled at Quigley, unable to contain his delight. Quigley just smiled and nodded his head. Reznik was recruited once again, along with Winston Greene who'd had previous experience working in his uncle's restaurant in Jamaica. The two screws on official guard duty were Jessop and Challis, just like before. Munro arranged the place settings so that the Major sat across the table from Charlotte and he sat opposite Felicity Morris. The Major wore a white regimental dinner jacket, adorned with an impressive array of war medals and ribbons and Felicity wore a red dress that would not have looked out of place on the ballroom floor of the first *Come Dancing* show ever televised. In Charlotte's case, less was more and she looked absolutely stunning in a simple off-the-shoulder, emerald green dress with a single string of pearls around her neck. Munro wore a brand new chef's jacket and trousers, acquired by Quigley from Tommy the Tout, his fix-it man in C Wing. Unable to take his eyes off Charlotte, Munro's heart was racing as he took his place at the table.

Reznik served the first course and much to Munro's delight, he refrained from his Bogie dialogue. Conversation was hard work at first, before erupting miraculously into life, midway through the second course. Greene and Reznik were coping superbly and by the time the dinner was over, everyone was getting on famously. That is, until Reznik served the coffee. As instructed by Munro, he served the guest of honour first. Unfortunately, the birthday girl dropped her guard, smiled at Reznik and said thank you. Reznik stared at Felicity with a blank look in his eyes then switched into Bogart mode. '*Many people are going to die before this is over and it's up to us who don't to make sure their deaths ain't for nothing.*'

Reznik couldn't have chosen a more intimidating quote, if he'd tried. Images of Reznik throttling his wife in front of the television set, swam around inside Felicity's head, she recoiled in horror, eyes bulging, her napkin pressed against her mouth. Reznik smiled, bowed politely, turned on his heels and left.

'That man's crazy, Bernard! Stark, raving, fucking bonkers!' she growled. 'Sorry everyone, pardon my French.'

The Major interjected, tactfully changing the subject. 'The food was wonderful, Munro. Give my compliments to the chef.' Amused by his own witticism he chortled like a schoolboy.

'Thanks, sir. I'll mention it to the chef when I see him. I'm sure he'll appreciate it. Compliments from the patronage have been few and far between of late.'

'Bernard Morris!' snapped Felicity. 'Bend your precious bloody rules for once in your life. Offer Munro a brandy with his coffee.'

'No thanks, Mrs. Morris. I'll stick to water,' said Munro. 'You're very thoughtful.'

'Isn't this dinner bending the rules, sir?' said Charlotte, giving the Major a knowing look.

'Good heavens no, Miss Blake. How could you suggest such a thing? It's simply an initiative I've taken to bolster Munro's rehabilitation programme,' he muttered. 'It's all above board and strictly in the line of duty.'

'Oh, you're such a boring old fart, Bernard,' scoffed Felicity. The gin was starting to kick in. 'Stop trying to make out that you're the one who's doing the man a favour.' She gazed lovingly into Munro's eyes. 'Munro's the one who has done us the favour. The meal was superb darling, you're so damn talented!' She raised one eyebrow. 'And so bloody handsome, it's not true!'

Charlotte dived in before Munro could reply. 'Did your husband tell you about my discovery?'

'Discovery? No he didn't. He doesn't confide in me about anything, my dear' she said, glaring at the Major. 'What exactly did you discover, my dear?'

'I shan't bore you with all the details. I went undercover and confronted the girl who testified that it was Munro who stabbed her boyfriend. She admitted to me that it was she and her boyfriend who attacked Munro and that he's innocent,' said Charlotte.

'Good God!' gasped Felicity, staring daggers at the Major, her mouth hanging open.

'Do you hear that, Bernard? Munro's innocent! What the hell are you going to do about it?' she barked.

'There's nothing I can do, my dear. Legally there are no grounds for appeal. And even if it went to a re-trial, the girl would only have to deny that she ever spoke to Miss Blake. It's a no-win catch twenty-two situation. My hands are tied!'

Felicity looked at Munro, her eyes brimming with warmth and affection. 'I knew it. You're far too handsome and far too gifted to be a vicious killer. Oh, you poor darling, I feel like taking you in my arms and hugging you till all the pain you must be feeling, ebbs away.'

The Major raised his eyebrows.

'Actually there is something we could do,' said Charlotte. 'We could tell the police what we know and ask them to interrogate Ashley Roper. There's a chance she may crack under pressure. It's a long shot but it's worth trying.' She looked at the Major. 'But it will need *your* approval, sir.'

'Don't worry, my dear. Bernard, will see that you have it. Won't you, Bernard!' she barked, glaring menacingly at the Major.

The Major closed his eyes, threw back his head and sighed. 'A letter of approval will be on my desk tomorrow morning, Miss Blake.' He leaned forward, eyebrows raised. 'But it's important you realize that if nothing comes of this, Munro will have no other alternative but to bide his time and wait for parole.'

'That's a risk I'm prepared to take, sir,' said Munro.

'That's the stuff, Munro!' cheered Felicity. 'I love to see a man who's got spunk. Prison life hasn't emasculated *you*!' She leaned across the table and placed her hand on his, eyes smouldering. 'That would be such a waste.'

'I'm sure Munro would be much happier if we didn't discuss his bodily functions at the dinner table, Felicity,' said the Major, fiddling nervously with his bow tie.

119

'Bodily functions!' she shrieked with laughter. 'You've got a nerve. The last time you had a bodily function worth talking about was on the evening of our silver wedding anniversary.' Felicity rolled her eyes to the heavens. 'And that was seven years ago.'

The Major stared at her open-mouthed, a hurt look on his face.

'More coffee, anyone?' said Munro, coming to the Major's rescue.

'No thanks, Munro. I'll have a brandy.' She glared at the Major. 'Make it a large one.'

'I'd like to propose a toast,' said Charlotte. 'Here's to Munro.'

'To Munro and freedom!' cried everyone, but none could out-cheer Felicity.

'I think this is turning out to be the most exciting birthday party I've ever had!' she trilled, clapping her hands together. 'We'll have you out of here and back on television in no time, Munro!'

'My television days are well and truly over Mrs. Morris. Far too many bad memories I'm afraid and far too much alcohol. All I want is to keep my nose clean and qualify for parole.' Munro glanced at Charlotte, smiled warmly and rose from his chair. 'Sit tight everyone. I have a surprise for Mrs. Morris.'

'For goodness sake, Munro, do stop calling me Mrs. Morris. You make me sound like a bloody charlady.' She smiled at Munro, eyelashes fluttering seductively. 'Now that you're an *innocent* man, my darling, you may call me, Felicity,' she drawled, stressing the word *innocent* for the benefit of the Major's ears.

'I'll come and help you, Munro,' said Charlotte. She stopped in her tracks and glanced at the Major for approval. 'Sorry sir. I presume that will be ok?'

'Carry on, Miss Blake,' he sighed, staring daggers at his wife. 'Nobody else around here takes a blind bit of notice of me, so why should you!'

Munro and Charlotte dashed to the kitchen.

'Reznik, Greene, wait outside while Munro and I sort out the surprise for the Major's wife. Help yourself to food and take some through for Jessop and Challis.'

After loading up a tray with food, Reznik and Greene closed the door behind them and Charlotte fell into Munro's arms.

'You look good enough to eat, Miss Blake,' he said, looking into her eyes. 'You'll make a delicious addition to my next menu.'

'Coming from such an accomplished chef, I'll take that as a compliment, kind sir.' She cupped his face in her hands and showered him with kisses.

Stolen moments later, she pushed him away, holding him at arm's length.

'I'll never give up trying to clear your name. Promise me you'll never give up, Munro,' she said, choking back the tears. 'Promise me you'll be strong.'

'I promise,' he whispered, gently brushing a tear from her cheek.

Challis threw open the kitchen door.

'You two not ready yet?' he chirped, fragments of rice flying from his mouth as he spoke.

'We're ready, Challis. Miss Blake had something in her eye, that's all. Do me a favour, switch off the lights in the meeting room while we light the candle on the cake.'

'Switch off the lights?' Challis shook his head disapprovingly. 'Don't know about that Munro. Not planning a break-out are you?' he guffawed. 'I'll have to slap the cuffs on you if you are.'

Charlotte rolled her eyes.

'Of course we're planning a break, Challis. I was just about to open the bloody window for him. Now, stop behaving like a damn clown and switch off the lights,' she snapped, resentful of his slovenly tone.

She lit a solitary red candle and placed it in the centre of the heart-shaped chocolate cake. Munro carried the cake into the meeting room, followed by Charlotte, Jessop, Greene and Challis all singing happy birthday. The Major stood to attention and joined in. Felicity threw her arms in the air, wailed like a banshee and burst into tears, the alcohol had finally taken its toll and she swayed unsteadily in her chair.

'Speech! Speech!' yelled everyone.

Felicity blew out the candle at the third attempt, sat back in her chair and opened her mouth to speak. Everyone waited and watched agog. A strange vacant expression crept over her face. It was evident that the lights were on and there was no one at home. Her eyelids grew heavy and flickered to a close, and like a felled pine tree, she collapsed face first into the cake.

Dressed to kill, Yvette paced the room at The Plaza Hotel waiting anxiously for Bryan's return. It was 8.15 pm and he was long overdue. She sensed something was amiss because he wasn't answering her calls. At 9.15pm she rang reception.

'Is there any sign of Mr. Donaldson yet? He should have been here over an hour ago and I'm very concerned.' she said, unable to mask the fear in her voice.

'I certainly haven't seen him madam, but I only came on duty fifteen minutes ago. Please hold, while I consult with the hotel manager, Mr. Fitzroy, perhaps he knows where Mr. Donaldson might be.'

Yvette lit a cheroot and toyed nervously with the fringe of her hair while she looked at herself in the mirror.

'Good evening, madam. Montgomery Fitzroy here. Mr. Donaldson checked out at 6pm this evening. He settled the bill and said you would be checking out at noon tomorrow.'

'He did what?' shrieked Yvette.

'He checked out, madam.' Fitzroy laughed. 'Madam's mind must be playing tricks on her. Surely, Mr. Donaldson told you what he was doing?'

'Is this some kind of a sick fucking joke?' screamed Yvette, hysterically.

'Not to my knowledge, madam,' said Fitzroy, courteously. 'If it is indeed a prank, then Mr. Donaldson did not make me party to it.'

Yvette slammed the phone down and dashed across the room to check inside Bryan's wardrobe, it was empty apart from the hotel coat-hangers. Yvette felt terribly alone and a cold shiver ran down her spine. She threw a coat across her shoulders and rushed downstairs to confront Fitzroy.

'Did he say anything before he checked out?' she demanded. 'Did he leave a message for me? A forwarding address… a phone number… anything!'

'He left no forwarding information whatsoever, madam. However, he did say that he'd enjoyed his stay at the hotel very much and complimented me and my staff on the high standards we attain,' said Fitzroy, beaming proudly. Fitzroy had yet to grasp the gravity of the situation. 'Is anything wrong? Madam looks a trifle peaky. Perhaps madam would like a refreshing glass of mineral water or a cup of soothing Camomile tea?'

'Is anything wrong?' Yvette screamed, hysterically, tears rolling down her face. 'Did you take a master's degree in *understatement*? You fucking moron! Things couldn't get more fucking wrong if they tried! Two and a half million quid wrong!' she screamed, before collapsing in a heap at his feet.

By the time the fraud squad detectives had finished interviewing Yvette, they were far from being optimistic about their chances of tracing her money and even far less optimistic about tracing Bryan.

'I can't believe you handed over all that money to a man you've only known for six months, Mrs. Munro.' DI Wilson shook his head slowly from side to side. 'This bloke was a real professional, Mrs. Munro, false passport, ID, credit cards, the works. He's even taken your Mercedes. We'll want you to come down to the station at some point and plough through some mug shots. How can we get in touch with you?'

Yvette didn't hear a word he said, she sat shell-shocked, zombie-like, staring into space. She'd been taken for every penny by the only man she'd ever really loved.

'Mrs. Munro.' DS Fitch tugged gently on the sleeve of her coat. 'How can we get in touch with you, Mrs. Munro?'

Despite her disturbed and highly emotional mental state it slowly dawned on her that she was not only penniless but homeless too. She burst into tears. 'How could he do this to me? We could have been so happy,' she wailed, rivers of mascara running down her face.

Now that Fitzroy fully understood the reason for her outburst in the hotel lobby that evening, he was deeply sympathetic and handed her a large brandy. 'I think she's had enough for one night Inspector Wilson. Leave your card with me,' said Fitzroy, who'd assumed the mantle of guardian angel. 'I'll see to it that Mrs. Munro calls you tomorrow morning. Right now, it's important that she rests. God only knows how she must be feeling.'

One of the female desk clerks, a blonde, bespectacled Polish girl named Greta, ushered her into the room and sat with her until the doctor arrived.

'The sedative will ensure you get a good night's sleep, Mrs. Munro. I suggest you see your own doctor as soon as possible,' he advised.

'A good night's sleep you say. Hah! Are you fucking kidding? Is every fucker in this hotel a comedian?' She waved her hand at him dismissively. 'Just get out of my room and leave me alone!' she screamed. Greta stood transfixed, too scared to move. 'That means you as well four-eyes. Both of you fuck off and leave me alone!' She rolled over onto her side and stared at Bryan's empty wardrobe. 'How could you do this to me, Bryan? How could you do this to me?' she wailed, repeating the same thing over and over again until finally she fell into a deep, sedative-induced sleep.

It was 11am when Yvette came to and the harsh reality of what had taken place hit home. In the grip of an unnatural chill, her nerves shot to pieces, she couldn't stop her hands from shaking. She stood under the scalding hot shower to try and get warm, but her teeth chattered like castanets and goose bumps erupted over her flesh. She dressed, packed her things, went downstairs to the restaurant and ordered a strong, black coffee.

'Will that be on your room number madam or would you prefer to pay cash?' said the waitress.

'Put it on room number 397.' whispered Yvette, as she signed the slip without looking up. Cash! She wasn't sure if she had any. Panic stricken, she dived into her handbag and pulled out her purse, her hands were shaking as she opened it to reveal three crisp one hundred pound notes, a parting gesture from Bryan. Yvette's tears flowed freely as she pictured the look on his handsome face when he walked out of their room the night before and despite everything, she was still not convinced of his treachery. She told herself he would realize that he'd made a terrible mistake and walk back into her life.

'I'm sorry to bother you madam, but you no longer have a room number,' said the waitress, looking somewhat embarrassed as she placed the tray on the table.

'Oh yes! I forgot about that,' said Yvette, opening her purse. She threw a one hundred pound note on the salver. 'I'd hate Mr. Montgomery Fitzroy to think I was doing a runner over one measly, fucking cup of piss-poor coffee!'

The waitress nodded politely and started to place the coffee items on the table.

'Stop fussing! I'll do that!' said Yvette, with a dismissive wave of her hand.

'Does madam require anything else?'

Yvette smiled at her 'No. Madam doesn't require anything else. Madam just wants to let you know that she won't be leaving you a tip!'

The waitress nodded politely then walked away.

Not leaving a tip reminded her of Herb, he was far too parsimonious to indulge in such profligate practices. Herb! Of course! The light bulb inside her head sparked into life. Fat Herb, the devoted clown, the man whose heart she broke and whose love she spurned. Herb wouldn't turn her away. He loved her. Herb worshipped the ground she walked on. He'd welcome her back with open arms. Desperate times call for desperate measures and as far as she was concerned, this was any port in a storm time. She left the hotel and climbed into a taxi. Herb had rented the same office for nineteen years, purely because it was dirt cheap. The fact that it was located in the outskirts of the city, on the fringes of an abandoned industrial park didn't bother him in the slightest, saving money was all that mattered and Yvette and money were the only deities he ever truly worshipped. She climbed out of the taxi and pressed the buzzer on the intercom.

'Cohen Enterprizes,' said the fragile voice.

'Rebecca. I'd like to see Mr. Cohen,' said Yvette.

'And who shall I say wishes to see him? Mr. Cohen's on the telephone at the moment.'

'Tell him it's Yvette.'

'Yvette! Oh, please forgive me. I didn't recognize your voice,' she gasped.

Seconds later a buzzer sounded and the security door latch opened with a click. The ancient lift juddered and clattered like a railway goods wagon all the way to the third floor. The doors parted with a screech to reveal a still plump but marginally leaner and hollow-eyed, Herb. Yvette's cruel departure had clearly taken its toll. Despite looking apprehensive, his adoring eyes gleamed with a mixture of love... and huge dash of hope.

Yvette threw herself into his arms. 'Oh Herb!' she gasped. 'Herb, I couldn't stay away any longer. I'm so sorry I hurt you, I'll never leave you again, I promise.' She cupped his face in her hands and rained kisses over him. Herb sobbed like a baby.

'I knew you'd come back, baby!' he mumbled, overcome with emotion and finding it difficult to speak. 'I knew you'd come back!'

Herb shouted through to his aged secretary. 'Rebecca, I'm going home for the rest of the day and I'm not to be disturbed.' He turned, stared at Yvette, and shouted again. 'Rebecca, I won't be back in the office for the rest of the week. I've a lot of important personal business to catch up on. So don't disturb me on any account. Not on any account, is that clear?' He winked at Yvette.

'Yes, Mr. Cohen.' sniffed Rebecca, wiping her tears. 'I hear you loud and clear. Don't worry. I'll make sure you're not disturbed, Mr. Cohen.'

The reunited love birds emerged from the lift in the underground car park and climbed into Herb's Bentley. On the journey to the penthouse, Yvette stroked the nape of his neck and he was in paradise. Herb was so happy it never entered his head to ask her why she'd arrived at his office in a taxi and not in her Mercedes.

When she entered the penthouse, everything was more or less as she had left it, the stale aroma of Herb's Havana cigars, the strong scent of his cheap aftershave, the familiar volume of afternoon light pouring through the windows and the smell of burnt toast. Herb had a thing about burnt toast, ever since an old Jewish tailor had told him 'If you want to keep a woman happy in bed my boy, eat plenty of burnt toast, it puts zip in your putz.' Herb made coffee and they sat at opposite ends of the sofa smiling at each other. They were the personification of the Beatles lyric... *deep in love, not a lot to say.* He reached across and stroked the back of her hand. Yvette lowered her head in a false display of contrition and whimpered. She knew he would fall for that because it was so out of character. Herb was lapping it up. It was hard to imagine that this was the same broken man that she'd dumped so callously.

'Before you say anything baby, let me say that I don't want to know what happened. If you want to talk about it, fine. If not, that's fine too. I'm just so happy that you've come home to me. That's all that really matters. Your happiness and our future together are all that matters, baby.' Herb squeezed her hand. 'Welcome home, baby. God, I've missed you so much.'

Yvette burst into tears and threw her head on his lap. 'Oh, Herb, I feel so ashamed of the way I treated you,' she said, lying through her teeth. 'I'll make it up to you, my darling. I promise.'

Herb stroked her hair and smiled, she'd called him *darling*, and that was something she'd never done in all the years he'd known her. Aroused by her touch, her smell, the sound of her voice and the warmth of her breath on his thigh, Herb had one thing on his mind. However, making love with Herb was the last thing on *her* mind. She took immediate and evasive action.

'I'm absolutely shattered, darling. Would you mind if I took a long soak in the bath and had a nap afterwards?' she whispered.

'Er, no baby,' mumbled Herb, unable to hide his disappointment. 'You go right ahead. Take as long as you like. I'll be right here when you need me. You call baby and I'll come running,' he chuckled, mocking his own subservience.

She kissed him on the cheek before heading for the bathroom.

'Hey baby!' he called after her, 'Let's eat out tonight. What do you fancy, Italian, Indian or Cantonese?' Herb raised his voice. 'Did you hear what I just said, baby?'

She sat in the bathroom, shuddering at the fawning tone of Herb's voice and pretended not to hear him. A forlorn figure trying to stem the flood of tears, she felt trapped, lost and terribly alone. She yearned for Bryan to call her. To tell her he was sorry and that it was all a bad joke. To tell her he had their flight tickets for New York in his hand and that he was sending a taxi to bring her to the airport. To tell her he loved her. But in her heart she knew that wouldn't happen. Yvette had no other choice than to tie herself to Herb. Like a female rattlesnake tied to a plump desert rat, sooner or later something would have to give and she was determined it wasn't going to be her. She was also well aware that Herb was going to be diving between her legs at the first opportunity and the thought made her flesh crawl. The idea of someone else other than Bryan between her legs didn't bear thinking about. But even she, with all her feline cunning wouldn't be able to keep him at arm's length forever. She decided that when the time came she'd be so shit-faced drunk, she wouldn't notice.

On the stroke of 11am, DS Percy Rudge banged on Ashley Roper's front door. He looked like a man whose haemorrhoids were giving him serious gyp.

'I'm coming. Don't knock the fucking door down!' screamed Roper, as she yanked open the door. She had a sheet draped around her and a smouldering roll-up hanging from the corner of her mouth. Rudge waved his identity card in her face.

'What the fuck, do you and your copper bitch want with me, Rudge?' Roper started coughing. Retching, like an aged cat, gagging on a fur ball. When the coughing fit subsided, she walked towards Rudge, placed one hand on his shoulder and jettisoned the contents of her mouth past his ear, into the car park below. 'You won't find any drugs or stolen gear in here, Rudge,' she wheezed, still finding it difficult to speak. 'You're wasting your fucking time.'

'I'm not here looking for drugs or stolen goods. And I'm not making an arrest. I'd like you to come down to the station and answer a few questions about the Danny Gordon business, that's all. You can have a lawyer present if you wish,' said Rudge, with the enthusiasm of a stunned slug.

'Lawyers! What would I want one of them for, Rudge? All they're good for is taking your money!'

A gangly, bleary-eyed youth with a swastika tattoo on his neck emerged from the bedroom, completely naked, his more than considerable manhood swinging between his skinny legs. Rudge and the WPC gawped open-mouthed, unable to mask their amazement.

'Big innit,' Roper smiled, noting the look of envy on Rudge's face. 'When God was dishing them out, Jimbo picked the biggest one in the box, because he thought they were for eating.' She looked at Rudge. 'If you want to give your copper bitch a real birthday treat this year, you should send her round here, Rudge. Jimbo'll put a bigger smile on her face than a box of Milk Tray ever will.' She turned to the WPC. 'Sorry, bitch. I didn't mean to build your hopes up. Jimbo wouldn't screw a copper's bitch like you, if you paid him. So it looks like you'll just have to make do with your vibrator.'

'What's Mr. and Mrs. Filth want, Ash?' said Jimbo, still half-asleep.

'Rudge and his bitch want to ask me some questions at the station, Jimbo,' she said with a smile, snuggling up to him. 'If you ask me, they just wanted to look at your cock.' She ran her fingers up and down its more than considerable length.

Jimbo yawned. 'Wake us up when you get back Ash. I'm going back to me bed.'

'Get dressed Roper. I haven't got all day,' barked Rudge, growing impatient.

'Keep your hair on, Rudge. Oops, I forgot. You ain't got none.' She chuckled to herself as she slammed the bedroom door behind her. Rudge stared in the mirror, frantically patting his comb-over.

No words were exchanged until they reached the police station where the WPC ushered Roper into an interview room. Charlotte remained in the corridor to observe from behind the one-way glass. The constable standing with her shook his head from side to side.

'Rudge won't get much out of that one. I was at the same school as her. Psycho Roper we called her. Mind you, nobody dared say that to her face. Just about everybody in the school was terrified of her. She was into everything, drugs, stolen property, prostitution, porn, and boy did she love violence. She's a smart one though, hasn't even got a criminal record.'

'You're joking,' said Blake, looking stunned, her eyes fixed on Roper through the glass.

'No, I'm serious, Miss Blake. She's always managed to keep one step ahead of the police. The detention centres and nicks must be full of innocent people who've taken the rap for her just because she forced them to. The whole bloody family's crazy.

The old man's doing a stretch for GBH and her mother, a hopeless junkie, is being kept alive on a life support machine in the county hospital. None of them are what you'd call normal. Two years ago, her younger brother, Harold, signed up with a band of mercenaries. He's out in Africa right now, killing people on a daily basis. Harold was her enforcer when he was here.' He turned to Blake. 'If you don't mind me asking, what's *your* interest in her?'

'I'm hoping she'll confess to perjury.'

The constable raised his eyebrows. 'You've got no chance of that, I'm afraid. Ashley Roper isn't the confessing type. She's never owned up to anything in her life and never will. It's not in the Roper genes.'

Minutes later, Rudge walked into the interview room and sat at the desk.

'About fucking time!' Roper snarled, nodding at the clock on the wall. 'Do you think I've got fuck all else to do than to sit in 'ere looking at the blank walls?'

Rudge ignored her. 'Does the name Gemma McArdle mean anything to you?'

The name struck a chord, igniting a spark of recognition in Roper's eyes. 'No! I've never heard of her,' said Roper, lighting a roll-up. 'Why? Has she left me some money in her will?'

'No, nothing like that, she claims to know you?'

Roper glared menacingly at the one-way glass. And even though Roper couldn't see her, Charlotte could feel her eyes burning into her.

'Well I don't know her!' She ground the roll-up into the floor with the sole of her shoe. 'Look Rudge! What the fuck has all this got to do with Danny getting stabbed?' she snarled.

'Gemma McArdle claims that she met *you* in the Ring O Bells several weeks ago. She claims you got drunk and told her that you and Danny Gordon attacked Anton Munro with intent to rob him and that Danny fell on his own knife during the scuffle. She claims you boasted about lying in court just to get Munro sent down.'

Roper lit another roll-up. 'So that's why I'm here? Some fuckwit feeds you a load of bollocks and you drag me in for questioning.' She blew smoke in his face. 'You're a joke Rudge!' She rose to her feet and walked over to the one-way glass. 'I know you're out there watching me, bitch. You lying cow!' She inhaled long and hard on the roll-up before stubbing it out on the glass.

'Get back to the table!' yelled Rudge.

Charlotte was growing impatient with Rudge's soft line of questioning. Roper was running the show, toying with him, doing as she pleased. He wasn't applying any pressure at all, just going through the motions. Frustrated and angry, she stormed into the room.

Roper jumped to her feet. 'This is her, ain't it? You ain't been getting enough cock missus, that's you're trouble.' Roper leapt to her feet. 'What gives you the right to tell lies about me? What harm have I ever done you?' She turned on Rudge. 'You put her up to this, didn't you!' she snarled, contemptuously.

'I'd like a word with you, in private, DS Rudge,' demanded Charlotte, ignoring Roper.

Rudge pursued Charlotte into the corridor, clearly annoyed by her untimely interruption and the belligerent tone of her voice.

'You have absolutely no right to enter that room unless invited, Miss Blake. Try that again and I'll end the proceedings.'

'End the proceedings! Don't make me laugh. From where I'm standing the proceedings haven't even started yet. She's lying, detective! Can't you see that she's lying?' screamed Charlotte. 'Start probing for God's sake! Put her under pressure. Start doing your job! An innocent man's life is at stake here!'

'Don't tell me how to do my job, Miss Blake. Remain here in the corridor. Enter that room again and I'll have you escorted from the building.'

Rudge went back into the room and sat down.

'You're certain that you have no knowledge of the incident that Gemma McArdle claims took place in the Ring O Bells?'

Roper rolled her eyes to the heavens. 'Have I been talking Chinese or what? How many fucking times do I have to I tell you something before it sinks in, Rudge? I don't know her! I've never laid eyes on her! And I don't have a fucking clue what she's on about!' she roared, banging the table with her clenched fist to stress each point.

Charlotte could see that Rudge was getting nowhere. She threw open the door and ran into the room.

'Watch yourself, Rudge! The mad cow's back! She wants to spank you for being a naughty boy,' she jibed.

Charlotte leaned across the desk, completely out of control. 'Tell the truth, damn you!'

'Get out!' yelled Rudge, motioning for the constable to take her away.

'An innocent man is rotting in jail because of you! You evil, lying, degenerate bitch!' screamed Charlotte, as the constable dragged her from the room.

'Fuck you, bitch! Whoever you are! That murdering Paki bastard, Munro, got what he deserved!' hissed Roper, defiantly.

Roper leaned back in the chair, placed her feet on the desk and nonchalantly blew smoke rings into the air. 'Where the fuck did you get that loony from, Rudge?' A smirk crept across her face. 'She ain't one of your relatives, is she?'

'She's the woman who claims to have met you in the Ring O Bells.'

'Are you taking the piss? A posh tart like her wouldn't last five minutes in the Ring O Bells before she was tumbled. She's off her fucking rocker!' She stubbed out the roll-up on the desktop.

'She claims she was undercover, disguised as one of the locals,' said Rudge.

'Now I know you're taking the piss. We'd have spotted a mummy's girl like her a mile off.' Roper stood up. 'I've had enough of this bollocks! Either you charge me or let me leave *now!* Or are you hoping I'll suck your little, withered truncheon first, before you'll let me go?' she smirked, wriggling her pinky at him.

'Get out of here!' barked Rudge, dismissing her with a wave of his hand.

Roper reached the door, unable to resist a final parting shot. 'I've been wondering how you got all those little craters in your face, Rudge. Didn't your dad have a dart board at home to practice on, when you was a kid?'

'Get out!' screamed Rudge, leaping out of the chair. 'You vile, bitch!'

Rudge entered the holding cell where the constable had taken Charlotte.

'That was pathetic Sergeant! You made no attempt to put that lying bitch under pressure. You made no attempt to offer her a leniency deal if she told the truth. What's the matter? Does the *truth* bother you? Worried you'd be found to have arrested the wrong man? Policemen like you turn my stomach!' She glared at him, a look of contempt etched on her face. 'An innocent man is rotting in jail because you didn't do your job properly and haven't got the balls to make amends.'

Rudge turned and walked away, speaking over his shoulder.

'Both you and Governor Morris will receive a copy of my report in a few days, Miss Blake. Don't bother to close the door on your way out.'

Charlotte left the police station in tears. Munro's last chance of freedom had slipped through her fingers and she blamed herself. She knew they would never be together.

'I did warn you, Miss Blake,' sighed the Major, looking out the window. 'That's it now for Munro. His goose is well and truly cooked. His only hope of leaving here is parole. You *must* focus on that now. Make sure he responds in a positive manner, to what will undoubtedly be, a most bitter disappointment. You must drill it into him that if he applies himself appropriately, the time will pass quickly.'

'That police officer was pathetic, sir. He didn't interrogate Ashley Roper, he chatted with her. I'm surprised he didn't ask her which hair salon she used.' Frustration spilled over as Blake slammed her fist on the table. 'Rudge knows Munro is innocent! He's just covering up his own ineptitude.'

'That may be so, Miss Blake. Unfortunately, there's nothing that we can do.' He sat drumming his fingers on the desk. 'Now we both have a problem. You have to break the bad news to Munro and I must tell my wife.' He rolled his eyes to the heavens.

Blake rose to leave.

'Oh, before you go Miss Blake, just one more thing. It's become very apparent to me that your emotional involvement in this case goes above and beyond the normal line of duty.' He leaned back in his chair and clasped his hands. 'I saw the way Munro looked at you when we had the dinner party and I saw the way you looked at him. Take the advice of an old warhorse, Miss Blake. Keep your head down and watch your back.'

'I don't know what you mean, sir,' said Charlotte, trying hard to look bemused.

'Oh, I think you do, Miss Blake. I may be much older than you, but I'm a long way off from being senile. You're walking on very thin ice as far as your career is concerned. I'd tread very carefully, if I were you.'

Blake could feel the colour rising in her cheeks, she turned and left.

By the time she reached her office Charlotte was in tears. Her mind in turmoil, she was dreading the meeting with Munro. As soon as he entered the office, Munro could see that things had not gone to plan. Charlotte was crying.

'You don't have to say a word,' he said softly. 'You gave it your best shot.'

She walked from behind the desk and closed the blinds. 'I'm so sorry, Munro!' she sighed, wrapping her arms around him.

'Hey! Whatever happened to not giving up? I need you in my corner more than ever.' he whispered, wiping the tears from her eyes.

'I know, I know. You're right,' she said, wiping her nose with a tissue. 'I feel so foolish and so bloody inept. I believed there was an excellent chance that Roper would crack. How could I have been so grossly naïve?' She paced the office, going over everything in her mind.

Munro took her hand. 'Hey, stop beating yourself up. It's not your fault. It was *my* decision to take the chance. Not yours. Hey. At least we know now, that it's going to take a lot more than interrogation by the police, to make Roper tell the truth.' Munro shrugged dismissively. 'Anyway, *mackerels* don't happen overnight!'

'Mackerels.' She smiled. 'Don't you mean *miracles?*'

'No, I mean mackerels. I was quoting Bruno, a dyslexic set designer who worked on my TV show. He was a lovely bloke, very sensitive but had a tendency to get upset at the slightest thing.' Munro chuckled. 'We were running behind schedule and the producers and I were giving him a hard time. So he threw a big hissy and stormed off the set. Everyone presumed we'd seen the last of him. But no, we couldn't have been more wrong. Bruno turned up on set two hours later, brandishing a large hand-painted placard. It read *…Give me a break, mackerels don't happen overnight!'*

They both laughed and fell into each other's arms. Just being together, holding and caressing seemed to ease their pain. She held him at arm's length, smiled and shook her head from side to side.

'You're totally unrecognizable as the wanton, belligerent, foul-mouthed man who walked into my office two and a half years ago. You've changed Munro and you've changed for the good. I always felt that there was a decent man inside you screaming to get out.'

'You've certainly got that right.' he said, with a wry smile. 'I've been screaming to get out of here for over two years.'

'You know that's not what I meant, Munro.'

'I've got you and Quigley to thank for that.' He held her at arm's length. 'It's easy for me to recognize the difference that falling in love with you has made. You're in my thoughts, all the time and you've given me new hope… You've given me something to live for.' he said, gently stroking her cheek. 'As for Quigley, well that's a bit of a mystery. I know he's influenced me a great deal, but I can't pin it down to anything in particular. He's a man of very few words and only talks when he feels there's something worth talking about.' Munro chuckled. 'I'm sure the other lifers think that because we share a cell, we're chatting all the time, but we're not. We can go days without speaking to each other.' Munro paused. 'I know this may sound silly… but I feel safe when I'm with him. I've never known anyone like him. Quigley's friendship means so much to me.'

'I love you, Munro,' she whispered, slipping her arms around his waist.

'And words can't describe how I feel about you,' he said, pulling her close. Their lips met and for one exquisite stolen moment their deepest fears were dispelled.

Quigley handed Munro a cup of whisky. 'That's a tough break, Munro. Not what the doctor ordered, eh?'

'To be honest Quigley, I can't really say I expected anything else. Not from Ashley Roper. She's a nasty piece of work that one. Nothing scares her,' he said, with bitter resignation in his voice.

'We're all *scared* of something, Munro. Everybody has a tender spot. All you have to do is keep prodding away till you find it. And when you do find it, they'll beg you not to prod it anymore.' said Quigley, with the authority of a man who was speaking from practical experience. The cold, steely look in his eyes, suggested to Munro that Quigley was referring to the painful demise of Bela Petrescu, the man who brutally raped his granddaughter.

'At this moment in time, Munro, the million dollar question you must ponder over, is will Miss Blake wait for you?

'Only time will tell Quigley and I've plenty of that. At least six years by my reckoning and that's *only if* I get parole.'

'So, where do you go from here?'

'Well, I don't know about you, but I'm going to the canteen for some pig swill. Coming?'

'Might as well. My favourite pie and mash restaurant is closed for refurbishment and as luck would have it my credit's still good in the prison canteen.'

Senior Officer, Jack Dobson was on duty when they arrived at the entrance to the canteen, he approached Munro. 'The Governor told me what happened, Munro. Hang in there, something will turn up. You never know what's around the corner.'

'Thanks, Jack. That's what everyone keeps telling me.' Munro laughed. 'There's been that many corners in my life, I'm beginning to think I was born in a maze.'

Reznik was sitting at the only free table, and not surprisingly he was on his own.

'A luncheon date with Warsaw's answer to Humphrey Bogart is the last thing I need,' sighed Munro.

'Leave it out, Munro. The man's harmless. The least you can do is humour him and let him have his bit of fun,' said Quigley, nudging Munro in the ribs. 'Adam Reznik arrived in Kingswood the same day I did. All this loony business is just a front. There's far more to him than meets the eye, believe me.'

Reznik's top lip was already in Bogart mode before they sat down with their trays.

'*You don't have to be a genius to see that all our troubles, don't make a big pile of beans in the topsy-turvy troubled world we live in.*'

'I couldn't agree more, Adam. How's it going?' asked Quigley, with a friendly smile.

'Fine, Mr. Quigley, just fine. I've been meaning to ask you. *Have you ever been stung by a bee that wasn't alive?*'

Quigley, winked at Munro. 'No Adam, I can't say I have. But I've been stung by live wasps a few times.'

'I don't mind wasps! *But the thing I hate most, is leeches… slimy, dirty little things!*' said Reznik, his Bogie lip working overtime.

'I never asked you if you enjoyed helping out at the Major's dinner party, Reznik. Did you have a good time and did you try my curry?' said Munro, hoping for a non-Bogie reply, but he should have known better.

'It was ok, I suppose. *A burger at the football match beats roast dinner and Yorkshire pudding at the Savoy.*'

Quigley interjected. 'Tell me Adam. Don't you ever tire of sharing your life with Humphrey Bogart?'

'Don't be silly, Mr. Quigley!' scoffed Reznik. 'We keep each other company. Though, I have to admit it can get a little crowded sometimes. But most of the time we get on fine. Mind you, he does like to push his weight around. He tells me to do things!' he said, nodding his head pensively.

'He tells you do things?' Quigley's curiosity was aroused. 'What kind of things?'

'Oh, like the time he told me to strangle my wife. Bogie and I were watching one of our favourite movies on television one night, The Treasure of the Sierra Madre. Then out of the blue, my wife walks in and switches the TV over to another channel. I looked at Bogie and he looked at me and said... If you don't strangle that inconsiderate bitch, I will. So I jumped out of my chair and strangled her.' Reznik grinned like a mischievous schoolboy.

Quigley burst out laughing. 'You're nothing but a scoundrel, Adam Reznik. I bet you tried that one on at your trial.'

'You should have seen the look on the judge's face,' said Reznik, chuckling hysterically as he slapped the tabletop with the palms of his hands.

Much to Munro's relief, a welcome silence fell over the trio and Munro and Quigley picked at their food for a time. Reznik's eyes never left Munro for an instant, an ordeal that proved to be far more unnerving than his Bogie dialogue. When they decided to call it a day Quigley and Munro rose from the table in unison.

'See you later, Reznik'

Reznik reached across the table and took hold of Munro's hand.

'If there's gold up in those mountains, how long do you think it's been there? Billions and billions of years, I reckon. So why

the big rush? Waiting for just a few days isn't going to make much difference,' he said with a shrug of his shoulders.

Quigley intervened when he saw that Munro was lost for words.

'We'll remember the wisdom of those words, Adam. Make sure you look after yourself now, do you hear? And keep an eye on Bogie for us.' Quigley squeezed Reznik's shoulder affectionately.

'Thanks for sitting with Bogie and I. We truly appreciate your thoughtfulness.'

'I agree with the Major's wife. He's stark raving mad!' whispered Munro, as soon as they were out of hearing distance.

Quigley laughed dismissively. 'Adam Reznik is just as sane as you and I, Munro. He's playing a game, that's all. It's how he passes the time in jail. Everything he says has a relevance to what's happening around him. Think about what he just said to you. He deliberately chose a piece of dialogue that relates to your current situation. He's telling you to be patient and that things will work out in their own good time. All the pushing and prodding isn't going to make things happen any quicker. Adam Reznik was one of many Polish fighter pilots who defended these shores during the Second World War. He fought with great courage and was decorated on three occasions, for bravery above and beyond the call of duty. I feel sorry for displaced persons like Reznik. Imagine how he and his fellow countrymen must have felt when they discovered that Churchill and Roosevelt had sold them out at the Yalta Conference in 1945 by allowing Stalin to claim Poland as part of the Soviet Union. Those people had just fought a war to rid themselves of Nazi oppression only to find they were mere chattels of the Soviets. If that's not a perfect example of how politicians will kick you in the teeth, when it suits their political agenda, then I don't know what is. And when most of the Poles decided to stay in Britain rather than live under Soviet control they struggled to be accepted by the very people they had risked their lives for. Reznik throttled his wife, of that there is no doubt, but that doesn't mean he's stark raving mad. Sometimes rage can take hold of a placid man and make him lose control, it can happen to anyone. *It happened to me.* I'm sure there were far more complex reasons that led to him throttling his wife. Nobody kills their wife for switching TV channels.'

As they walked through the relaxation area Quigley nodded at the television set. A reporter was talking about the genocide taking place in Rwanda. Quigley shook his head. 'All over the world, there are so called *sane* people, killing other people, as we speak. You don't have to be crazy to kill someone. Look at the millions of innocent people the pedlars of greed continue to slaughter. Each one of them, enthusiastically aided and abetted by gutless, corrupt, morally bankrupt, self-serving political and religious leaders. They may not personally cause the famine, drop the bomb or pull the trigger but at the end of the day, *they* make the decisions. In my book, that makes *them* accountable and makes them no different to all the other cold-blooded killers who seek to destroy, not only people's lives but also their families. They should burn in hell.'

7

Yvette had been living with Herb for three months and had yet to divulge the true extent of her insolvency. Herb was aware that her car had been stolen, but that was all. As usual, the insurance company were ducking and diving to avoid stumping up the cash so she was still some way off from placing a lodgment into a bank account that had been rendered redundant by Bryan. Living with the fear that she might run out on him at any moment was Herb's Achilles heel, a weakness that Yvette ruthlessly exploited. Herb was far too scared to pry into her personal finances. Instead, he continued to buy her love and continued to shower her with expensive gifts, clothes and his undying devotion. It was the middle of the afternoon when Herb returned to the penthouse unexpectedly, Yvette was out on a shopping spree. As he was sifting through the mail, the phone rang. It was an irate client and his knickers were in a twist. With the phone wedged between his ear and shoulder he listened to the disgruntled client while he ripped opened an envelope, paying no attention to the name of the addressee. The letter was addressed to Yvette and it was from her bank manager. Herb stood mummified, reading the letter.

'I'll call you back Jerome, I'm in the car at the moment and the bloody traffic police are out in force today. Yes, of course, I'll call you back within the hour, I promise. Yes, Jerome, I promise. I'm sorry Jerome. But I must go now. Bye.'

The missive contained all the standard toadying bank manager corporate policy bullshit, expressing his deep regret about the theft of her money and wondering when and if she was ever going to start making deposits again. If not, then he would close the account. The painful realization that Yvette had come back to him out of nothing more than desperation, reached inside his ribcage like an invisible hand and ripped his heart out. Herb poured himself a large whisky, lit a cigar and stared at his reflection in the mirror.

'You were her meal ticket, Herb. Nothing more than a lousy meal ticket,' he growled through clenched teeth, squeezing the glass so hard it shattered. He pulled a handkerchief from his jacket pocket, wrapped it around his wound, took the house phone off the hook and switched off his cell phone. Herb crossed the room, closed the blinds and sat in the darkened room, swigging whisky from the bottle to drown his sorrows. When the bottle was empty, he crashed out on the sofa in a drunken stupor.

On her return, Yvette entered the room laden with packages. Herb was still asleep and the room smelled like a public bar. She placed the packages on a chair, pulled back the blinds and threw open a window.

'Close that window!' growled Herb, slowly getting to his feet.

The aggression in his voice terrified her. 'What's wrong, darling?' she stammered nervously. 'What on earth's got into you? Why are you speaking to me like that?'

Herb walked towards her and waved the letter in front of her face. 'You scheming, two-faced, lying whore. You've used me for the last time!' When she saw the bank's logo on the letterhead her jaw dropped. She backed away, eyes popping out their sockets.

'You shouldn't have opened my mail, Herb!' she gasped, trying to go on the offensive.

'This is my apartment. *Mine,* do you hear?' he screamed. 'I'll open whatever the fuck I want to open!' He ripped the letter into pieces and threw it in the air. Herb inched ever closer, fists clenched, grimacing, his face contorted with hate.

'Herb darling, I can explain!' she pleaded. 'I love you Herb! I've always loved you! It's always been you, Herb!'

'Love!' he screamed. 'You don't know the meaning of the word! How the hell can you claim to love someone when you're incapable of giving?'

Minute beads of sweat glistened on her forehead as she struggled to find the magic words that would calm him down. Her perfume was so strong he could taste it and the desire to fuck her raged inside him. Tears in his eyes, he reached out, and in one violent downward motion, ripped the dress from her body. Yvette took his hand and placed it on her breast, a strange calm fell over him as he stared at the body that had given him so much pleasure.

'Make love to me, Herb,' she whispered, hoping that a fuck would abate his rage. 'You know you want to, my darling.'

Herb picked her up in his arms, carried her to the bedroom and threw her on the bed. With her legs apart and a smug smile of triumph on her face Yvette watched him undress. Herb slid between her legs and drove into her, with all the fury of a man possessed. This wasn't the considerate lover she knew so well, the man between her legs was a grimacing, savage beast. She cried out in pain as he lunged into her, over and over again, till the sweat dripped from his brow, his face a contorted mask of contempt, angry and unfeeling. Just as she reached the point where the pain was unbearable, he climaxed. Without saying a word, he rose from the bed and walked into the bathroom. She could hear him sobbing. Nerves shattered from the ordeal, she lit a cheroot, hands trembling uncontrollably. Fifteen minutes or so elapsed without a sound.

'Are you ok, darling!' she called out, praying that he'd slashed his wrists with his treasured straight-razor, a sixteenth birthday present from his father, Caleb.

Herb emerged from the bathroom minutes later, a broad smile on his face, still naked, apart from the dressing gown cord draped around his neck. He lay beside her and while his lustful eyes studied every curve of her body, he stroked her nipples with the tassel and kissed her breasts.

'Thank God!' she gasped. 'You scared the life out of me, Herb!' she sighed, much relieved that the drama was finally over. 'So, big boy, you want to play kinky with the cord, huh?' she cooed.

'You could say that,' he said with a smile, repeatedly stretching the cord until it snapped taut between his clenched fists. Far from being over, the drama was about to begin.

'No Herb! Please God, no!' She shook her head from side to side. 'Don't come near me, Herb! Please, Herb, stay away from me! Stay away from me! Mother of God, please help me!' she screamed hysterically, clutching the sheet around her breasts.

Panic stricken, she tried to scramble from the bed. He lunged, grabbed her by the ankle and they tumbled to the floor. 'Don't fucking come near me!' she howled, clawing at his face. He pinned her down, took the silk panties that were lying on the floor and crammed them into her mouth. Yvette's muffled pleas fell on deaf ears. The gentle, loving Herb she once knew had gone absent without leave and was unlikely to return to base camp ever again. Sobbing like a baby, he gazed lovingly into her terror stricken eyes, wrapped the cord around her neck and pulled it tight. Yvette's legs jerked frantically until every spark of life had left her body. An eerie silence fell over the room, broken only by the sound of Herb's irregular breathing as he struggled to his feet. He spent the night sitting on the chaise longue by the window, staring at her lifeless form. Come daybreak, he placed her corpse on the bed, cleaned himself up and drove to the office.

'You look very pale this morning, Mr. Cohen. Is anything wrong? Goodness me! Your face! It's covered in scratch marks!' gasped Rebecca, concern etched on her face.

'Yvette and I had a little bit of a row last night.' He shrugged his shoulders. 'She blew her top because I opened one of her letters by mistake, Rebecca. It wasn't deliberate I assure you. But it's resolved now and everything is just fine.' Herb smiled and wiggled his eyebrows. 'I'm taking her out for a romantic candlelit dinner this evening.'

He picked up the mail from the in-tray, went into his office and emerged moments later.

'Rebecca, why don't you take the day off? Go and do some early Christmas shopping.'

'I don't really do much shopping at Christmas, Mr. Cohen. You're the nearest to family I have you see. You're the only person I ever buy a present for.'

'Well, give me a miss this year, Rebecca. That's an order.' Herb opened the office safe and reached inside, emerging with a wad of banknotes. 'Here's three thousand pounds, buy yourself something special. Go on now. Get the hell out of here, before I change my mind.'

Rebecca's response was a mixture of elation and sheer astonishment. This was most unlike the miserly Herb she'd known for nineteen years and she suspected that all was far from well. However, this didn't stop her from dashing off before he could change his mind. As soon as Rebecca had left the office, Herb poured a large whisky and gazed out of the window at the brooding skyline, the black clouds reflected his mood entirely. Several glasses later, he locked the office and drove to the penthouse. When he walked into the lounge he could smell Yvette's perfume, it felt like she was still alive and part of him wished she was. Now that she was dead, he missed her more than ever. Even when she dumped him for Bryan, he never felt this empty and alone. He lit a cigar, poured a whisky, strolled into the bedroom and switched on the bedside lamps. What had once been a beautiful face was now a grotesque death mask and Yvette's long delicate fingers, stiffened by the onset of rigor mortis, had set like hideous talons. He sat beside her and stroked her hair, reminiscing.

'We had some good times didn't we, baby.' He paused. 'No, I stand corrected. We had some *wonderful* times!' he enthused, smiling sorrowfully through the tears. 'Remember the time in Vegas when that guy came up to you... What was his name now? Cletus something... Cletus Balfour, yes that's it. Cletus Balfour said he'd pay you fifty thousand dollars for a fuck. The arrogant hillbilly prick! I soon put that inbred fucker in his place!' Herb paused to unfasten his shirt collar and remove his tie before continuing. 'Then there was the summer in Cannes, when that French model thought I was a movie director and wouldn't leave me alone. At least not until you followed her into the ladies room and gave her a slap. Yeah baby, we certainly had some great times.' He rose from the bed and paced the room, deep in thought, talking to himself. He turned to Yvette and slapped his hands together, a huge smile on his face. 'The Plaza de Toros de Las Ventas in Madrid! We were seated in the second row when you opened your legs. The picador was so distracted, he and the horse were tossed up in the air by the bull!' Herb looked questioningly at Yvette. 'Tell me the truth, baby. Did you really forget to put on your panties before leaving the hotel that morning?' He sat down beside her, shaking his head from side to side. 'You could be one very naughty girl when you wanted to be. My God, you looked stunning that day.' He placed his hand on hers. 'You looked stunning every day, my sweet. I loved to walk into a restaurant with you by my side and see every man in the place looking at me enviously. I felt ten feet tall. Perhaps if I'd told you that, you'd have treated me better.'

149

The smile drained from Herb's face. 'Please baby, please don't look at me that way.' He turned his head away, biting into his clenched fist. 'You drove me over the edge. There's only so much a man can take. You treated me like dirt for years and I never complained. Now look what I've done to you. Oh, dear God, please help me! Please bring her back to me.' He sat for some time, head cradled in his hands. Then rose to his feet, closed her eyelids and pushed her tongue back into her mouth. 'Forgive me, baby. Please forgive me.' he kissed her tenderly on the lips and draped a silk sheet over her body. When he reached the doorway he looked back. 'Sleep well, baby,' he whispered. 'I'll always love you.'

He began humming the song *'I guess I'll always love you'*, switched off the lights and closed the door behind him. Herb walked slowly across the lounge towards the balcony, flicked open the door latch and stepped outside. The wind was fierce and biting cold but Herb didn't feel a thing. He leaned against the balcony parapet smoking his cigar, watching the neon lights and Christmas illuminations that lit up the cityscape. Assembled in the building forecourt, fifteen hundred feet below, a Salvation Army brass band together with the St. Dominic's male voice choir, delivered a rousing arrangement of *Good King Wenceslas*. Herb waited patiently for Yvette's favourite, *Silent Night*. As soon as it ended, he leaned forward, rolled gently over the parapet and tumbled into the void. Seconds later, he hit the paving slabs with a sickening crunch, bringing the ensemble's rendering of *The Holly and the Ivy* to an untimely and horrific end.

Yvette's murder and Herb's suicide were big news. It was Quigley who first mentioned it to Munro. 'At least your wife's demise will save you the trouble of applying for a divorce.'

'Your cynicism never ceases to amaze me, Quigley,' said Munro, shaking his head, a wry smile on his face. 'Honestly,

Quigley, the thought never entered my mind. Daft as it may seem, I feel sorry for them. Yvette had this innate ability to drive you to distraction without even trying. That's why I'm convinced it was she who drove Herb off the rails. Murder isn't Herb's scene, Quigley. Herb worshipped the ground she walked on, he wasn't a violent man.' Munro laughed. 'I've seen Herb jump onto a chair when a mouse ran into his office. It's funny the way things turn out, Quigley. If you'd told me about this, six months ago, I'd have been doing cartwheels and the champagne corks would have been popping.' Munro shrugged his shoulders. 'But those days are long gone. I don't feel rage anymore, Quigley. I just feel regret for the way I've screwed up my life.'

Quigley peered at him over the top of his spectacles. 'Think about it for a moment, Munro. If you hadn't screwed up, you wouldn't have met Miss Blake. So perhaps you should start counting your blessings.'

Quigley slapped the newspaper with the back of his hand. 'According to this, she lost all her money in a finance scam. Some fly-by-night Casanova took her to the cleaners. The reporter says and I quote... *he got away with everything except the gold fillings in her teeth.*'

'It was *my* money he got away with, *not hers*. And she only had *one*,' said Munro.

'Only, *one* what?' said Quigley, looking puzzled.

'She only had *one* gold filling.'

Quigley nodded appreciatively. 'Nice to see you've got your pedantic head on today, Wurzel.'

Quigley was spending more time in the prison sick bay than in his cell, the headaches were getting worse and he was also suffering from bouts of drowsiness, nausea and blurred vision. It was decided that he should attend the neurology department at the County Hospital. Handcuffed and placed under the watchful eye of three armed guards, he was placed in a private room. After three days of primary tests, a doctor he'd never seen before entered the room. Quigley could tell by serious expression on his face that he was not the bearer of happy tidings.

'Good day, Mr. Quigley, we haven't met, my name is Richard Prendergast, I'm the resident neurosurgeon. I'll get straight to the point. It's not good news, I'm afraid.' Prendergast clipped four images to a light-box. 'These are the scans that were taken after you were assaulted thirteen months ago. As you can see, there is no indication whatsoever of anything abnormal.' He replaced them with four others. 'These are the latest scans. It's this area here where the problem lies.' He tapped the spot with his pen. 'It's a tumour, it's malignant and it's a bloody big one.' He switched off the light-box and sat in the chair by Quigley's bed. 'To say that you must have been in considerable pain would be a gross understatement. I trust you would agree.'

'I wouldn't argue with you on that one, doc,' said Quigley, forcing a smile.

'I strongly advise that we operate straight away to remove the bulk of it and follow that up with an intensive course of radiotherapy.'

'The gamma knife treatment, eh doc! My dad had that. It did nothing for him, other than keep him hanging around a little bit longer. Building up everyone's hopes just for the big let-down.' Quigley took a sip from the beaker that was on his bedside table.

'Shoot from the hip doc. What are my chances of beating this?'

Prendergast looked at him anxiously. 'That's a tough one, Mr. Quigley. At best, I'd give you a 10% chance.' He paused for reflection before continuing. 'Possibly less, because of where the tumour is sited.'

'How long have I got, if I don't have the treatment?'

Prendergast took a deep breath. 'Three or four months, five months tops. It's nigh on impossible to predict these things accurately, Mr. Quigley. Each person is different. Some people have a greater resilience than others. I've seen people defy all the odds and live longer because they have such a strong desire to live.' He sighed. 'They do however, succumb to the inevitable eventually.'

Quigley turned away and gazed up at the ceiling. 'I'll give you my answer tomorrow, doc. Thanks for being straight with me. Now, if you don't mind, I'd like to be alone.'

Prendergast rose from the chair. 'Whatever your decision, Mr. Quigley, I shall support you. In my line of work, one cannot afford to be judgmental. When all is said and done, it's *your* life, and *you* are the one who is dying. The final decision *must be yours.*' He sighed, resignedly. 'I'm sorry I couldn't be more help, Mr. Quigley. I'll speak with you tomorrow morning.' Prendergast turned away and left the room.

The door opened moments later and Sister Kennedy entered the room, followed by a nurse pushing a dinner trolley. She told the nurse to leave.

'What would you like for dinner, Mr. Quigley? And I'm not talking hospital grub here, I'm talking outside caterers. You can have *anything* you want and it's on me,' she said, smiling from ear to ear.

A smile crept over Quigley's face. 'You're having me on.'

'I've never been more serious, Mr. Quigley.'

'I can really have *anything* I want?'

'That's what I said.' She stood with her arms folded across her chest.

Quigley's eyes lit up. 'There's something I haven't had in years.'

She stared at him disapprovingly. 'You may be in a private room Mr. Quigley, but I can't arrange for that sort of thing. I'd lose my job.'

'No Sister. Not that!' he chuckled. 'I'd love pie and mash with green liquor from Ernie Bishop's Nosherie. It's up a little side street, just off Market Square. Do you know where that is?'

'No, but I'm sure the taxi driver will know. Consider it done Mr. Quigley.'

'Thanks, Sister. You're a star.'

'You're the star, Mr. Quigley. I followed your trial in the newspapers. What that beast did to your granddaughter was inhuman. And I've yet to meet anyone, male or female who condemned your actions.' She began to sniffle. 'I'm so sorry that it's come down to this, Mr. Quigley,' she said, shaking her head. 'Life just isn't fair, believe me. I see it here, every day and it breaks my heart.'

'Come on now, Sister Kennedy. I bet you get one hell of a buzz when one of your patients walks out the front door with a big smile on their face, fully cured and a long healthy life stretched out before them. Surely those moments of triumph must make it all worthwhile.'

'Yes, it does help, Mr. Quigley. But, only a little bit. The way I see it, the good days act in the same way that painkillers do for a migraine sufferer. The headache will vanish for a time, but you know deep down that not before too long, another migraine will arrive.' She rolled her eyes upwards. 'Oh God, you must think I'm such an old misery guts,' she gasped.

'On the contrary, Sister Kennedy, I think you're marvellous. Now pull your finger out and send someone to fetch that pie and mash!'

'Oh God, I'm such an old blether! You must be starving by now!' She spun on her heels and shot out the door. Forty-five minutes later she entered the room carrying a tray. Quigley's eyes lit up as he lowered his head to smell the pie and mash.

'I've died and gone to heaven, Sister. I can't tell you, how much I've missed this! When people tell you that ambrosia is the food of the gods, don't believe a word.' He pointed at the food with his fork and smiled. 'This is the food of the gods, believe me.'

'Stop talking, man and dig in before it gets cold. You, daft old bugger.' She turned to leave and shouted over her shoulder. 'Just leave the tray on the table when you're finished. A nurse will pick it up later.'

Prendergast entered Quigley's room at 10am the following morning. Quigley was seated at the side of his bed, reading a magazine.

'Have you reached a decision, Mr. Quigley?'

'I have doc,' he said, placing the magazine on the pillow. 'I don't want the treatment. My family's been through the mill with one thing and another over the past seven years. It's time for me to put an end to it. They've suffered enough, especially my daughter Connie and her husband.'

'I had a feeling you might say that.' Prendergast sat on the edge of the bed. 'It's a small consolation but are you aware that under such unfortunate circumstances as yours, medical parole is virtually guaranteed? You'll still be subject to the mandatory security provisions, but at least you'll be able to find a hospice that is closer to your daughter's home.'

'I wasn't aware of that, doc. Connie's going to take this bad. I don't know how I'm going to tell her. We've always been very close, you see. She's my eldest.' Quigley smiled proudly. 'She loves her dad.'

Prendergast stood up. 'If you wish, I could speak to her.'

'No, doc.' Quigley shook his head. 'Connie has to hear it from me. But, thanks for offering.'

'I wish there was more I could do for you, Mr. Quigley.'

'Don't beat yourself up doc. You can't win them all.' He sat upright and shook his hand. 'You people do a great job here and that Sister Kennedy's one hell of a woman!'

Prendergast nodded and headed for the door. Quigley called after him.

'I've had time to do a lot of thinking while I've been in here, doc.' Quigley took a deep breath. 'Rightly or wrongly, I've been banged up for seven years. And I've learned that life is great when everything is hunky-dory. But when it isn't, as in my case… no freedom, cut off from your loved ones, missing out on your grandchildren growing up, family get-togethers, birthdays and that sort of thing, dying doesn't seem so bad.'

Quigley was transferred to Kingswood the following day and his first port of call was the governor's office.

'I'll set the wheels in motion straight away and apply on your behalf for medical parole. Please be patient, Quigley, these things can take time. However due to the extreme and most unfortunate circumstances, I'm sure there will be no objections from the Parole Board and the Home Secretary too, for that matter,' said the Major.

'There's just one thing, Major Morris. I don't want any of the staff or inmates to know the *real* reason why I'm leaving Kingswood. Especially Munro, he's got enough on his plate right now, as you well know. As far as everyone's concerned, I'm just being transferred for further scans and tests.'

The Major looked surprised. 'I don't have a problem with your request, Quigley. If that's what you really want, it's the least I can do.'

Quigley rose from his chair. 'I bet you didn't think you'd be getting rid of me this soon, eh!'

'No Quigley, I didn't,' he sighed. 'I just wish it was for different reasons.' The Major looked at him a trifle nervously. 'It's a terrible predicament that you find yourself in, Quigley. I trust it wasn't a direct result of the assault on you by O'Farrell.'

Quigley smiled. 'No, Major. I saw the scans they did after the assault and they were clear. It was nothing to do with that, so you can sleep comfortably in your bed at night. Nobody will be banging on your door demanding your head. Your unblemished reputation as Governor is intact.' Quigley paused. 'I still think O'Farrell should have been prosecuted for assault though. Anyway, what's done is done and it isn't going to change a thing as far as my current situation is concerned.'

Quigley reached the door and turned. 'What are the chances of using your phone, Major Morris? I'd like to speak to my daughter, Connie. She doesn't know about any of this yet and it'd be nice to speak to her without a prison officer standing next to me, listening to every word.'

'No problem at all, Quigley. Help yourself, old chap. I'll leave you alone. Take as long as you like.' The Major left the room to wait in Shenstone's office. Fifteen minutes later, Quigley emerged looking somewhat downcast. 'Thanks, Major Morris. Much appreciated. My daughter had to put the phone down when I told her. Poor girl, she's distraught. We're so close, you see.'

'The next time you wish to speak to her, Quigley. Tell one of the officers on duty that you need to see me urgently,' said the Major, with an assuring nod of the head.

Jessop ushered Quigley to his cell, where Munro was busy polishing a pair of shoes.

'Polish mine, while you're at it! They could do with sprucing up,' said Quigley.

'Quigley!' yelled Munro, excitedly 'How did it go?'

'Not exactly how I hoped it would. I'll be going back to undergo more tests in a week or so. Not one of the specialists can put his finger on where the problem lies. It could take a couple of months before they sort it out. That said, there is an upside, it gets me out of here for a while and I won't have to look at your miserable face every day. So it can't be all bad.'

'Well I'll be damned! Some blokes have all the luck!' Munro threw the polish brush at him. 'I wish it was me! All those gorgeous nurses fussing over me twenty-four hours a day, breakfast in bed every morning, tucking me up in bed at night and after lights out probably a little bit of hanky-panky!'

'That's a thought you should share with Miss Blake? It would make her day, to hear that,' said Quigley, as he removed his shoes and tossed them at Munro's feet.

The Major kept his word. Quigley's medical parole was prioritized and approved within two weeks. He would be transferred to the Saint Ignatius Loyola Hospice, just three miles away from where Connie lived.

'They're packing me off to hospital tomorrow, Munro.'

'That's a bit sudden, isn't it?' said Munro, looking disappointed. 'You've only just got back.'

'The sooner I sort this out the better. It's been dragging on. Apparently they've just had a new scanner delivered from the States. It looks like I'll be their guinea pig.'

'Do you know how long you'll be gone for?'

'The specialist can't really say how long it's going to be.'

'I'll miss you.'

'Yes, the same here, son. Help yourself to my books and what's left of the whisky. I've had a word with Tommy the Tout.' Quigley winked. 'He'll keep you topped up with a regular supply of the amber nectar.'

'Thanks, Quigley. Drop me a line once you get settled in. I'll get the Major to fix it so that I come and see you. If he doesn't cooperate then he can forget about me doing any more dinners for him and his missus.' Munro wiggled his eyebrows. 'I can't see

158

him refusing though, because she thinks the sun shines out my ars... er, bum.'

Quigley smiled, said nothing and stretched out on the bed. An air of solemnity fell over the cell, which lasted until lights-out. The following morning Munro said farewell to Quigley and went straight to the canteen for breakfast. He sat with Reznik and Rocky.

'Mr. Quigley, he go this morning, huh?' said Rocky, his glum expression more appropriate for a funeral.

'Yes, Rocky. Mr. Quigley he go this morning.' Munro replied flatly, pushing the food around the plate with his fork.

'Mr. Quigley, he very nice man. He always say hello to Rocky. Not like other cons. They don't take the time of day with nobody and only care about themselves. Only yesterday, I say to Reznik, I miss Mr. Quigley when he go away. I suppose you miss him too, eh?'

'Yes, I miss him too Rocky. He's the only *real* friend I've ever had.' Munro's eyes welled with tears.

'*I came into the world when you gave me a kiss. And when you went away I died. But while you were with me, loving me, I was alive,*' said Reznik in Bogie fashion.

Munro stared at him. Quigley was right. Reznik wasn't crazy, he was razor sharp.

'You're a big fan of Quigley. Aren't you Reznik?'

'Very much so Mr. Munro and if a man like Mr. Quigley has seen fit to offer you his hand in friendship, then you are indeed, a very lucky man.'

Munro was stunned. This was the first time he'd ever heard Reznik speak normally, let alone make real sense.

'What happened to Bogie?'

'Nothing happened to him, Mr. Munro. Nature called, that's all. He just stepped out for a pee.' Reznik winked. 'He'll be back in a couple of shakes.'

Munro and Rocky burst into fits of laughter.

'Are you planning on doing any more dinners for the governor, Mr. Munro?' said Reznik.

'Not that I know of, why do you ask?'

'I'd like to help you again, if I may. It's good fun.' His face lit up. 'And I love scaring the shit out of the governor's wife,' he said, rubbing his hands together like a mischievous schoolboy.

'Hey! Don't forget me,' said Rocky, his face like a puppy dog begging for scraps. 'When I was a young kid, back home in Palermo, I work in my grandfather's bakery. I make the best bread in all of Sicily!'

Munro pulled a face, deliberately taking his time to reply. 'Ok. Consider yourselves hired.'

Rocky cupped Reznik's head in his hands and kissed both cheeks.

At 1.30am Ashley Roper staggered out of the Ring O Bells with her arm wrapped around Jimbo's waist. He struggled to keep her upright as they zigzagged their way through the deserted precinct, heading in the direction of the high-rise flats that littered the hillsides of Belle Vale, like ugly tombstones. Roper pulled Jimbo into a doorway, where she unbuttoned his coat and unfastened his flies. She rummaged eagerly inside his trousers and withdrew his erect cock. Roper dropped to her knees and took it in her mouth, her head jerking expertly back and forth, while Jimbo moaned with pleasure.

Roper got to her feet. 'Now, doggy me!' she gasped impatiently, turning her back on him. She bent forward with her arms outstretched and leaned against the door. Jimbo hoisted her coat and skirt above her waist, pulled her panties below her knees and drove into her, over and over again. She gasped with every thrust until she climaxed and fell to her knees.

'But, I haven't come yet!' complained Jimbo as she pulled up her panties.

'That's your tough luck!' barked Roper, adjusting her clothing. 'I'm fucking freezing and I want to go home!'

'Fuck you Ash! You're a selfish bastard when you want to be!' he moaned, his face a picture of disappointment. He stepped towards her. 'C'mon Ash, let me finish, I was just about to come.'

Roper pulled a knife on him. 'If you don't back off, right now, I'll cut that off!' she snarled, nodding at his erect cock. The look on her face, the menacing tone of her voice and the knife in her hand made an immediate impact, the cock that moments earlier had stood so proud and tall, now hung between his legs, a mere shadow of its former self. Looking like the poster boy for peevishness, Jimbo tucked it away, zipped up his flies and stormed off for the safety of the Belle Vale hills.

'Aaah, true love never runs smooth,' said a voice. 'We're not interrupting anything are we?'

Startled, Roper looked up. Two heavily built men were smiling at her. They were dressed the same; black overcoat, white shirt, grey tie, black trousers and shoes. Built like oxen, they were the type you wouldn't want to tangle with.

'Fucking pervs!' screamed Roper, squaring up defiantly. 'Looking for cheap thrills are you?'

The men laughed and walked towards her.

'I'll give you a thrill you won't forget in a hurry!' she bellowed, brandishing the knife in her outstretched hand. 'Come any closer and I'll cut your fucking balls off!'

Still smiling, the men inched closer until they were towering over her. Roper was silent, breathing heavy, her eyes darting frantically from one man to the other. She backed off slowly and found herself trapped against the shop door. She took a deep breath, preparing to scream and before she could utter a peep, a right hand crashed against her jaw and Roper fell to the ground, unconscious.

One of the heavies threw her effortlessly over his shoulder and carried her to a black Range Rover that was parked nearby. Two other men of similar stature and dress code watched their progress from another vehicle. One of the assailants removed her coat, placed a blindfold over her eyes and sealed her mouth with gaffer tape while the other, bound her arms and legs. After dumping her on the back seat they drove off, the other vehicle following close behind. Two hours later, Roper was conscious when they pulled off the dual carriageway into an abandoned industrial estate. With gaffer tape across her mouth she was finding it difficult to breathe through her nose, years of snorting cocaine had taken its toll. The driver stopped outside a warehouse unit and flashed the headlights. The graffiti strewn roller-shutter door clanked slowly upwards and the cars rolled quietly inside.

'Nobody saw you?' said the man, who opened the roller-door.

'No. That shit hole is deserted. Even the rats have left.'

One of Roper's assailants carried her from the car and dumped her on top of a workbench. 'Get the whisky out, George. This could be a long night and I'm bleeding freezing,' he said, blowing furiously into his cupped hands.

Connie placed the flowers in the vase, alongside the framed photo of Quigley and his granddaughter Linda. She looked at the photo and smiled. 'I love that photo, dad. Brighton wasn't it?'

'Yes. One of the best holidays we ever had. Me and Linda were inseparable that fortnight,' said Quigley, with a warm smile.

'It's lovely having you nearer to home, dad. It's a smashing place and the nurses seem nice.'

'Yes, sweetheart, the nurses are top drawer, every one of them. It can't be easy, working in a place where people are dropping dead every day.'

'Don't say that dad! It upsets me!'

'It doesn't exactly fill me with cheer.'

Connie sat on the bed, and took hold of his hand. 'How long do you reckon, dad?'

Quigley took a deep breath. 'Three weeks, Connie. Just three weeks.'

Connie pulled a tissue from her bag and blew her nose, then walked over to the window.

'How's Daichi doing at university?' said Quigley. 'Big lad now, I bet.'

'He's the same size as his dad,' she said, indicating his height with her hand held above her head. 'He's doing really well with his studies. They made him captain of the rugby team last week. He's a tough bugger, really gets stuck in when he tackles.' She paused to wipe her eyes. 'The pollen from those flowers isn't half giving my sinuses gyp,' she said, sniffing repeatedly. 'He misses his granddad. He's always asking how you are.'

'I miss him too, Connie,' sighed Quigley. 'It must be at least four years since I last saw him.'

'No dad, it's been six years.'

'Have you told him about me?'

'No I didn't. You specifically asked me not to. I told him you're having treatment for a chest virus, that's all.'

'That's good. I don't want him thinking about me when he should be focusing on his studies.' Quigley yawned like an old lion. 'Sorry Connie! Marvellous isn't it? Lying in bed all day makes me drowsy. I reckon I must sleep for at least eighteen hours a day.'

'I'll go then, dad. You have a nap. I'll pop back in the morning.'

Connie put on her coat and kissed her father goodbye. He grabbed hold of her hand.

'Have I been a good father?'

She threw her arms around him. 'Oh dad, don't be so silly. You've always done your best for us. You're a wonderful father. We all respect and love you.' Tears welled in her eyes. 'I don't know what we'll do when you go, dad.'

'Now who's talking silly? You'd all do just fine, Connie.' He kissed her tenderly on the top of the head.

She rose from the bed, kissed him on the cheek and headed for the door.

'Connie!' he called after her. 'Ask the screw with the big nose and the shifty eyes to pop in and see me.'

'How are the screws treating you?'

'Ok, I suppose. A bit over enthusiastic at times. They've been assigned from a local nick and aren't anything to do with Kingswood. They don't know me from Adam.'

'I thought I hadn't seen them before. See you soon, dad. Love you.' She smiled and blew him a kiss.

The screw in question, a tall serious looking character with a huge nose, walked in after Connie had left. 'What is it Quigley?'

'I need a favour, Mr. Sheridan.' Quigley pulled a sheet of paper from underneath his pillow and handed it to him. 'Phone the Governor at Kingswood. I've written his phone number at the top of the page. All you have to do is read the message to him, word for word. It's very important that you do that.'

Sheridan read the note. 'No problem, Quigley. Is there anything else?'

'Now that you mention it, there is something,' said Quigley, adjusting his pillow. 'I'll be dead in a few weeks and the only way I'll be leaving this hospice is in a pine box. Now, I know you blokes on security have a job to do. But do you really have to search my visitors so thoroughly and talk to them like they were criminals?' Quigley smiled. 'It's me that's the big bad wolf. Not them.'

Sheridan remained silent while he considered Quigley's request.

'Ok, Quigley. Providing you give me your word that nothing iffy's going on. I've a wife and three kids and I don't want to lose my job.'

'You have my word, Mr. Sheridan,' said Quigley, with an appreciative smile as they shook hands.

After receiving the phone call from Sheridan, the Major sent for Munro right away.

'I received a phone call today from the officer who is responsible for keeping an eye on your friend Quigley. He wants to see you. He only has three weeks to live.'

'What? Three weeks! I thought he was just having tests!' Munro was distraught. 'When will I be able to go and see him?'

The Major fiddled with his tie, rose from his chair, walked over to the window and stood with his back to Munro. He cleared his throat nervously.

'I'm afraid that the rules are clear regarding such matters, Munro. Quigley isn't family. I'd lose my job if I allowed you to visit him. Besides, the Saint Ignatius Loyola Hospice is too far away which makes the security risks much higher. It would be different if you were visiting him at the hospital down the road,' he mumbled, apologetically.

'He may not be my flesh and blood! But he's the *only* family I have, Major! For pity's sake give me a break here. I shouldn't even be locked up in this godforsaken place! Quigley is dying and he's asked to see me! Doesn't that count for anything?' Munro begged, tears in his eyes. 'Please, in the name of all that's holy, please let me go and see him before he dies.'

'I'm sorry, Munro. I am also very much aware of the high regard you have for Quigley. But my hands are tied. There's no way I can authorize such a visit.' The phone rang, much to the Major's relief. 'I'm sorry Munro. I *must* take this call. Please see yourself out. And calm down, there's a good chap.'

Munro stormed from the room and slammed the door behind him, cracking the glass panel. The smile faded from Winston Greene's face when he saw the anger in Munro's eyes. He said nothing on the way back to the cell. Munro threw himself on the bed and stared at the ceiling, his hands clasped tightly behind his head. Angry demons, he thought long dead, rose from the grave to torment him. He jumped to his feet.

'Let me out of here you bastards! Let me out of here!' he roared, pounding the cell door with clenched fists until it ran with his blood.

Minutes later, soaked in sweat, he dropped to his knees, sobbing like a baby, physically and emotionally spent. Challis opened the door and stepped inside, closely followed by Greene. Both men looked shocked.

'Jesus, Munro,' said Greene. 'You gone bust up your hands man.' He bent down to assist. 'Why you do such a crazy thing?'

Munro said nothing, cradling his bloody and swollen hands across his chest.

'Give me a hand, Winston. He'll have to go to the sick bay,' said Challis, hoisting Munro to his feet.

'What brought this on, Munro?' said Doris, as she bandaged his hands.

Munro said nothing and stared into space, his mind was elsewhere.

'You're lucky you only broke your little finger,' she said, shaking her head. 'It's not the one you pick your nose with is it?' she joked, trying to inject some levity into the proceedings.

Munro remained taciturn.

'It's mostly bruising and cuts. You'll be all right in a few weeks. Providing you don't start beating up cell doors again,' she said, peering over the top of her spectacles.

Munro swung his legs from the table and headed for the door.

'Don't bother thanking me, Munro. I'd hate to put you to any trouble.'

Munro said nothing, closed the door behind him and asked Greene to take him to Charlotte's office.

'What happened?' asked Charlotte, concern written over her face.

'It's Quigley, he doesn't have long to live and he's asked to see me. The Major says he can't authorize the visit,' sighed Munro, looking distraught.

'Oh, god!' she said. 'I'm so sorry, Munro.' She looked at his hands. 'Is that what this is all about?'

'I'm not family.'

'Oh, I see,' said Charlotte, the penny having finally dropped.

'I must see him before he dies, Charlotte. I can't let him down.'

Charlotte smiled. 'Leave it with me, Munro. There's something the Major hasn't considered in all of this. He just needs to be reminded of it, that's all.' She held his bandaged hands. 'For God's sake keep your temper under control. If it hadn't been for Challis and Greene you'd be on report.' She leaned over and kissed him tenderly on the lips.

'You'd better go now, Munro. I've much to do.'

'When will you know if it's OK for me to go?'

'It's hard to say.' She giggled. 'Wasn't it you who once told me that *mackerels* don't happen overnight?'

Alone in the kitchen, Felicity Morris gazed from the kitchen window, studying the young gardener's every move, as he trimmed the hedge, stripped to the waist. Her fertile imagination, running riot. Just as she was getting to the juicy bit, the phone rang in the hallway.

'Bollocks!' she moaned and scurried to pick up the phone.

'Hello, Felicity Morris, speaking,' she barked.

'Hello, Felicity. It's Miss Blake, here. Is anything wrong? You don't sound very pleased.'

'Hello, my dear. No, nothing's wrong, nothing that a phone extension in the kitchen wouldn't resolve.'

'Phone extension in the kitchen? I don't understand.'

'Take no notice of me, my dear. It's only the ramblings of a frustrated, middle-aged woman. Besides, if I told you you'd be horrified. It's the warm weather. It does strange things to my hormones. How I survived in the Middle East is beyond me. What can I do for you?'

'I wonder if I could drop by and see you, later today. I've something very important that I need to discuss with you.'

'I knew it! You're going to marry that gorgeous man, Munro!' she trilled.

Charlotte laughed. 'No, it's nothing like that. But it does concern Munro and I need *your* help. Will 4.30 suit you?'

'4.30 will be fine, my dear. Oh, I do love a little bit of excitement and intrigue! Being married to Bernard is like living with a Trappist monk. Talk about dull! My God, I've had more excitement watching a coffin lid warp.'

8

Due to the blindfold, Roper's ears were the only means she had of determining what was happening. A lighter clicked and someone lit a cigarette, it was a foreign brand, strong and scented. She heard the smoker walk away. At the far side of the room, a door opened and closed, followed by muted laughter and the murmur of indistinguishable conversation. They hadn't brought her here for the good of her health and her imagination was running riot, for the first time in her life she was terrified. The toughest bitch in town's veneer was crumbling away by the second, her body trembled uncontrollably and warm tears seeped from beneath the blindfold that covered her eyes. Three hours or so later, she heard approaching footsteps, a man picked her up, threw her over his shoulder, carried her across the room and dumped her on the floor. Roper gulped in the welcome air as the gaffer tape was ripped from mouth. With the blindfold removed, her eyes were drawn to a solitary light bulb which shone over a sunken vat of greenish yellow liquid. She squinted, straining to get a look at her captors but they remained hidden in the shadows and her eyes were still adjusting to the light source.

'What do you want with me?' croaked Roper, hoarsely, her throat parched. There was no answer. One of the men cranked a handle and a pulley bearing an animal carcass clunked into motion. The suspended carcass inched slowly along a steel track until it hung over the vat. The man pulled a lever and the carcass dropped. The vat of liquid bubbled and spat violently as it consumed the carcass, sending feint wisps of yellow smoke into the air.

'Amazing stuff, nitric acid!' said her captor, shaking his head. 'It's hard to believe that in less than four hours there'll be nothing left. Not a single trace.'

Roper was quick to assess the significance of the demonstration. 'Oh, fuck no! Please no! Don't put me in there! Jesus! Don't put me in there!'

One of her captors dragged her by the feet across the concrete floor, hooked her legs to the pulley and hoisted her into the air.

'Naaaaw! Pleeease! Fuuuck! Naaaaw!' she screamed, shaking her head violently, eyes jumping out their sockets.

The pulley clunked to a stop when she was over the vat. She peed herself, her urine sizzling violently as it hit the acid.

'I wouldn't wriggle about like that if I were you. This equipment hasn't been used in years. It might fall to pieces at any time,' he warned her, before walking away. Two hours later, a man carrying a cup of coffee approached her. She recognized him as one of her assailants from the shopping precinct.

'Please. Can I have some water?' she begged.

'That depends on the answers you give me,' he said, with a smile. 'Anton Munro?'

'What about him?' she stammered, her voice trembling.

'You tell me,' he said, still smiling.

'I don't know anything about him,' she said.

The pulley clicked and she inched slowly downward towards the vat.

'No! Stop! Please stop!' she wailed like a distraught baby crying for its mother.

The smiling man repeated the question. 'Tell me what you know about Anton Munro?'

'I don't know what you're driving at!' she squealed. 'Please! Stop this fucking machine!'

The pulley stopped four feet short of the vat. She could smell the heat rising from the acid which was still disposing of the animal carcass.

'I think you know exactly what I mean,' he said, nodding to the man who was operating the pulley.

'No, stop!' she screamed. 'I lied in court and got him sent down.'

'Now why would a lovely, gentle girl like you, want to do something nasty like that?'

She shook her head. 'I don't know. Out of spite, I suppose,' she whispered, meekly.

'Spite, eh. I wouldn't have thought you capable of such a thing. You don't look the type,' he said, shaking his head. 'Telling fibs just to get an innocent man locked up for life. No, I don't believe you. You're taking the blame for someone else. A sweet girl like you could never do such an evil thing as that.'

'Please, stop torturing me like this and tell me what it is you want from me,' she whimpered, anxious to end her torment.

'Let's say, for argument's sake, I decide to let you go. What would you do?'

'I wouldn't do *anything*! Honest, I wouldn't breathe a word about this to the filth!'

'That's not the answer I'm looking for!' he barked, no longer smiling.

'Please! I'm not lying, I wouldn't say a word!' she squealed.

'That's still the wrong answer,' he said, as he pulled a packet of Gauloises from his pocket and lit a cigarette.

'Please! Just tell me what the fuck you want me to do and I'll do it! Just don't put me in there! I'll do anything you want! Anything! I don't want to die!' she screamed, weeping uncontrollably.

Her captor flicked the cigarette butt into the acid and walked away. An hour or so later, another man emerged from the shadows and the pulley clunked into motion, carrying her sobbing frame away from the vat. He removed the binding from her arms and legs, sat her in a chair and threw her coat across her lap. 'Don't move!' he barked. Thirty minutes later, the smiling captor emerged from the office sipping whisky from a plastic cup.

'This is what I want you do, Ashley.'

Roper's eyes opened wide when she heard her name.

'You seem surprised that I know your name. Well don't be, because I know everything there is to know about you and your dysfunctional family.' He smiled the smile of a man who took pride in the thoroughness of his work. 'I know the pubs you use, who fucks you and I even know when you take a piss.' He placed the half-smoked cigarette in her mouth. 'Now where was I? Oh, yes. Later this morning, we'll drop you off at the offices of The Gazette newspaper. You'll go inside and ask to speak to one of their reporters. You'll tell the reporter how you lied in court to get Munro sent down. Then you'll go straight to the police headquarters and you'll tell them what you did.' He looked at her swollen jaw. 'Should the police ask about the swelling, you tell them you got mixed up in a bar room brawl last night. The judiciary bodies take exception to people who commit perjury, so it's a foregone conclusion that you'll get sent down and the maximum penalty is seven years. However, I'm pretty sure they'll take into account that you've decided to come clean, so it's very likely you'll only get five years tops. If you're a good little girl while you're in the slammer, eat all your greens, wash behind your ears and don't push drugs, I reckon you'll be free as a bird in three years.' He smiled. 'If you don't do *exactly* as you're told.' He glanced menacingly at the vat of acid. 'Bath nights for you, my darling, will never be the same again.'

Roper nodded nervously and coughed, choking on the cigarette.

'Silly thoughts of running away, hiding, fleeing the country, plastic surgery and a new identity may be bouncing around inside that cunning little head right now.' He lit another cigarette. 'Just remember one thing. We're the best at what we do and we *will* find you. Think about it. What's three years in the slammer compared to no years on the planet?'

'I'll do everything you want me to do,' she whispered, resignedly, eyes downcast.

'One last thing, before you go. You're a bit of a villain in your own right and you know the score. Answer one question for me. Why do you think I'm *unconcerned* that you know what I look like?' he said, smiling smugly.

Head bowed, hands trembling, she tugged nervously at the buttons on her coat. 'It's probably because, the filth don't have your face on file?' Her voice was shaking. 'And... if my confession doesn't appear in tomorrow's paper... you'll come after me.' She paused to clear her throat. 'And after you've done me in, there's no chance the police will ever find you.' A button fell from her coat and rolled across the floor into the shadows.

'Bingo! I knew you weren't just a pretty face!' he said, stubbing out the cigarette underfoot. He reached across and placed his hand on her swollen cheek. 'Some of our boys don't know their own strength. Put a packet of frozen peas on that as soon as you can, it'll take the swelling down.' He turned and walked away, talking to her over his shoulder. 'Everybody gets free dental treatment when they're in the slammer. So if I were you, I'd have some bridgework done on that missing tooth. Not only will it improve your smile, it will also increase your chances of finding a girlfriend. Three years is a long time to remain in a state of celibacy.'

Charlotte sat in the lounge at the Major's house waiting for Felicity to arrive with the coffee.

'This is so exciting!' trilled Felicity. 'What's it all about?'

Charlotte told her about the Major's refusal to grant Munro permission to visit the dying Quigley.

'Oh! That man can be so infuriating! Bloody rules! He lives by his damn rules! Our whole life together has been governed by a series of bloody rule books! Don't you worry, my dear, I'll have a word with him. Munro shall visit his friend or my name's not Felicity Abigail Morris.' She screwed up her face as if she had a bad taste in her mouth. 'Morris is such a dull, common surname, don't you think? It makes me sound like the wife of a window cleaner. It certainly doesn't complement Felicity Abigail.' She raised one eyebrow and admired her reflection in the mirror. 'I was meant for better things. I should have married someone with the name Churchill or better still, Mountbatten. Yes, Felicity Abigail Mountbatten, oh I do like the sound of that. It has such a noble and distinguished ring to it, don't you think?' She glared at Charlotte. 'When Bernard and I first met, I asked him what he would do when he left the army. My heart missed a beat when he told me he was going to get a job in Whitehall. I had visions of attending grand dinners, mixing with the leading politicians, foreign ambassadors, rubbing shoulders with members of the aristocracy.' She raised her eyes to the heavens. 'When his big opportunity finally arrived, he failed the bloody psychometric test. The results showed that he was too bloody honest, too rigid in his thinking and not devious enough by far! I am what you might call, the 3D's. Dissatisfied, disillusioned and distressed. I'm the wife of a bloody prison warden and you can't get further away from Whitehall and the aristocracy than that!' She leaned closer to Charlotte, a mischievous look of intent etched upon her face. 'Mark my words, darling. If Bernard Morris doesn't do as I say on this matter, I shall be looking for a new fucking surname!'

It was 7.30pm when the Major entered the house, dumped his briefcase by the coat stand, hung up his jacket, removed his shoes, donned his slippers and ambled along the hallway towards the kitchen. 'I'm home darling.' he called, pushing open the door, only to find the kitchen in darkness and devoid of all mouth-watering aromas. This was Tuesday and Felicity always cooked cottage pie on a Tuesday. The Major simply adored Felicity's cottage pie. So much so, that apart from when on active service, he'd eaten cottage pie on Tuesday evening for the last twenty five years. When he switched on the light, there was a note stuck to the oven door. His initial disappointment lessened, anticipating that all he had to do was warm up the pie in the microwave. The note read... *There's a tin of pilchards in the cupboard. Pilchards on toast should be fun. I'll be back later. Enjoy. P.S. Make a mess at your peril.*

The Major was practically in a state of mourning over the demise of his cottage pie. However, his Commanding Officer had spoken and orders must be obeyed. He prepared his pilchards on toast, placed it on a tray, carried it through to the lounge and ate in funereal silence. At 11.15pm, Felicity's car pulled up outside. When she entered the hallway, the house was shrouded in silence. The faint strip of light, shining through the gap at the bottom of the lounge door, was the only indication of life. She walked in to find the Major fast asleep, he was snoring loudly. On the coffee table to his right, stood a whisky bottle, it was half full and the room reeked of pilchards.

'Bernard! Wake up!' she yelled, poking his chest.

'Y-Y-Y-Yes colonel, the mortars are in position, sir!' he stammered, slowly emerging from a deep sleep. She poked him again, much harder this time. He opened his eyes and sat upright in the chair. 'Oh, it's you, dear.' he croaked, clearing his throat.

'Yes, Bernard, it's me! Where were you tonight, on the Suez Canal?'

'Er, no dear. Palestine,' he mumbled. 'Colonel Galbraith had just asked me to set up a mortar position with three of the chaps…'

'Bugger, Colonel Galbraith!' she screamed, throwing her coat over the back of a chair. 'Why, are you refusing to let Munro visit his one and only friend?' She sneered disapprovingly. 'A friend who is dying, I might add. Have you no heart?'

The Major's jaw dropped. 'Who told you about that?' he squealed, eyes bulging.

'Never mind who told me. Why can't he visit his dying friend?' she screamed.

'He's not family. The rules clearly state that…'

'Fuck the rules, Bernard!' she roared, eyes hanging out of their sockets. 'For all I care, you can take your rule book, roll it up into a neat little tube and shove it up your arse! I've had it up to here with you and your damn fucking rules!'

'But, I don't make the rules, dear.' he said, scratching his chin nervously, the colour draining from his face by the second.

'So! Munro's not family, eh!' she said, a menacing look in her eye as she stabbed his chest once more with her finger. 'If you don't fix it so that Munro visits his *dying* friend,' she rasped, placing emphasis on the word dying. 'There will be someone else I know who won't be family.' She stood upright, towering over him. 'Make it happen, Bernard!' she said, patting the top of his head with her hand. 'If you don't, I'll be out that bloody door by the weekend.'

She stormed out of the room and went upstairs. The Major looked like a mortar shell had just landed in his fox hole. He poured himself a more than generous whisky and knocked it straight back.

The following afternoon, Munro was called into the Major's office. 'I've some good news for you, Munro. You may visit Quigley, after all,' he said, clearing his throat.

Munro's face lit up. 'Brilliant! How did you manage it? I thought everything was set in stone,' said Munro, vigorously shaking the Major's hand.

'Let's just say I found a loophole and leave it at that, Munro. When do you wish to go?'

'What about tomorrow? Is that too soon?'

'No that's fine. Don't let me down, Munro. Don't do anything silly.'

'You can rely on me sir, I won't let you down. I've my parole to think of.'

Felicity rang Charlotte. 'Bernard crapped himself when I threatened to leave him. I wish you'd been a fly on the wall.' She howled with laughter. 'The last time I saw him look so shell-shocked, was in Aden, when an ammunition truck blew up outside the Officers Mess.'

'Thanks, Felicity. This means so much to Munro.'

'Anytime darling, just promise me one thing. When you see Bernard, please don't laugh. I've put him through the wringer over the last few days. I don't want him joining Kamikaze Kent in sick bay.'

'Don't worry, Felicity. It'll be our little secret.'

A Black Maria pulled up outside the entrance to the Saint Ignatius Loyola Hospice at precisely 11am on Thursday morning. Munro's escort handed him over to Officer Sheridan who was busy laughing and joking with the receptionist at the check-in desk. Sheridan draped a towel over Munro's arms to conceal the handcuffs and took him to Quigley's quarters. As they meandered through the hospice corridors, it was very evident why Quigley was here. Munro's heart was heavy as he opened the door and the first thing that hit him was the perfumed scent of flowers. Quigley's room looked like a florist's shop.

'Cheer up, Munro. Anyone would think it was you, who was dying,' said Quigley, clearly delighted to see him. Munro removed the towel and draped it over a chair. 'What the heck have you been up to?' said Quigley, when he saw the bandages on Munro's hands.

'Oh, it's nothing. I had an argument with a cell door, that's all,' said Munro, taken aback by how thin Quigley looked.

'Blimey! It looks like the door won. Come and sit over here. I've missed the banter.' Quigley patted the bedside chair. 'And for goodness sake lighten up. It's making me depressed just looking at you.'

Munro smiled and hugged him. 'Are you in much pain?'

'No. They're giving me morphine tablets. But, only in small doses, just enough to stave off the pain. I've told them I want to be alert when the time comes. Connie will be with me, you see. I don't want her staring at a living corpse for hours on end. If you know what I mean.'

'How long have you got?' whispered Munro.

'Blimey. You don't beat about the bush, do you?' Quigley cleared his throat. 'Three weeks, maybe four.' He nodded at the flowers and chuckled. 'I keep telling my family to send me flowers, *after* I'm dead. Not while I'm still alive, but they don't listen.'

Munro was not amused.

'Thanks for the bouquet.' Quigley nodded at the vase of red roses by the window.

'Bouquet?' said Munro, looking puzzled.

'Yeah, they're from you and Charlotte.'

'That's Charlotte's doing, Quigley. She didn't say a word to me about it.'

'And there I was thinking what a nice considerate bloke you turned out to be.' Quigley shook his head, feigning disappointment.

'I've missed you, Quigley,' said Munro, trying hard to raise a smile.

'Missed *me*? God, you really don't have any pals, do you?' Quigley reached out and ruffled Munro's hair. 'I'm only kidding, son.'

'By the way, you *were* right about Reznik, he isn't the nutter he makes out to be. He's just stringing everyone along. Which reminds me, Reznik and Rocky send their regards and they're going to be helping me at the next dinner party I do for the Major and his wife. Oh, yes, Jack Dobson hopes that...' Munro stopped, realizing the sentiment contained in the message.

'Jack Dobson says what? Come on lad, spit it out!'

'He hopes you get well soon,' said Munro, lowering his voice. He stood up and walked to the window. 'How come everyone thinks you're just having tests, Quigley?'

'Because that's what I wanted everyone to think, Munro. That's exactly what I told the governor to tell them. It's nice to see he kept his word for once. Good for him. It's about time he did something right.' Quigley adjusted the pillow and folded his arms. 'Carry on then, who else has messages for me?'

'Challis, Jessop, Greene and Doris from sick bay say hello. Oh, I almost forgot... Charlotte sends her love and a big kiss.'

'How are you and that girl doing?'

'Fine, Quigley, really fine. If anything, our love is stronger. I don't know how she managed it but she pulled a few strings with the Major, so that I could make this trip. I'm not family you see.'

'That's good to hear. You hang in there, that girl's a bit special. Just you wait and see, time will fly by and you'll both be walking up the aisle before you know it.'

'I wouldn't be in this position if it hadn't been for you and Charlotte.'

'We all need a little help from time to time, Munro. When all is said and done, it's you who's made it happen. The position you find yourself in now, is far from ideal, but it's a step in the right direction. Don't throw it away. Grab it with both hands. But most important of all, be patient, just like Adam Reznik said.'

Quigley's voice was steadily growing weaker and his eyelids growing heavy, finally fluttering to a close as he dropped into a deep sleep. Munro took hold his hand and sat for thirty minutes or so, studying his face and listening to the sound of his breathing. As his eyes wandered around the room, he noticed the framed photo on the bedside table. It was a signed photograph from Quigley's granddaughter, Linda and she was exactly as he described her. Beautiful, with loving eyes and a smile that could make the sun shine on a grey day. His heart aching, tears welling in his eyes, he bent down and kissed Quigley goodbye. He opened the door to leave and as he turned to look at his friend, a voice inside his head told him he'd never see him again.

One of the men standing by the Range Rover clicked his fingers. Roper looked up. He motioned for her to get in the car. She rose from the chair, somewhat unsteadily and climbed in. It was 8.00am when they pulled up outside the offices of *The Gazette*. Roper got out of the car, weaved her way between the marching hordes of office bound pedestrians and stopped at the revolving doors. She turned and looked back at the driver. He smiled and made a waving gesture with his hand. Pale and still shaken by the ordeal, she pushed open the doors and stepped inside. Roper approached the reception desk.

'May I help you?' said the receptionist, looking her up and down, somewhat disapprovingly.

'I want to speak to one of your reporters.'

The receptionist picked up the phone. 'Hi Bryan, there's someone here who'd like to speak to you.' She looked at Roper. 'And your name is?'

'Never mind what the fuck my name is. Just tell him to get his arse down here, if he wants to get on the front page.'

Three minutes later, Bryan Dimmock approached the reception desk. The receptionist nodded in the direction of Roper, who was standing by the window, gazing aimlessly at passers-by.

'I'm Bryan Dimmock, what do you want to speak to me about?' he said. There was a distinct judgmental tone to his voice as he eyed her up and down.

'I want to tell you how I lied in court to get an innocent man sent down for murder and when I'm finished with you, I'll be going straight to the filth to turn myself in.'

'What's big news about that? That sort of thing goes on every day.' He shrugged his shoulders, clearly unimpressed.

'The man in question happens to be Anton Munro, the TV chef,' said Roper.

Dimmock's eyes lit up. 'In that case, you better come with me.' He stopped at the reception desk. 'Gladys, I'm not taking any calls, until further notice.'

Two hours later, Roper left The Gazette offices and walked the half mile or so to Longbank Police Station. Due to serious nature of the matter, it was Chief Inspector Lawrence Daykin who dealt with the situation. The following day, Ashley Madonna Roper was on the front page of the evening edition of *The Gazette*. The banner headline read *"Roper confesses to perjury! Munro, innocent!"* Several archive photographs of Munro in his celebrity heyday and one of a glum Ashley Roper sporting a very swollen jaw, punctuated the article. After the story broke, Longbank Police Station and Kingswood Prison were besieged by every gossip-mongering, gutter-press newshound in the country.

Two days later, after five years wandering alone and forgotten in wilderness, Munro was back on the front pages, nationwide.

It was 10.15pm when Munro returned from visiting Quigley and as he stepped from the Black Maria he was summoned to the governor's office. The moment he walked through the door a jubilant Charlotte threw her arms around his neck. 'It's happened, Munro! The miracle we've been praying for has actually happened!' Tears of joy rolled down her cheeks. 'She's confessed!'

'Who's confessed?' said Munro, glancing at the Major who was grinning like a loony.

'Ashley Roper!' She handed Munro a copy of the Gazette.

Munro scanned the story, a look of disbelief on his face. He slumped in a chair and let the paper slip from his grasp onto the floor. Charlotte smothered his face with kisses.

'I do hope this extreme display of affection is all in the line of duty, Miss Blake,' said the Major, as he handed Munro a glass of whisky. 'This, Munro, is one of the finest, most expensive and extremely rare single malts ever to emerge from a Scottish distillery. I drink it *only* on special occasions. And this is certainly the *most special* of occasions. Here's to you old chap and to your pending freedom!'

Munro took a sip from the glass and smiled at Charlotte. 'Very special and extremely rare, she certainly is, sir. And might I add, incredibly, tasty!'

Shenstone popped her head around the door. 'There's a Sir Norbert Grantham on the phone. He wishes to speak to you urgently, Mr. Morris.'

'Sir Norbert Grantham! What in God's name can he want? Good lord! Put him through.' The Major dashed to his desk and slapped the phone against his ear. 'Hello, Governor Bernard

Morris here. How may I be of service, Sir Norbert?' he said, in an ingratiating tone.

Unable to contain her joy, Charlotte kissed Munro openly and without concern. Phone call over, the Major placed the phone on the receiver and poured another round of whisky.

'My beloved amber nectar's disappearing fast.' he wailed, holding the bottle against the light to check the level. He sat on the edge of his desk, took a sip from the glass and stared at Munro. 'I can only presume that you've sold your soul to the devil, Munro. That was none other than Sir Norbert Grantham QC. He's one of the best barristers that money can buy and he's been asked to represent you at the court of appeal.'

Munro furrowed his brow, looking bemused.

'This is madness, I've never heard of the man, *until now*! And who the hell asked him to represent me?'

'He didn't say, Munro. But you'd be insane not to accept the offer. Sir Norbert Grantham has represented members of the aristocracy for goodness sake, and now he wants to represent you.' It was the Major's turn to look bemused. 'Tell me the truth, Munro?' He narrowed his eyes. 'You've made a pact with old Beelzebub, haven't you?'

'If only it were that simple. Making a pact with the devil would be far easier to explain,' said Munro. 'But this has got me completely baffled.'

'Think carefully, Munro,' said Charlotte. 'You could have met him when you were working for the television network. A BAFTA presentation dinner in London, perhaps? You must have attended many of those.'

Munro shook his head and laughed. 'Oh, yes. I attended lots of those. I have three BAFTA's. But I was so drunk I can't remember a thing about the dinners or who was there. I passed out once and the host told everyone I was ill and had been rushed to hospital, overcome by a mystery virus. I'd gone to hospital alright, but it was to have my stomach pumped. I almost died of alcohol poisoning that night.'

'Well whatever you've done it's certainly working, Munro.' said the Major, looking puzzled. 'Are you absolutely sure you've never had dealings with Sir Norbert Grantham?'

Munro shook his head. 'I'm absolutely sure, sir. I've never heard of the man. This is as much a mystery to me, as it is to you.'

The Major pointed his finger at the floor. 'One thing's for sure Munro, your demonic cloven-hoofed friend down there, is working bloody damn hard on your behalf.'

As the Major poured the last of the whisky, he uttered an exaggerated painful sigh and dropped the empty bottle into the litter bin.

'I propose we hold a celebration dinner on your behalf, Munro. That's if you don't mind cooking the food.' He glanced nervously at Charlotte. 'Please forgive me, I meant to say, a celebration dinner for you *and* Miss Blake.' The Major tapped the side of his nose and gave her a knowing look. 'Remember the day I told you I wasn't senile?'

'Only too well, sir,' said Charlotte, bowing her head in acknowledgement.

The Major gazed out of the window with his hands clasped behind his back, rocking on the balls of his feet. 'Felicity will be absolutely delighted when she hears the good news!' he chuckled.

'What's wrong Munro? I thought you'd be jumping around. You don't seem at all happy,' said Charlotte, looking slightly concerned.

'It's all such a shock,' said Munro, running his hands through his mane. 'It's all so sudden.' He squeezed her hand. 'I am happy, believe me, Charlotte. It hasn't sunk in yet, that's all.'

'By the way Munro, you still have prisoner status, I'm afraid. Nothing's changed in that respect. But rest assured with Sir Norbert Grantham at opening bat, you'll be free as a bird in a few weeks' time. Of that you can be sure.' The Major lit his pipe. 'I wonder what brought about the change of heart from that Roper woman?' he said, peering through pale blue clouds of tobacco smoke.

Charlotte jumped in. 'That bitch doesn't have a heart!'

'I've been thinking about that too, sir. It just doesn't add up.' said Munro, shaking his head. 'She isn't the confessing type.' Munro looked at Charlotte. 'What do you think?'

'As far as I'm concerned, all that really matters is that she has confessed. I'm not interested in the reasons *why*. All I care about is you and your freedom. Nothing else matters to me.' She walked across the room, folded her arms and gazed out of the window. 'But, I have to admit, it does seem most out of character. Apart from being an evil bitch, she's the most, loathsome and racist woman I've ever had the misfortune to encounter.' Charlotte shuddered.

'Perhaps, Ashley Roper was *persuaded* by your old chum, Beelzebub. Perhaps he made her a *devilish* offer she couldn't refuse,' said the Major, sucking air through his teeth.

Charlotte dived in. 'I doubt that Beelzebub would want her anywhere near him, sir. That vile bitch would put him out of a job.'

When Munro left the Major's office, Jessop was waiting to shake his hand. 'That's brilliant news, Munro! Everybody in the nick's talking about it!'

'Thanks, Jessop. I can't wait to tell, Quigley.'

Three days later Munro was taken by Challis to the governor's office. He was greeted by the Major and introduced to a tall distinguished looking gentleman who was seated at the Major's desk studying a case file.

'Aah! Munro. Allow me to introduce, Sir Norbert Grantham QC.' said the Major, in an over familiar manner that brought a frown to Sir Norbert's brow.

'I'm very pleased to meet you, Mr. Munro.' Grantham extended his hand.

'Sir Norbert. The pleasure's all mine, believe me,' said Munro.

The Major was grinning inanely at Grantham and looked like a retard that had just peed in his pants. Grantham cleared his throat repetitively, hinting that they needed privacy.

The penny dropped. 'Right then, I'm sure you both have lots to discuss. So I'll leave you to it. If there's anything you need, Sir Norbert?' said the Major, bowing like a Chinese waiter. 'I'll be next door.'

Grantham waited until the Major had left the office.

'Please. Take a seat, Mr. Munro. Do you have any questions?'

Munro settled into a chair. 'Yes, I do. Why are you representing me?'

'*Why* I'm representing you is of no relevance, Mr. Munro. The fact, that I am representing you, is all that really matters.'

'Don't misunderstand me. I'm extremely grateful, Sir Norbert. But don't you think that I have a right to know?'

'The *only* thing you have a right to Mr. Munro, is legal representation. And in your case that happens to be me.'

'Why, the big secret?' Munro shrugged his shoulders. 'What do you have to hide?'

Grantham closed the file, folded his arms and sat back in the chair with his eyes fixed on Munro. 'You may rest assured Mr. Munro that I have nothing whatsoever to hide. What if I were to tell you that you have a benefactor who apart from paying me an obscene amount of money wishes to remain *anonymous*? Would that be sufficient information to satisfy your curiosity?'

Munro thought about it for a few moments.

'Since you put it like that, you leave me no choice but to respect my benefactor's wishes. And whoever pays the piper calls the tune, right?' Munro smiled mischievously. 'And if my benefactor is paying you an obscene amount of money, then I can only presume that your brand of musicianship doesn't come cheap. Please correct me if I'm wrong, Sir Norbert.'

Grantham smiled. 'That's a very astute observation, Mr. Munro. My musicianship does not come cheap. But one has to bear in mind that the quality of my musicianship is unsurpassed and I have a large orchestra to support.' He lowered his eyebrows and glanced at his wristwatch. 'Now, Mr. Munro, may we proceed? I've been invited to banquet at Windsor Castle this evening and I don't wish to be late.'

Three hours of intensive discussion ensued, concluding with Grantham packing his briefcase. 'Right we are, Mr. Munro. The court of appeal date has been set for three weeks tomorrow. If there's anything else I need to talk to you about, prior to that, I shall be in touch. Somehow, I don't think it will be necessary, but one never knows.' They shook hands and Grantham headed for the door. 'I almost forgot. My client, your *mysterious* benefactor, would like you to have this.' Grantham handed him a roll of banknotes. 'It's six hundred pounds. Purchase a smart suit and other bits and pieces for the big day. I'm sure the governor would be happy to arrange for a local supplier to come in with a selection of clothing that you may choose from. Appearances matter, believe me.'

'Thanks, Sir Norbert. I can't express how grateful I am.' Munro smiled. 'Oh, by the way, should you feel a Corgi humping your leg at the dinner table tonight, just smile and think of England.'

9

Just as Munro had promised, Reznik and Rocky were chosen as waiters for the celebratory dinner. Felicity eyed Reznik with a mixture of fear and morbid fascination which was exactly the response he had hoped for. The atmosphere at this dinner, unlike those previous, was one of joyous celebration and remarkably tension free.

'That strange little foreign man, the one that's not right in the head. He keeps smiling at me.' whispered Felicity, out the corner of her mouth.

'He's just being friendly, darling. That's all.' said the Major, dismissively.

'Why hasn't he been doing that silly Humphrey Bogart nonsense?'

'I don't know, Felicity. Perhaps he's not in the mood.' said the Major, unable to mask his annoyance.

At which point, Reznik placed the main course in front of her. Felicity nodded her thanks. Reznik nodded courteously and walked away. When he reached the door he stopped, looked at everyone in turn until his eyes came to rest on Felicity. Everyone held their breath as Reznik opened his mouth to speak.

'*So that's how it is! Everything's as clear as the nose on your face. You want the bandits to come and get me. You'd love that, wouldn't you? It wouldn't bother your conscience one little bit.*'

When he'd finished he turned and left the room.

Munro burst out laughing and everyone but Felicity followed suit. 'I don't see what everyone finds so funny!' moaned Felicity.

'That man is bloody insane.'

'He's just having a bit of fun, Felicity. He's really quite harmless. Believe me.' Munro assured her.

'He gives me the creeps!' She shuddered and pulled a strange face.

'Are you enjoying the food?' said Munro, quickly changing the subject.

'It's superb, as always, Anton.' she said, smiling at him appreciatively across the table. 'Will you start a restaurant when you return to the outside world?'

'No. I don't have the finances and I doubt if the banks would be keen on giving me a loan. What people say about mud sticking is true, I'm afraid. Don't believe anyone who tells you different,' said Munro. 'Despite my innocence, you can be sure that a lot of people will still regard me as a convicted killer.' He glanced at Charlotte. 'We'll just have to wait and see.'

'And what about you, Charlotte dear, I'm sure you must have *plans* in the pipeline,' said Felicity, smiling mischievously and wiggling her eyebrows up and down.

'I believe you're referring to, *wedding plans,* Felicity?' she said, glancing at Munro. 'It's something we've yet to discuss. Munro has an appeal to win first. We're not looking further ahead than that.' Charlotte lowered her gaze. 'It probably sounds crazy, but we're not counting our chickens.'

'Balderdash, Miss Blake,' groaned the Major. 'With Sir Norbert Grantham leading the assault on the enemy lines, it's a foregone conclusion! Stop worrying.' He reached for the wine. 'Anyone care for a refill?'

With a smile on his face that would have put Winston Greene to shame, Rocky entered the room carrying a tray of desserts and singing *'O Sole Mio'* under his breath. He served the ladies first, politely muttering *mi scusi, mi scusi* to each of the diners as he placed the dessert bowls on the table.

'What's that scrawny little man in for, Bernard?' said Felicity, as she scooped a heaped spoonful of mango kulfi into her mouth.

Munro was first to respond. 'Rocky arrived in England many years ago. He married an Irish girl, a bus conductress named Sadie. Things went well for the first six years and they had two kids, a boy and a girl. Suddenly, she started behaving strangely, not wanting sex, staying out all day when the kids were at school, coming home late from her friends and that sort of thing. Rocky realized that something fishy was going on. So instead of going to work one day, he hid in a cupboard until she left the house. He trailed her to a flat that was just a couple of streets away. When a man opened the door, she threw her arms around his neck, kissed him and disappeared inside. Rocky waited for fifteen minutes or so before climbing the stairs to the flat. He turned the door handle and stepped inside. The first sounds he heard were those of his wife moaning with pleasure. There was a wooden baseball bat lying in the hallway. He picked it up, walked into the bedroom and clubbed his wife and her lover to death. Apparently the affair had been going on for years.'

'Good lord! He doesn't look strong enough to swing a breadstick let alone a baseball bat!' said Felicity, shaking her head in disbelief.

'That's an uncannily appropriate choice of comparison, Felicity,' said Munro, smiling. 'When Rocky was a youngster growing up in Palermo, he worked in his grandfather's bakery.'

The Major interjected. 'Size isn't everything, my dear.'

'Oh, how I wish that were true!' sniped Felicity, rolling her eyes to the heavens.

The Major glared at her before continuing. 'Rage can give some people superhuman strength. I saw it in 1954, during the Mau Mau uprising in Kenya. Some of those terrorist chaps were barely five feet tall and had no trouble running through the jungle like the clappers, toting machine guns that were bigger than they were.' he said, nodding his head, the horrified expression on his face suggested that it was far from being an enjoyable experience.

'What would you do, Felicity, if you found your husband in bed with another woman?' said Charlotte.

'Haaa! Haaa! Don't be silly, my dear. The last time *Bernard* was in bed with a woman, other than me, was when he was being breast-fed by his mother!'

'Have another glass of wine, my dear.' said the Major, scowling.

After coffee had been served, *without incident*, Reznik entered the room carrying a large bundle in his outstretched arms. All conversation stopped immediately as he walked the length of the table until he reached Munro. Felicity, her eyes glued to Reznik, fiddled anxiously with her napkin. Reznik placed the bundle in front of Munro, stepped back from the table and cleared his throat.

'Ladies and gentlemen,' said Reznik, bowing and smiling at each of the diners in turn.

Felicity kicked the Major. 'He's not talking like Bogart,' she whispered. 'What's wrong with him?' The Major held his finger to his lips, bidding her to stop talking.

'When Mr. Munro first asked me to assist at his dinner parties, I had no idea it would be so much fun. I only accepted the invitation in the first place, because I thought it might provide me with an avenue of escape.' He pointed at the windows. 'As you can see, I'm still here! The bars on the windows are too strong.' He chuckled and winked at Munro. 'This is my way of saying thank you, Mr. Munro. It is with the greatest of pleasure that I present you with this token of my regard. *Please*, open it up.'

Gasps of astonishment erupted when Munro untied the string and opened the sack to unveil a beautiful sculpture of an eagle. Wings spread majestically, its regal head gazing skyward and a salmon clasped in its mighty talons. Reznik's ingenious use of paint had given the alabaster sculpture a bronze look. Felicity's open-mouthed expression resembled that of the salmon as the other diners broke into a spontaneous round of applause. Reznik stared at Munro, waiting for a response, an eagerly expectant look on his face.

All the derogatory comments he'd made about Reznik in the past, came back to haunt him. 'I don't know what to say,' muttered Munro, almost apologetically. 'It's beautiful. You have a great talent, Reznik. Thank you so much. I shall treasure it always.'

Reznik placed his hand on Munro's shoulder. 'The eagle represents freedom, Mr. Munro. It symbolizes the freedom that I hope will come your way in the not too distant future.'

Reznik stared menacingly at Felicity and his top lip started twitching. '*I'm warning you, keep your hands off my donkey!*' he Bogied.

Felicity smiled the smile of someone who'd had one glass of wine too many, she leaned back in her chair totally unruffled and looked Reznik straight in the eye. Her top lip started twitching.

'*What buggering Badges? We don't have any buggering badges! Bugger you mate! I don't have to show you any buggering badges!*' she Bogied.

Reznik saw the delicious irony in Felicity's choice of dialogue, the Mexican bandit leader's words to the anxious prospectors in The Treasure of The Sierra Madre. This was Reznik's favourite Bogart movie and the one which was key in the violent demise of his wife. Felicity had done her research perfectly and ensured that in true Reznik fashion, the dialogue was totally inaccurate. Everybody burst into fits of laughter, apart from the Major. He sat staring into space, his mouth hanging open in disbelief, stunned by his wife's remarkable recitation.

After the diners had finished admiring Reznik's artwork, the Major pinged the side of his glass with a spoon. An expectant hush fell over the gathering as he rose to his feet.

'Well Munro.' He paused and cleared his throat. 'I feel quite sad knowing that this is the last Kingswood dinner party. Felicity and I have enjoyed them so much. In the three plus years that you've been here...' He paused to sip some water, before continuing. '...we've had our differences, but you've taken it all in your stride and without malice.' He lowered his gaze. 'It hasn't been plain sailing for you by any means. Only you know what it feels like to be wrongfully imprisoned and then to lose your mother in such a dreadful manner.' He took a deep breath and stuck out his chest. 'Let's hope there are only blue skies ahead for you and Miss Blake. God knows, you both deserve it.'

A hug fest ensued. Felicity seized Munro around the neck, planted a long lingering kiss on his lips and whispered. 'Knock 'em dead in court, Anton.' The words were no sooner out of her mouth when she realized what she'd said. 'Please don't take that literally, my darling or you'll wind up in here again.'

Three days after the dinner party, Ashley Roper was led from the dock in handcuffs, by two WPC's. Ashen faced, hollow-eyed, shoulders bent, gone was the confident strut, a five year sentence for perjury was already taking its toll. Old foes and victims lined the public gallery to gloat over her long awaited comeuppance but they were mindful not to let it show. They knew that with good behaviour Roper would be back on the streets in three years. So it would have been very foolish of them to invite future reprisals. It wasn't until Roper was out of sight that the party hats and whistles came out and the celebrations commenced. With Munro's court of appeal hearing imminent, the timing of Roper's incarceration could not have been better.

As instructed by Sir Norbert, arrangements were made for Munro to kit himself out with a new outfit for the big day. Munro had the looks and physique to make factory overalls look chic and as he stood in the Major's office on the day of the appeal, dressed in a non-brand off-the-peg, black double-breasted suit, grey herring bone shirt, black tie and shoes he could easily have been wearing something by Armani.

'I'm sorry about the handcuffs, Munro,' whined the Major, apologetically.

'They'll be gone by the end of the day,' said Charlotte, snaking her arms around Munro's waist. 'You look great, Munro,' she whispered, proudly. 'Just make sure you come back to me, when it's over.'

Munro smiled anxiously. 'Keep your fingers crossed,' he said, before kissing her tenderly on the lips.

The Major checked the time on his wrist watch and nodded to Challis and Greene. They escorted Munro from the room and into the waiting Black Maria.

'When we reach the Crown Court, we won't be able to go through the main entrance!' shouted the driver. 'It'll be heaving with arseholes from the media. I've already phoned ahead so we can get in through a side entrance. A motorcycle escort will meet us at the junction of Farrington Street and guide us in!'

When they turned into the side street at the rear of the Crown Court, it felt like they were entering an electrical storm, as flashing camera lights lit up the grey sky. Press photographers and fans alike, were applying the shotgun approach and taking photos of anyone and anything that moved. It didn't matter whether people were going in or coming out, it was open season and everyone was fair game.

After a brief meeting with Sir Norbert they took their place in the courtroom and the proceedings commenced. Three hours later, the Right Honourable Lord Justice Lewington pronounced that Munro was innocent of the charge of murder and could leave the court as a free man. There were cheers from the public gallery and a frenzy of flashlights erupted into life, as Munro hugged Sir Norbert. In order to secure the best vantage point for Munro's departure, the rabid newshounds scrambled from the press gallery and the unfortunates who stumbled were trampled underfoot. However, their exuberance was to go unrewarded. Munro departed in the Black Maria just as he arrived, from the back door, only this time he was minus the handcuffs.

'My missus will be proper made up about this, Munro. That autograph of yours will be worth a packet now!' heehawed Challis, his eyebrows wiggling like a ventriloquist's dummy.

Greene phoned the Major. 'Munro's a free man, sir. Yes. Everything went like clockwork. We're heading back now. Munro? He's fine, sir. Not saying much. Probably hasn't sunk in yet. Tell him what, sir? Sorry I can't hear you, sir. You're breaking up, sir. Miss Blake says what, sir? Ok, I'll tell him.' Greene put his phone away and reached out to shake Munro's hand. 'Congratulations, Munro. Couldn't happen to a nicer fellah! Miss Blake sends her love.'

Greene shook Munro's hand and smiled. 'Jessop will be delighted when he hears the news!'

Emotionally and physically drained, Munro didn't bother to reply. He closed his eyes and leaned his head against Greene's shoulder. Charlotte was waiting at the reception point when they arrived at Kingswood. As soon as Munro stepped down from the vehicle she threw herself into his arms. The guards who were present, whooped and cat-called like spotty adolescents. Blake and Munro clung to each other until they reached the Major's office. Felicity was the first to greet him, tears of joy rolling down her cheeks.

'Come here, you gorgeous hunk,' she sobbed, throwing her arms around his neck and planting a kiss on his lips.

'Good show! Munro,' cried the Major. 'What's it like to be a free man?' he asked, handing Munro a glass of his treasured Scottish malt.

'It hasn't sunk in yet,' said Munro, somewhat flatly. 'I keep thinking that Challis will walk into my cell and wake me up.'

'Waking you up will be my job from now on,' said Charlotte as she threw her arms around his waist and pressed her head against his chest like she would never let him go.

'I don't understand why I feel so drained,' said Munro, looking a trifle bemused.

'Nervous exhaustion and stress old boy!' said the Major. 'I used to see it all the time when I was in the army. After three or four days lying in wait for the enemy, waiting for an attack to commence, I've seen chaps keel over, just like that.' The Major snapped his fingers. 'Some of those young conscripts were dropping like flies when the pressure was on.'

Felicity raised one eyebrow and scowled at the Major. '*Yes*. I know from personal experience, exactly how they must have felt.'

Munro drained the glass and handed it to the Major. 'Well, I guess there's no point in hanging around.' He took hold of Charlotte's hand. 'I guess it's time to go?'

'I think so,' said Charlotte, with a smile.

'Where will you be staying, Munro?' said the Major, innocently.

'He's taken a room at the YMCA!' snapped Felicity, shaking her head in disbelief. 'He'll be staying with Charlotte, of course!' She looked up to the heavens. 'Please God! Give me strength!'

Charlotte interjected to save the Major further humiliation. 'Munro will be staying with me until we decide what to do.' She smiled at the Major. 'Thanks for giving me the time off, sir.'

'Think nothing of it, Miss Blake.' spluttered the Major, still reeling from Felicity's verbal onslaught.

When Charlotte's car pulled up at the security checkpoint, a guard motioned for her to wind down the window. 'I'd climb into the boot if I were you, Munro. The media are outside. Should they spot you, your chances of getting through unmolested are zilch. You can always get out once you're down the road a piece.'

'Officer Davis is right, Munro. If they see you in the car with me, we'll never get a moments peace.' Charlotte gritted her teeth and growled. 'God, I hate reporters!'

Munro climbed into the boot. Cameras flashed as Charlotte drove slowly though the baying mob of newshounds. Like locusts descending upon a cornfield they milled around the car, faces pressed against the windows, eyes bulging hungrily, searching for anything that might give them a clue as to Munro's whereabouts or lead to a story. Charlotte smiled innocently, shrugged her shoulders and drove away. A mile down the road she pulled to a halt, released the boot catch and Munro climbed out.

'Don't worry,' he said, massaging the back of her neck. 'This will all have blown over in a few days' time.'

The happy couple spent a blissful two weeks together, venturing from the sanctuary of Charlotte's flat, only when it was absolutely necessary. And when they did go out, it was always under cover of darkness. It amused them to see that one of the national tabloids was offering a thousand pounds reward to anyone who knew of Munro's whereabouts. Fortunately, the campaign had to be abandoned after one week, because of the countless calls from cranks that were jamming the switchboard.

When Charlotte returned to Kingswood, she found a note taped to her office door. *Miss Blake, Please see me, without delay. Governor Morris.* The Major was on the phone when she walked into his office. He waved his hand beckoning her to take a seat. As soon as the call had ended he adjusted his tie and cleared his throat with a series of loud nervous grunts.

'Ah! Miss Blake. It's good to have you back,' he said, toying nervously with the red paper clip container on his desk. 'I've some bad news, I'm afraid. Cedric Quigley passed away peacefully in his sleep at 11.30pm last night. He'll be cremated at Broadlands Crematorium on Saturday.'

'That's only six days away. Munro will be devastated.' Her eyes welled with tears. 'We both knew it would be soon. But that doesn't make it any easier to accept. He was like a father to Munro.' She dabbed at her eyes with a tissue. 'I'll tell Munro as soon as I get home. I'd prefer to be there with him when he finds out. God only knows how he'll react.' She shook her head. 'It's just one thing after another.'

Later that day, Charlotte opened the door to her flat and was immediately greeted by the wonderfully exotic aroma of the evening meal that Munro had prepared for them. The smile fell from his face as soon as he saw her. She threw her arms around him, her head pressed against his chest.

'What's wrong?' he asked, kissing the top of her head.

'It's Quigley...'

'When?' he asked, anticipating what she was about to say before she could finish.

'Last night. Peacefully, in his sleep. He's being cremated on Saturday.'

Munro was inconsolable and wept uncontrollably. It seemed for a time that she was holding a heartbroken child in her arms and not a grown man.

'Can you find out what the arrangements are?' he said, once he'd regained his composure.

'Yes, Munro, I'll do that first thing.'

Delayed by heavy traffic on the motorway, Munro and Charlotte were running late and as they pulled off the road into Broadlands Crematorium, two heavily built men wearing black overcoats were standing at the gateway. Munro presumed they were there to ward off anyone from the press who might dare to make an unwanted appearance. Both men acknowledged them with a single nod of the head as they drove by. The hearse was pulling slowly away as they drove into the car park and by the time Munro and Charlotte entered the small chapel the Quigley clan, were already seated, so rather than draw attention to themselves and interrupt the proceedings, they sat at the back. After the vicar had said a few words, a handsome man in his mid-thirties, strode to the lectern and delivered a glowing tribute to his father. As the strains of The Pearl Fishers Duet sung by Jussi Bjorling and Robert Merrill filled the chapel, heads bowed as the coffin glided slowly away and the red velvet curtains closed behind it. Quigley was gone. Tears rolled down Munro's cheeks as he made the sign of the cross. Munro and Charlotte were the last to leave and when they stepped outside Connie was speaking to the man who'd delivered the tribute.

'Thanks for coming, Munro. Dad will like that,' she said, with a welcoming smile. 'This is my brother, Bryan.'

'Hi, very pleased to meet you Bryan. This is my partner, Charlotte.'

'I've heard a lot about you, Munro,' he said, with a firm handshake and a cheery grin. 'How does it feel to be a *free man* once again?'

'Words can't describe it, Bryan.' Munro paused. 'I know it's a cliché, but you never fully appreciate your freedom until it's been taken away from you.'

'I'm happy to take your word on that, Munro. Personally, it's an experience I could well do without.' Bryan glanced at Charlotte. 'Dad said she was beautiful. You're a lucky man, Munro.'

Munro looked at Charlotte and smiled. 'Yes, I am.'

'It's never easy losing someone you love, especially a father,' said Charlotte, with sadness in her eyes.

Bryan nodded resignedly. 'None of us live forever.'

Connie butted in. 'Bryan. Take Charlotte to see the beautiful floral tributes that dad received. I'd like a quiet word with Munro.'

Bryan nodded courteously, took hold of Charlotte's hand and they sauntered off towards the Garden of Remembrance. Connie and Munro strolled in the opposite direction until they reached a large oak tree. Connie reached inside her handbag, withdrew a large envelope and handed it to Munro.

'Dad wanted you to have this.'

Munro looked bemused as he opened the envelope. He glanced at the content and looked even more bemused. 'This letter says I have a Swiss bank account. It says I have one million, five hundred pounds!' gasped Munro. 'There must be some mistake. I don't have two pennies to rub together. And I certainly don't have a Swiss bank account.'

'It's not a mistake, Munro. Believe me, it's *your* bank account.'

'This doesn't make sense. I've *never* had a Swiss bank account!' Munro gave her the envelope.

'No, Munro. It's definitely *your* bank account and it's definitely *your* money. Or what's left of it,' she said, handing the envelope back.

Munro looked mystified. 'I'm sorry. This doesn't make sense.'

Connie pointed to a bench that was sheltered by a natural canopy of rambling roses. 'Let's sit down and I'll explain,' she said, with a wry smile. Connie inhaled deeply through her nose. 'I just love the smell of roses. Don't you?'

'I haven't really had the opportunity to smell flowers over the last few years. But you're right, they do smell wonderful. It beats the smell of body odour and disinfectant any day,' said

Munro, still staring at the envelope, shaking his head from side to side.

'It's the money that *your* wife gave to Bryan,' she said, lighting a cigarette.

'I still don't understand.' Munro shrugged his shoulders. 'Why would Yvette have given Bryan money, to give to *me*? I'm the last person she'd want to give money to.'

'She didn't. Bryan conned her into thinking she was taking part in a big investment deal. You must have read about it in the papers.' She looked over at the crowd of people gathered outside the chapel, a man with shoulder length blond hair was approaching, she waved and he waved back. 'Bryan's one of the best con-artists in the business, if not *the* best. We set it up for him to get his foot in the door by rescuing your wife from a mugger. She fell for Bryan hook line and sinker. 'My knight in shining armour' she called him. Bryan's been beating women off with a stick, since he was fourteen.' She laughed. 'And from what I read, you had similar problems.'

She reached out and held Munro's hand. 'All we wanted to do was recover your money. It was never our intention that the con would end so tragically. That's not the type of business we run. Next thing we know, that Herb geezer she was shacked-up with flips his lid and bumps her off.' She rolled her eyes. 'Then, he decides to go sky-diving from the balcony of his penthouse without a parachute.' She paused to dust some cigarette ash from her sleeve. 'We've never ripped anyone off that wasn't corrupt or crooked.' She laughed and lit another cigarette. 'And in today's world we haven't been short of rich pickings. Don't be thinking that we're some kind of a vigilante group. We're not. Helping you was dad's idea, not ours. And we've always done what dad told us to do, ever since we were kids. To pull off a con of that magnitude takes time and time is money. The money in your Swiss bank account is what remained *after* we deducted our expenses and a handling fee.' Connie placed her hand on Munro's knee. 'It really is *your* money. The money those two cheated you out of when you hit the skids. Dad figured that setting up a bank account in Switzerland would be the best way for you to benefit and evade the prying eyes of the Inland Revenue.'

The man with the shoulder length blond hair arrived. He smiled at Connie and Munro in turn.

'This is my husband Kioshi, he's Japanese,' she said, her eyes glowing with affection.

'Pleased, to meet you, Kioshi.' Munro reached out and shook his hand.

Kioshi bowed courteously. 'I'm very pleased to make your acquaintance, Mr. Munro. Connie's father told us, all about you. You were a good friend to him.'

'He was the only true friend I ever had,' said Munro, his voice cracking with emotion. 'I'm sorry for your loss. I also, feel like I've lost a father.'

'In Japan, death is just one of many stepping stones in life, Mr. Munro. Connie's father has gone to a better place. We don't mourn his death. We celebrate his life.'

Kioshi looked at Connie and smiled. 'The vicar has given the urn to Teddy. We should leave soon.'

'Good. I'll join you shortly. I haven't finished with Munro just yet.'

Kioshi bowed and left.

'How did he lose his eye?' said Munro.

'It happened when he was a thirteen-year-old kid in Osaka. His parents ran a small restaurant and were being forced to pay protection money to the Yakuza. Business was bad and they couldn't pay. The Yakuza weren't content with shooting his mother and father, they shot Kioshi too. Luckily for him the bullet passed through his eye and out the back of his neck. When he was fully recovered, he lied about his age to get a job on a merchant ship. He worked his way around the world, until he reached Britain.' She paused, watching Kioshi in the distance, a warm glow in her eyes. 'He sees more with one eye than most of us do with two. I met him at a club in London. It was love at first sight.' She smiled at Munro. 'Dad told me you know quite a lot about love at first sight, Munro.'

'He told you about that did he?' said Munro, smiling.

'Dad told me everything. We have no secrets in our family.'

'Yes, I certainly know all about love at first sight,' said Munro glancing at Charlotte who was standing outside the chapel talking to Bryan and other family members.

'We have a son Daichi, he's at university.' Connie lowered her eyes. 'And you know all about our daughter, Linda.'

'Yes. Your dad was never the same after that.' Munro took her hand. 'When Linda died, part of him died also.'

'The old Japanese lady you saw in the chapel is Kioshi's grandmother, Aeko. We brought her back with us, after Kioshi and I were married in Osaka. She's one hundred and two next birthday, never had an illness in her life and still has all her marbles.' Connie rose to her feet. 'Is there anything else you'd like to know, before we head back?'

'Yes. There's something that's always troubled me. Well, not exactly troubled me, it's a suspicion that I've held concerning the O'Farrell incident. Was it your dad who arranged all that?'

Connie smiled. 'No! Dad knew nothing about it. O'Farrell was *my* doing. It's the first time any of us have acted without consulting dad first. I witnessed what he did to my dad and there was no way I was going to let him get away with that. We've always looked after our own people, Munro. You hurt one of us and you hurt us all. That's our strength. It was Kioshi who took care of O'Farrell.'

Munro raised his eyebrows, recalling what happened to O'Farrell.

'I can see you're shocked, Munro.' Connie smiled sardonically. 'What you have to realize is that in some Japanese cultures, ruthlessness is tempered by honour. Fear and anxiety are regarded as grave offences. Retribution aside, Kioshi was giving O'Farrell an opportunity to show courage in the face of adversity and redeem himself for all the shameful things he had done throughout his life.'

They rose from the bench and strolled back to the chapel. 'Why haven't you asked me about Ashley Roper, Munro?' Connie picked a flower head from a rose bush and held it to her nose.

Munro stopped in his tracks. 'You mean you...you didn't...not her as well?' Munro's mouth hung open. 'You did, didn't you?'

Connie chuckled. 'Yes Munro. We got to Ashley Roper as well. Dad was sure she'd crack if we pressed the right buttons. My brother Teddy handled that job. There's nobody more persuasive than him when he puts his mind to it. Kioshi told me he's seen Teddy reduce grown men to tears without laying a finger on them.' She looked at Munro, inviting further questions but none were forthcoming.

'Hiring Sir Norbert Grantham was also dad's idea. He didn't want to leave anything to chance. Yes Munro, it'd be fair to say that one way or another, you've kept us pretty busy over the last two years, albeit inadvertently.' She stopped to place the flower in Munro's buttonhole. 'It was dad who was responsible for your mother's headstone. That's what started him on the Munro Crusade.' She smiled. 'That's what he used to call it. One small gesture of friendship set the ball rolling, I suppose. Dad believed you were innocent and felt sorry for you, Munro. He could see how cut up you were, not only by your mother's death but also because you didn't have the money to pay for a headstone yourself.'

'Your family, have done so much for me, Connie. I'll never, be able to repay you.' said Munro, looking troubled.

'Dad knew you'd say something like that. He told me to tell you that the only way you can repay him is to look after Charlotte and make her happy. Dad really admired her. He said she'd got grit. She reminded him of my mum, in that respect.'

When they reached the others, Teddy handed the urn to Connie. She turned to Munro and Charlotte.

'That's it then. The party's over and now it's time to move on. So, we'll love you and leave you.' The sun broke through the mist and she looked skyward. 'It's funny how things turn out. One minute everything looks bleak and the next... you know what I mean.' She wrapped an arm around Charlotte. 'Thanks for coming, Charlotte. You've certainly got your work cut out, looking after old *Catastrophe* here,' she said, smiling.

'*Catastrophe*?' said Charlotte, looking bemused.

'You'd better ask him,' said Connie, nodding in Munro's direction. 'He'll be able to tell you all about *Catastrophe*.'

Munro and Charlotte watched the fleet of black Range Rovers pull slowly away, until the last one had passed through the Broadlands gateway. They walked in silence to the car.

'You and Connie were talking for a long time,' said Charlotte, in the way that women do when they're curiosity has got the better of them.

'Yes, she did have a lot to say. They're such nice people. I find it impossible to think of them as criminals. Nice ceremony wasn't it?' said Munro, deliberately avoiding her reference to Connie.

Charlotte nudged his arm. 'Come on, spill the beans, Munro. What did Connie have to say?'

'Not now. I'll tell you all about it when we get home. Just keep your eyes on the road.'

No words were exchanged and an uneasy veil of silence descended. Munro could taste the tension as Charlotte shuffled around in the driver's seat, muttering to herself, cursing under her breath at every careless driver and pedestrian who crossed her path. She was perilously close to breaking point when Munro's resistance appeared on the ramparts and waved the white flag. He asked her to pull over at the next lay-by.

'Not so long ago, Adam Reznik told me I was a very lucky man to have Quigley as a friend,' he said, handing over the envelope that Connie had given to him. 'Adam Reznik's never been more right about anything, in his entire life.'

'I trust the funeral went well?' said the Major, clearing his throat.

'Exceptionally well, sir. They're quite a remarkable family. Nothing like I expected them to be.'

The Major snorted. 'Don't be fooled by appearances, Miss Blake. Many years ago we had five Sudanese tribesmen in our camp. They used to help out doing odd jobs and a bit of translating when required, *everybody including me*, thought they were bloody marvellous fellows.' The Major leaned across his desk, eyes narrowed. 'One morning we discovered that the devious buggers had slit ten of our chap's throats while they were fast asleep then buggered off across the desert with one of our Jeeps and twelve boxes of hand grenades.'

Charlotte frowned. 'I didn't see any signs of hand grenades or slit throats on Saturday, sir. Only love, compassion and unity.'

That wasn't the response he expected and the Major cleared his throat, in the way people do when they're irked. 'What can I do for you, Miss Blake?' he said, po-faced.

She handed him an envelope. 'What's this, a wedding invitation?' he said, tearing it open.

'No. It's my letter of resignation.'

'Resignation?' he stammered. 'Have I done something to offend you, my dear?'

'On the contrary, Major Morris. Munro and I are moving abroad, that's all.'

'Abroad! Good lord! May I ask where?' The Major was becoming more flustered by the second and his face was starting to glow bright red.

'Switzerland.'

'Switzerland! Good lord! Do you ski?'

'Yes I do, but I don't know if Munro does. We're not going there for the skiing. We're toying with the idea of starting up a restaurant, an Indian restaurant.'

'Do you speak Swiss?'

'No, my French is excellent and Munro is fluent in both Portuguese and French, so that should stand us in good stead.'

The Major propped the letter against the lamp on his desk, sat back in his chair and drummed the desktop with his fingers. Something was clearly troubling him.

'This has all come as a bit of a shock, Miss Blake. Forgive my reaction. Of course I wish you both well in your new venture and I hope it works out for you. It's just that...' He hesitated. '...Switzerland is such a bloody long way for Felicity and I to travel for a curry!'

Charlotte burst out laughing when she realized the *real* source of his disappointment.

'You really think that Munro's curry is that good, huh?' she said.

The Major rolled his eyes and took a deep breath. 'The *best* I've ever tasted, Miss Blake. As you well know, I've travelled the world but I can truthfully say that I've *never* eaten anything that comes close to the wonderful food that Munro serves up. The man's a genius!' He stared at her, a frightened look in his eyes. 'God help me! Felicity will blame *me* for all of this.'

'Have no fear, sir. I give you my word that I'll speak with your wife before we leave and clarify our reasons for going abroad. Don't forget, I still have to work my notice.'

'Well, even on a professional note, I shall be sorry to see you leave, Miss Blake. It's been very nice having you around the place and of course your work ethic is first rate. Many of the prisoners have benefitted greatly from your help.' He shook his head. 'Felicity will also be sad that you're leaving. She's always telling me how she enjoys your little get-togethers.' Charlotte got as far as the door, when the Major called out.

'Before you waltz off to Switzerland, what are the chances of Munro making some curry dishes that we could put in our freezer?'

'I'd say not a hope. We've so much to do before we leave.'

'Ah well, no harm in trying,' he said, frowning like a little boy who'd just been told that his hamster must be put to sleep.

'Oh yes. I forgot to say that we'll be taking a long vacation first. Somewhere hot, probably Barbados,' she said, before closing the door behind her.

'Off to sunny Barbados, eh?' The Major reminisced, muttering aloud to himself. 'We used to have a Bajan chap in the regiment, a wireless operator. Now, what was his name? Ah yes, Livingston Stanley, that was it. A big fellow, lovely teeth, shoulders like an ox and a wonderful voice. Now what was that old Bajan song he used to sing?' The major rubbed his chin furiously until his eyes lit up. 'I remember now! It was called *'Inckle the English sailor'*. I wonder what became of big Livingstone.' He picked up the phone and dialed. 'Hello darling. It's your devoted spouse, Bernard speaking. You'll never guess what Miss Blake has just told me…'

Charlotte walked into the apartment and kissed Munro on the cheek. 'The Major wasn't too happy about me leaving. He does however send his regards and hopes that our new venture in Switzerland will be a great success.' She started laughing, uncontrollably.

'What's so funny?' said Munro.

Charlotte couldn't speak for laughing.

'Take your time, Charlotte. I've got all night.' Munro, leaned against the wall with his arms folded and a puzzled expression on his face.

Charlotte regained her composure. 'He asked *me* to ask *you*, if you would knock out some curries so that he could put them in the freezer,' she said, stifling her laughter with her hand.

'You have to admire his nerve,' said Munro, as he pulled her playfully onto the sofa. 'I've more important things to do than stand at a cooker all day making curry for the Major and his missus.'

'You've got that look on your face again, Mr. Munro.'

'And what look is that?'

'The same look you had this morning, last night, yesterday afternoon and every day before that,' she said, turning her head away as he tried to kiss her.

Munro grabbed the back of her hair and pulled her close, their lips were almost touching. 'You're the *only* person I know who can wipe that look off my face,' he whispered.

'Hmmm. And what makes you think that I want to wipe that look off your face, Mr. Munro,' she said, placing her index finger over his lips.

'That's easy.' Munro kissed her neck. 'I can see it in your eyes and the eyes are the windows to the soul.'

Munro rose from the sofa, hoisted her in his arms and carried her into the bedroom.

10

It was early in the evening and Munro had left Charlotte at home while he collected the groceries from the supermarket. She was reading when her phone rang. Thinking it was Munro calling, she rummaged through her bag in search of the phone. When it came to cell phones, Charlotte was just like every other woman, the phone was buried at the bottom of her bag, underneath mountains of *stuff*. The sort of *stuff* that only women would think about hanging on to… food recipes torn from magazines, out of date discount grocery vouchers, cosmetics, notebooks, various wallets and purses, address books, old diaries, deodorants, more cosmetics and lots more *stuff*.

'Hello. Who's calling?' she said, unable to recognize the number.

The voice at the other end was cheerful and had a familiar ring to it. 'Hello, Miss Blake, Officer Henry Jessop here. Remember me? I work at Kingswood prison. I hope you don't mind me calling you. I got your number from Governor Morris' secretary, Mrs. Shenstone.'

'Oh yes. I do remember you, Henry. Munro always spoke highly of you. What can I do for you?'

'Is Mr. Munro with you, at the moment?'

'No, I've sent him to the supermarket.'

'Haa, haa! I love it!' said Jessop, chuckling. 'No need to ask who wears the trousers in your house!'

'I'm expecting him back soon. Do you wish to speak with him?'

'No! That's the whole point of me calling *you*. Some of the lads and I have had a whip round. We want to buy him something to remember us by. My name was drawn out of the hat, so it's my job to purchase the gift. Unfortunately, buying gifts isn't exactly my forte. I've seen some nice identity bracelets in Temple Brothers on King's Street. Look, Miss Blake, I know this is short notice, but if you could see your way clear to pop out and meet me, you could help me to choose the bracelet. The shop's closed now, but all you have to do is look at the selection on display in the window and pick one out. You know what Mr. Munro likes far better than I do. You'd be doing all the lads a huge favour.'

'That's such a lovely gesture, Henry. It's no trouble at all. I'll meet you there in twenty minutes.'

Charlotte rang Munro to tell him she was popping out to the late night pharmacy for some *ladies things* but there was no reply. She left a note on the coffee table.

King's Street was ten minutes brisk walk from Charlotte's flat. When she arrived outside the shop, a man was a standing in the doorway, there was no sign of Jessop. He flicked what remained of a cigarette into the street and waved to her.

'Thanks for coming, Miss Blake. I really appreciate this.'

'Oh. It's you, Henry. Please forgive me. I didn't recognize you without your uniform.'

'No problem, Miss Blake. It happens all the time.' He pointed to the bracelets on display. 'There they are. Which one do you think Mr. Munro would like?'

'How much do you have to spend, Henry?'

'We raised five hundred quid.' Jessop grinned proudly.

'Gosh! Munro must have *really* made a good impression on you all.'

'Oh, he's certainly done that, Miss Blake. He impressed me from the first moment I saw him. He's definitely something else, is Mr. Munro.'

Charlotte peered through the window. '*That one*, it has an Asian feel to it. Munro would like that because it would remind him of his mother,' she said, smiling.

Jessop looked disappointed.

'Sorry! Please forgive me, Henry. I'd didn't mean it to sound like that. He will of course *always* remember you and the other officers for your kindness and for thinking of him so fondly. Munro will be delighted when he receives your gift.'

Jessop laughed. 'I'm just pulling your leg, Miss Blake. I don't get the chance to be cheerful when I'm at work.'

'Yes! I know precisely what you mean. Kingswood isn't exactly the House of Fun.' She glanced at her wrist watch. 'Gosh, I really must dash, he'll be worrying where I've got to.'

'You walked here?' said Jessop.

'Yes. It's not very far. It'll only take me ten to fifteen minutes.'

'Come on. I'll give you a lift. I'm parked around the corner.' Jessop nodded in the general direction of his car.

'Thanks all the same, Henry. A brisk walk will do me good. Munro is always saying I don't get enough exercise,' she said, turning up the collar on her jacket.

'Please, Miss Blake, I insist!' He took hold of her arm. 'Please, let me drop you off. I'll feel better.'

Charlotte smiled, resignedly. 'Ok, then. You win. Thank you very much. You're very kind.'

They turned the corner into the side street and climbed into Jessop's beaten up Land Rover. 'You turn right and then second left after the traffic lights,' said Charlotte, pulling the cell phone from her bag.

Jessop turned left at the junction.

'No, Henry, I said *right.*'

Jessop snatched the phone from her hand.

'What do you think you're doing, Henry? Stop the car at once. Let me out now!' screamed Charlotte, frantically pumping the door-release button to no avail.

Jessop pulled a hunting knife from inside his jacket. 'Open your fucking mouth again and I'll leave you in such a state that even the magpies wouldn't pick at what's left. Now shut the fuck up. Do you understand? *Shut the fuck up!*' he roared.

Munro walked into the apartment and placed the shopping bags on the worktop.

'You take far too many showers, Charlotte. You're washing all your natural body oils away,' he yelled.

When he'd finished putting the shopping away, he pushed open the bathroom door. The room was in darkness.

'So much for you taking too many showers,' he muttered, under his breath.

Munro made a pot of coffee, sat on the sofa, picked up one of Charlotte's magazines and began thumbing through it. He spotted the note on the coffee table, read it and continued browsing through the magazines. Thirty minutes passed and she still hadn't shown so he gave her a call. She didn't answer. He waited another thirty minutes and tried again. There was still no answer. He threw on his jerkin and headed for the pharmacy. Charlotte was nowhere to be seen and none of the staff had seen her that evening. He dashed back to the apartment and tried phoning her yet again. There was a response this time.

'Charlotte! Thank God! Are you ok? I've been worried sick!' Munro's voice quaked with concern.

'Aah! Such loving concern, it's enough to make a grown man cry,' said the caller.

For a split second Munro thought he recognized the voice. 'Who is this? What are you doing with my girlfriend's phone?'

'Take my advice, sunshine. Never mind who I am and what the fuck I'm doing with her phone. If I were you I'd start worrying about what I might do to your glamour puss girlfriend!'

'Who is this? What have you done with her?' screamed Munro, his voice and his hands trembling.

'Haaa! Haaa! You'll find out who I am soon enough, pretty boy. As far as your glamour puss girlfriend is concerned, I haven't done anything *yet!*' The caller laughed. 'But don't take my word on that. I wouldn't trust me as far as I could throw me. If you know what I mean?'

'What do you want?' Munro was struggling to remain calm.

'Hmmm. What do I want? That's a tricky one.' He started singing. '*You can't always get what you want. But if you try sometimes, well you might find. You get what you need, oh yeah.*'

'Please. Just, tell me what you want. Please don't harm her,' said Munro, unable to hide the anguish in his voice.

'Look, you dumb fuck. The clue was in the song. It's not so much about what I *want*. This is more about *what I need.*'

'Ok! Tell me what you *need*,' pleaded Munro.

'I *need* you! I *need* you, you fuck!' the caller screamed.

'Where are you?'

'Before I tell you, I'd like to make one thing clear, come alone and don't get the police involved. If you *don't* do exactly as I say, you won't be able to recognize your glamour puss girlfriend when you see her. Believe me pretty boy. I make Hannibal Lecter look like Rupert the fucking Bear.'

'Please. Let me speak to her?' begged Munro.

'Who do you think you're dealing with here, the fucking Samaritans? Get your smelly brown arse down to the disused railway yard in Curzon Street. It's been fenced off for years and nobody ever goes there, not even the junkies and glue sniffers. If you look carefully, you'll find a piece of the chain-link fence you can pull to one side and squeeze through. Once you're through the fence you'll see a row of abandoned lock-ups. Only one of them has a sign hanging over the doorway, it says Barney's Auto Repairs. That's where I'll be. If you're not there by eleven o'clock your girlfriend will be dog food.'

Munro left for Curzon Street; parked the car and squeezed through the fence. The caller was right, the entire area was deserted. Apart from the drone of heavy traffic, streaming over the bridge that arched across the river, there wasn't a sound. The auto repairs sign hung by a single screw, partially blocking the doorway to the lock-up. Munro knocked on the door. There was no reply. The door creaked as he pushed against it and stepped inside. A candle glowed in the far corner. Munro inched his way towards the light, his heart pounding.

The grizzled face of an old vagrant appeared out of the darkness. 'Get the fuck out of here!' he croaked. 'I was here first! Find your own place!'

Munro's heart sank. He turned and left, punching Charlotte's number into his phone as headed back to the car.

'I see you found the place. And you didn't bring the police. I'm impressed,' said the caller.

'What's your game?' barked Munro.

'Game? This isn't a fucking game, pretty boy. I had to make sure you'd obey my instructions to the letter. And you did. So well done, teacher will give you nine out of ten for effort.'

'How do I know she's alive?'

'You'll just have to take my word for it. Your glamour puss girlfriend's far too busy fretting at the moment. You might say she's lost for words. Here's what I want you to do. Travel out of town on the main northbound carriageway. You'll come to a village called Linton on the Hill. Drive through the village for a quarter of a mile until you reach the first turn on your left. Follow the sign that says Brent Farm. Half a mile down the lane you'll see a big farmhouse, sitting on top of a hill. Open the gate, and make sure you close it behind you. When you reach the farmhouse, wait in the car until you hear from me. And remember, no funny business. And don't call this number again.'

Even though Munro's mind was in turmoil, he sensed that the caller was using Charlotte as bait to lure him in. That being the case there was every chance that no harm had come to her. The only reason he didn't contact the police was because the caller said the farm was on a hill and that being the case he'd spot the police coming, a mile away. He thought about calling Connie but he didn't have her phone number. That gut churning feeling of helplessness that he felt during his early months in prison resurfaced. He drove off and headed north out of town resigned to the fact that this was a problem that only he could resolve... or die trying. By the time he reached Brent Farm his only thoughts were of Charlotte. As instructed by the caller, he closed the gate behind him and made his way along a bumpy driveway until he reached the farmhouse. He switched off the engine and waited in the car. The only indication of life that he could see, an old beaten up Land Rover parked at the side of the barn. His phone rang.

'What do you want me to do?' said Munro.

'Leave the car and go into the barn. Wait for me there.'

Munro pushed open the barn door and the moment he stepped inside, a bomb exploded inside his head and he tumbled headlong into a black and silent void.

When Munro came to, his head felt like a blacksmith had been using it for an anvil. He was sitting with his back against a cellar wall and his wrists were fastened to an iron coupling above his head. As he struggled to his feet, a large rat squeezed through a broken window pane and scampered along the ledge towards him. The rat eyed him from his lofty perch with fleeting curiosity then disappeared through a hole in the ceiling. Munro struggled manfully to loosen the bonds but all his efforts proved futile. His mouth was parched and he was cold. Suddenly, the cellar door creaked open. Someone was standing in the shadows. Munro peered through the gloom to see who it was. The man lit a cigarette and Munro caught a glimpse of his face.

'It can't be! Christ! Is that you Jessop? Is that really you?'

'You certainly get yourself into some tight spots, Mr. Munro,' said Jessop, as he lit an oil lamp.

'How did you know I was here, Jessop? Cut me loose. Hurry man! Charlotte's been kidnapped. I must find her.'

Jessop pulled out a hunting knife and approached Munro. He unzipped Munro's jerkin, placed the point against his shirt and ran it slowly across Munro's chest. Munro screamed out. Jessop licked the blood from knife blade and smiled.

'Have you lost your mind? For fuck's sake, Jessop! What are you doing?' gasped Munro.

Jessop blew cigarette smoke into Munro's face 'Tell me Munro. Do you remember Danny Gordon?'

'Yes! How could I forget him? What's he got to do with this?'

'Danny Gordon was my brother.' Jessop leaned into Munro's face. 'And you fucking killed him!' he roared, holding the knife against Munro's throat.

The hatred in his distorted face brought an instant flashback. Jessop was one of the hecklers at Munro's trial. He was dragged from the public gallery by the police.

'But your name is Jessop, how can Danny Gordon be your brother?'

'Our old man died when Danny and I were kids. Our mother remarried and Danny being the youngest took the stepfather's surname. I was thirteen at the time and there was no way I was going to let them change *my* fucking name. Not for that drunken bastard! So I ran away!'

'But surely you heard about Roper coming clean. She told the court what *really* happened. Danny and Roper attacked me. It was an accident. I was cleared of all blame.'

'I don't give a flying fuck what some hoity-toity judge decided!' screamed Jessop. 'If you hadn't been there that night Danny would still be alive!' Jessop threw the knife at the door, piercing the old timber like it was cardboard. He smiled at Munro. 'Getting a job in the nick was the easy part. Being nice to you all the fucking time was the tough bit. I've lost count of the number of times I thought about opening your cell door and slitting your throat while you were asleep. Jessop wrenched the knife from the door. 'So there I was, biding my time, waiting for the right opportunity, then, bingo! Lady Luck shits a big turd of good fortune on your head from a great height and you're free as a fucking bird! It was just what the clap doctor ordered as they say in Belle Vale.' He pressed the knife against Munro's throat until he drew blood. 'And you know all there is to know about Belle Vale, don't you, Munro? '

Munro said nothing.

'That's where you killed my brother,' screamed Jessop. 'Say something, you cunt!'

Munro shook his head. 'It was an *accident*!'

Jessop pushed the point of the knife underneath Munro's chin and whispered in his ear. 'You'll be delighted to hear that I've got a couple of *accidents* lined up for you *and* your glamour puss girlfriend.'

'Please, Jessop. Don't do this. Let her go. She's never been party to any of this.'

'Little glamour puss makes Munro happy, doesn't she? Little glamour puss says she loves Munro, doesn't she?'

Munro nodded on both counts.

'Well then, that makes her a willing accomplice in my book.' Jessop rubbed his hands together. 'An accessory after the fact is how a judge would describe her and as I am the presiding judge in this courtroom, I find her guilty.' Jessop smiled. 'Now then, pretty boy. Which would you like to hear first, the good news or the bad news?'

Munro shook his head, fearing the worst had already happened to Charlotte.

'Don't go peeing in your trousers, pretty boy. Little Miss glamour puss is still alive.' Jessop turned his back, making the sound of a ticking clock. 'Tick tock, tick tock, tick tock... the clock's ticking. Good news or bad news, good news or bad news, good news or bad news?' He approached Munro. 'Can't make your mind up, eh? I'll start with the bad news then. Your glamour puss partner's going to get it first.'

Munro closed his eyes and shook his head. Jessop leaned into his face. 'Hmmm. Something tells me that you didn't like the bad news. But I can tell by your eyes that you just can't wait to hear the good news.' Jessop jumped about like an over-the-top game show host. 'Are you ready, pretty boy? The good news is... that I, Judge Henry George Jessop, have declared that you'll be there to watch! You lucky, lucky, lucky bastard! You'll have the best seat in the house when the curtain goes up!' He screamed hysterically and clapped his hands.

Then, like someone who'd just remembered they'd left a water tap running. Jessop stopped ranting and stared at Munro in silence, his mind elsewhere. He turned and walked to the door.

'All this excitement has made me a bit hungry, pretty boy. I'm just popping out to a service station for a cheeseburger.' He turned off the oil lamp and stood in the open doorway. 'I hope you're not frightened of the dark, Munro. I was scared shitless of the dark, when I was a kid. Our Danny was the same. We slept together most of the time. We'd lie in bed at night listening to mum crying and screaming when that drunken bastard was beating the shit out of her. Even now, I sleep with the light on.

Twenty-eight years old and still sleeping with the fucking light on. Is that sad or what? A shrink once told me it had something to do with that bastard stepfather. Psychosomatic something or other he called it. What the fuck do they know, eh? What the fuck, do those privileged, posh fuckers with their university educations know about life on a sink-estate?' Jessop slammed the door behind him, whistling as he climbed the stairs. Munro knew the tune well, the plaintive Irish ballad, *Danny Boy.*

Jessop's Land Rover coughed into motion and pull out of the farmyard and an eerie veil of silence descended over the building. Munro held his breath, listening for signs of movement that would tell him Charlotte was still alive, only to be greeted by the faint drone of traffic on the distant motorway. He pictured Jessop sitting at the service station, happy and smiling, talking to passers-by, the quintessence of innocence, as he nibbled his cheeseburger and fries. Suddenly his attention was drawn to a scratching noise above his head. He glanced up and fragments of crumbling masonry fell onto his face and mouth. The rat was back and it was gnawing through the brickwork beneath an air vent. Munro nudged some of the fragments into his mouth. They felt soft when he bit into them. The brickwork was old and crumbling. All was not lost, Munro started to work the coupling back and forth. After fifteen minutes of strenuous effort there were signs of movement. The cement around the coupling had started to crack. And before long, there was movement in the coupling itself. Munro's strength was waning fast and his wrists were lacerated with friction burns. The clatter of Jessop's Land Rover pulling into the yard spurred him into making one last frantic effort, this time the coupling moved considerably. Jessop entered the cellar with Charlotte in front of him, a strip of gaffer tape covered her mouth and her arms were tied behind her back. Munro didn't move as he watched Jessop light the oil lamp and dump Charlotte on a chair, her eyes bulging in their sockets as she stared at Munro from across the room. Charlotte was alive and as yet seemingly unharmed. For now, that's all that really mattered to Munro. He realized he'd have to unsettle Jessop to have any chance of catching him off guard.

'Look who's here to see you, Munro.' Jessop pointed at Charlotte. 'It's your little glamour puss, alive and well, just like I told you.'

'Charlotte. Don't worry. I'll get you out of this,' yelled Munro. 'Trust me. This lunatic's *bed wetting* days are numbered.'

The smugness drained from Jessop's face, he pulled the knife and held it against Charlotte's face. 'Pity about what happened to your mother, Munro. Not a very pleasant way to die. They say it's the toxic fumes that do the damage and not the flames. She probably died of suffocation before the fire burned her to a crisp.' He threw his head back and laughed. 'The fucking place must have smelled like a curry house when they found her.' Jessop stooped to whisper in Charlotte's ear. 'Crispy mother tikka was on the menu that day.'

Munro realized he was looking at the man who had burned his mother alive. A man he'd spoken to on a daily basis and someone he'd regarded as a friend. He wanted to rip the coupling from the wall and bury the shaft in Jessop's skull but too much was at stake and Jessop was standing too far away. This was not the time for futile heroics.

Jessop's smile returned when he saw the anger in Munro's eyes. 'Mind you, I don't think your mother passed out before the flames got to her, Munro.' He turned to Charlotte. 'I heard her squealing just after I dropped the match through the letter box. Just like a little piggy. Eeeeeeeeeeeh! Eeeeeeeeeeeh!' Jessop waved his arms in the air. 'Eeeeeeeeeeeh!' Jessop halted his theatrics and approached Munro. 'Where were you when your mother needed you, Munro? She was screaming your name.'

Jessop mimicked a female voice. 'Anton! Anton! Please help me! Why aren't you here to help me, Anton?'

Munro avoided all eye contact with Jessop and focused on Charlotte, pushing all thoughts of his mother to one side. If things were to go as he planned there would be plenty of time to exact retribution.

'Sorry Jessop, my mistake. It was sleeping in the dark that was your big problem, wasn't it? Not bed wetting. I can just see you now. You and that cry-baby brother of yours, cuddling up to each other, every night, scared out of your wits. Wondering if the bogeyman was going to come and take you away. Mummy, mummy come and save us! The bogeyman's in our room! Please mummy save us! But mummy couldn't come and save you because she was lying unconscious on the floor downstairs because your stepfather had battered her brains in!'

'Shut it!' screamed Jessop. 'Fucking shut it! Or glamour puss gets it now!'

'Tell the truth, Jessop. You enjoyed hearing your father beat the shit out of your mother didn't you? You jerked off while you were listening to it and you probably did Danny at the same time. It was the Jessop's version of Happy Families, father downstairs beating the shit out of mum while big brother Henry's tucked up in bed with little brother Danny, jerking him off in the dark. That's what it was *really* like, wasn't it?' screamed Munro. 'Tell the fucking truth! That's what it was *really* like, wasn't it!'

'He wasn't my fucking *father*!' screamed Jessop, foaming at the mouth, tears rolling down his cheeks. 'He was my *stepfather*! And don't you talk about my mum and our Danny like that!' Jessop ran at Munro with the knife.

In one movement, Munro wrenched the coupling from the wall striking Jessop on the side of the head. Munro's momentum sent him headlong into a pile of farming equipment, bringing it down on top of him. Jessop was unconscious by the time he hit the ground and lay on his back, blood pouring from a gash above his temple. Stunned and shaken by the fall, it took Munro several minutes before he could get to his feet. As he moved unsteadily towards Charlotte, she was shaking her head violently from side to side, her eyes jumping out of their sockets. Jessop had risen to his feet and was standing behind him, moving in for the kill. He lunged at Munro and plunged the knife deep into his shoulder. Munro fell to the ground, writhing in agony. Jessop stood over him and raised the knife again, this time there would be no mistake. Munro kicked out, striking him between the legs. Jessop groaned, dropped to his knees, the knife flew from his grasp and came to rest at Charlotte's feet. Both men scrambled frantically to reach it. Jessop got there first and as he tightened his grip around the handle, Charlotte raised her leg and brought the full force of her heel onto the back of his hand. Jessop squealed in agony and dropped the knife. Munro grabbed Jessop around the neck and they rolled across the floor, two wounded combatants punching, groaning, gouging in a desperate effort to gain the upper hand. During the heat of battle, a phone rang, it was coming from inside Jessop's pocket and it was Charlotte's ring-tone. Seconds later, the ex-army tones of Major Bernard Morris filled the air, providing a most macabre audio backdrop for the fight to the death that was taking place in the cellar. *'Sorry to bother you, Miss Blake. I can't find the report you did on George Cairns. The blighter's up before the parole board next week. Please give me a call when you get this message. I bet you're having a wonderful time. Felicity sends her love. Bye.'*

For a fraction of a second, Jessop was distracted by the sound of the Major's voice. It was all that Munro needed, he grabbed him by the hair and pounded his head on the floor until he lay unconscious. Munro rolled onto his back, exhausted and gasping for air, his chest rising and falling as if he'd just run a marathon.

Moments later, he got on his knees and crawled across the floor to cut Charlotte free.

'Are you ok?' he gasped, gently removing the gaffer tape from her mouth.

Charlotte threw her arms around him. 'Yes, yes, Munro,' she sighed, clinging to him like her life depended on it. Munro's shirt was soaked in blood and clung to his back like wet tissue paper. 'We must get you to a hospital.'

Ashen faced, Munro slumped in the chair and stared at Jessop's body. 'Your phone... it's in his jacket pocket... you must phone the police.'

Charlotte knelt down at Jessop's side, watching his eyelids for the slightest sign of movement. Cautiously, she reached inside the jacket and removed her phone. 'He's still alive,' she whispered, turning to Munro.

'Leave him there, for now,' he gasped. 'Hurry Charlotte, if I don't get a drink of water soon, I'll black out.' His voice was barely audible.

'There's a cold water tap on the ground floor,' said Charlotte. 'Do you think you'll be able climb the stairs?'

Munro smiled weakly. 'I'd go anywhere, for you,' he said, throwing his arm across her shoulder.

Charlotte locked the cellar door behind her and helped Munro climb the stairs to the ground floor.

While Munro quaffed his thirst at the tap, she removed her blouse, cut it into strips with Jessop's hunting knife and bandaged his shoulder. Only then, did she call the police.

'I know exactly where the farm is, Miss Blake. We'll be there in twenty minutes or so. An ambulance will be along too. Just leave Henry Jessop where he is. Do *not* go near him. We'll handle this from now on. In the meantime, try to keep your friend warm. From what you say he's lost a lot of blood. Do you know his blood group?'

'Yes constable. It's AB positive.'

'Ok. We'll be on our way in a few minutes.'

'Come on, Munro, one last push.' she said, placing his arm around her shoulder. 'It'll be twenty minutes before the police get here. You'll be more comfortable in the barn.'

Charlotte made a bed of straw for him to lie down on and cradled his head in her lap. Munro closed his eyes and fell into a fitful sleep. Mice scampered about in the shadows searching for food and everything was so tranquil, it was hard to imagine the ordeal they'd just been through. However, the welcome silence was short lived, when a chilling sound brought goose pimples to her skin. It was Jessop, and he was whistling *Danny Boy*. Charlotte ran to the door and peered through a knot hole. A lantern glow was gliding from room to room inside the farmhouse.

'For God's sake, wake up, Munro!' she whispered, shaking his arm. 'It's Jessop. He's managed to get out of the cellar and he's looking for us.'

Munro got to his feet. 'You must get out of here, Charlotte!'

'I'm not leaving without you, Munro.'

'You must, Charlotte. Please, get the hell out of here! Make for the road and wait for the police.'

'I'm not leaving you alone to face that animal! For God's sake, you can hardly stand up.'

'I've no intention of *facing* him. I'm going to hide. I must keep him here till the police arrive. If he gives them the slip our lives will be hell. We'll always be looking over our shoulders wondering when he'll show up.' He kissed Charlotte. 'I don't want to live like that. Now run, and don't look back... I love you.'

Tears welled in Charlotte's eyes. 'I love you so much it hurts, Munro.' She threw her arms around his neck, kissed him and ran.

Jessop roamed the farmhouse, lantern in hand, searching for his prey. The sound of Charlotte's footsteps had him rushing to the nearest window. He spat on the glass and rubbed away the grime and with one eye pressed against the window, peered into the darkness. There was nothing to be seen, other than the two vehicles and the barn opposite. Then just when he thought his imagination was playing tricks on him, he spotted a trail of blood. He followed it down the stairs and across the yard to the barn. Jessop kicked the door open, stepped inside and picked up a scythe that was leaning against a large crate.

'I can smell your fear, Munro,' he snarled. 'You're bleeding like a stuck pig, Munro and that little knife isn't going to do you any good. Not against this,' he giggled, staring wild-eyed at the scythe's curved blade. 'You're as good as dead, Munro, so why not show some bottle? Step out and face me like a man.' Jessop slashed the air with the scythe.

'What would a piece of lowlife scum like you know about being a man? You're the twisted pervert who enjoyed jerking off his little brother, remember,' yelled Munro, from the shadows of the hayloft.

'I'll cut your fucking heart out and feed it to the crows, Munro!' screamed Jessop. 'Stop saying stuff like that about our Danny.'

Jessop stood in silence, his ear cocked, listening for any sound that would betray Munro's whereabouts. Munro inched his way to the back of the hayloft.

'What's keeping you Jessop? Lost you're bottle? You gutless pervert!' yelled Munro.

As Jessop scaled the ladder to the hayloft, Munro dropped through a hatchway to the floor below, unseen. Jessop attacked the mounds of straw, slashing wildly. Each frenzied swing of the scythe, more maniacal than the last, until finally he dropped to his knees exhausted. When he realized that Munro had flown the coop, he wept uncontrollably. Minutes later he rose to his feet, walked to the pulley-door at the front of the hayloft and kicked it open. Crazy-eyed and foaming at the mouth like a rabid dog, he threw back his head and screamed into the night.

'You're a dead man walking, Munro! I'll find you and rip your fucking heart out!'

A burst of brilliant light sent Jessop reeling backwards, so powerful it almost knocked him off his feet. And as he tried to shield his eyes from the intense glare, a voice boomed-out through a loudhailer.

'Henry Jessop. This is the police. The barn is surrounded. Drop the weapon and place your hands behind your head!'

'Fuck you!' screamed Jessop, diving out of view.

As the ambulance sped off Charlotte took hold of Munro's hand. 'Munro. Can you hear me?' she whispered in his ear.

Munro opened his eyes and nodded his head.

'I love you,' she said, gently squeezing his hand.

'I love me too,' he whispered, with a smile.

All was quiet inside the barn.

Chief Inspector Terence Benedict addressed his men. 'Five more minutes, then we close in. We have it on good authority that he doesn't have a gun. Nevertheless, I want everyone to presume that he does have one. Do not take any chances. I repeat, do not take any chances. This man is violent and highly dangerous.'

'It's bloody quiet in there, sarge. I don't suppose there's any chance he could have done a bunk is there?' said a young police constable.

'Not unless, he's bloody invisible! We've got more men surrounding this place than Sitting Bull had surrounding General Custer at the Little Big Horn!' said the sergeant, eyes glued to the barn.

As soon as the five minutes were up, Benedict waved his hand in the air in a circular motion and the cordon of armed officers encircling the barn closed in. A marksman stationed at the bedroom window in the farmhouse, tweaked the sights on his rifle as two police constables kicked open the barn doors. There was still no sign of activity from Jessop. Two armed men rushed inside. Moments later, they emerged with their weapons lowered.

'He's a goner, sir!' the constable yelled.

'He *can't* be for Christ's sake! Keep looking man!' roared Benedict.

'Sorry sir! I don't mean that sort of goner, sir. I mean he's dead, sir!' The police constable tied an imaginary rope around his neck, tugged on it and stuck his tongue out, mimicking a person who'd been hanged.

Benedict dashed into the barn. And just like the police constable said, Jessop was a goner. He'd hung himself, his face grotesquely distorted beyond recognition.

Charlotte collected Munro from the hospital two weeks later.

'That's one strong man you've got there, my dear,' said the Sister, grinning from ear to ear. 'Mind you, I'll be glad to see the back of him. He never stopped moaning about the food.'

'He's just the same at home, Sister. Nag, nag, nag. I think I'll dump him for someone less demanding.'

'Thanks for all your help Sister,' said Munro, shaking her hand.

'You're welcome, Munro. Our aim is to please.'

A nurse trundled past, pushing a dinner trolley. Munro turned up his nose and sniffed the air disapprovingly. 'You could have fooled me, Sister!'

'There he goes again!' she said, turning to Charlotte. 'Get the big ingrate out of here, before I castrate him.'

Munro placed his hands on the Sister's shoulders and kissed her gently on the lips.

'Be off with you now,' she gushed, the colour rising in her cheeks.

Munro and Charlotte spent the following three weeks taking things easy, doing the simple things and enjoying each other's company. Their love was stronger than ever. When Munro received the final all clear from the hospital, they planned their move to Ticino in Switzerland. The money that Quigley had left him, simplified obtaining suitable premises for their restaurant, which they named, The Lugano Mahal. They also purchased a house in the foothills of Monte San Salvatore, a short drive away from the shores of Lake Maggiore. After three years of extremely hard work they had established a fine reputation for excellent cuisine and built up a patronage of not only the local populace but also celebrities from Geneva and as far afield as Milan. Business was booming and life was hectic, so hectic that the subject of marriage was never raised. They were successful, fulfilled and more than happy with their lot, the dark days of Kingswood Prison, Roper and Henry Jessop were but a distant memory.

Inevitably, the pressure of work began to take its toll, so Munro recruited a talented chef from Goa, named Raphael, who picked up where Munro left off. A local man, Carlo, quickly followed to handle all the managerial duties. It was time for a well-deserved break and rather than travel elsewhere they remained at their Lugano home. It was mid-July, the weather was beautiful and they were both relaxing in the gazebo.

'I can't believe how lucky we've been,' said Munro, smiling contentedly as he took a sip from a tall glass of ice-cold fruit punch.

'That we have, Munro. But I can't help feeling that the bubble will burst at any moment.'

11

At precisely 2.15pm the gates of Cranfield, open-prison creaked open to reveal a solemn Ashley Roper carrying a small hold-all, she was wearing a leather bomber jacket, jeans and white trainers. Prison life had clearly taken its toll, gone was the excess weight and the pink hair, her face was now gaunt and the hair cropped close to the skull. She strode purposefully towards the battered, white Ford Cortina that was parked out front. A powerfully built young man, wearing a short-sleeved camouflage patterned army shirt was lounging across the bonnet. He leapt to the ground and ran to greet her.

'Sis!' he yelled joyously, as he swung her around in his arms. 'Long time no see. Huh?'

'Guess so!' she mumbled flatly. 'Just get me the fuck away from this shit-hole.'

It was only when she got into the car that she noticed a very large and very bald African sprawled across the back seat. He was wearing a necklace of animal claws around his neck. As the car pulled away, she lit up a cigarette and turned to her brother.

'Where did you find Idi Amin?'

Harold looked into the rear view mirror and started laughing.

'That's my best mate, Bones. Bones and me have been through some real tough shit out there. He's saved my skin more than once. We're like brothers.' He looked over his shoulder at the unsmiling African. 'We're like brothers. Ain't we Bones?'

'That's the God's truth, Harry. That's the God's honest truth,' said Bones, nodding his head pensively, his voice like rumbling thunder. 'We is truly brothers in arms.'

'Well you ain't my brother and never will be,' she hissed, her mouth downturned. 'Why the fuck did you bring him along?' She glared at Harold. 'You know I can't stand darkies!'

'Look Ashley. Where I go, Bones goes. If you don't like it, you can catch a train.' Harold slammed his foot on the brake pedal and the car screeched to a halt. He reached across and pushed open the door.

She flicked her cigarette into the street, refusing to budge. Stared straight ahead and lit up another cigarette.

'Close that door and drive, you little bastard,' she snarled. 'If you don't, I'll cut your eyes out.'

Harold threw his head back, eyes bulging, veins standing out on his neck like rope cords, whining like a man in terrible pain, gripping the steering wheel so hard his knuckles turned white.

'I'll not tell you again,' she said, like a mother chastising a naughty child.

He reached over and closed the door. They drove for an hour and no words were exchanged.

It was Bones who brought the silence to an end.

'Wet your whistle, Harry's sister,' he said, passing a can of Carlsberg Special Brew to her.

She took the can, wiped the top with the cuff of her jacket and pulled the ring, took a long swig then passed it to her brother. He drained the can then tossed it out of the window.

'Harry said, you got a job for us,' boomed Bones, as he handed her another can.

'That was before I knew he'd have Idi Amin in tow,' she hissed, staring daggers at her brother.

'Well, it's just like Harry says, where he goes I go.' He placed a shovel-like hand on Harold's shoulder. 'If Harry wants me to stay out of it, that's OK with me.' He gave Harold's shoulder a gentle squeeze. 'We'll always be brothers.'

'Oh! For fuck's sake! I can hear the violins. Pass me a hanky so I can dry my tears,' she wailed.

'You don't understand, Harry's sister. What we got is more than just brotherly love,' said Bones, gently kneading the nape of Harold's neck.

She stared at her brother, open-mouthed. 'Oh no, please tell me I'm wrong!' She elbowed him in the ribs. 'Has Idi Amin been fucking you?'

Harold said nothing. She watched the colour drain from his face.

'Tell me I'm wrong!' she screamed.

Harold couldn't look at her.

'I don't believe it! My brother has a liking for Zulu cock. He's been out in Africa, butchering innocent people for a few quid and getting porked by Idi Amin in his lunch break!' She grabbed her bag. 'Pull over. Drop me in that pub car park. I need a drink!'

'Please, sis! Don't be like this. I want to help you,' he begged, grabbing her by the arm.

'It's you who needs help, you sad, sorry bastard! And take your clammy shirt-lifter paws off me!' She glanced over her shoulders and sneered at Bones. 'I know where they've been.'

She stormed from the car then paused to look up at the weathered pub sign. She bent double, laughing hysterically, then turned and yelled at Harold.

'Check out the name of the pub, little brother, it's The Gay Cavaliers. You and Idi Amin should make this your local.'

Harold gritted his teeth, slammed his foot on the accelerator and the Cortina screamed across the car park onto the main road, clouds of exhaust fumes swirling in its wake.

Roper burst through the swing doors and strode to the bar.

The barman, a small grey-haired man in his late fifties, didn't see her. He was busy stocking the shelves with soft drinks.

'What do I have to do to get some service in here?' she barked.

Startled, the barman jumped to his feet, banged his head on the bar and dropped a bottle of grapefruit juice on the floor.

'Sorry, love,' he said, in a broad Dublin brogue, his faced etched with pain. 'I didn't see you come in. You're the first customer today. What's your pleasure?' he said, trying hard to smile as he twiddled nervously with his red bow tie.

'Let's get a few of things straight, Paddy. Firstly, I'm not your love. Secondly, my pleasure is none of your business, you nosey old fucker. Thirdly, drop all this being nice to the customer shit, even when you can see that the customer is a right bad bastard! So move your skinny little red-face Mick arse and get me a snake bite, a large whisky and a bag of pork scratchings.' She scanned the empty room. 'I'll be sitting over there,' she said, pointing at the Wurlitzer Jukebox that stood on top of a wooden dais. The barman nodded and smiled meekly. She dropped her bag on the floor, dropped a pound coin in the slot and scanned the selection. There was nothing but country and western. She turned to the barman.

'Oi! Paddy! What sort of a pub is this? You got a load of cowboys living round here or what? Get your red-face Mick arse over here, quick. I want my fucking money back!'

The barman scurried over with her drinks, one in each hand and a bag of pork scratchings clenched between his teeth.

'Get your slobbery old gob off my scratchings!' she moaned, snatching the bag from his mouth.

The barman placed her drinks on the table.

'All that country and western shite is down to the gaffer's missus,' he said, rolling his eyes disapprovingly. 'She entered a contest two years ago in some magazine or other. She won an all

233

expenses trip to the Grand Ole Opry in Nashville.' He nudged Roper with his arm. 'The daft old cow came back believing she was Dolly Parton. She's got dyed blonde hair and big tits and there the similarity ends.' Demonstrating agility and balance that defied his years, he jumped onto a stool and looked out the window. 'Great! The car's not there, they've gone into town to do the shopping.' He jumped down and slipped a pound coin into Roper's hand.

'Punch-in A3 75,' he said.

Roper dropped the coin in the slot and punched-in the code. The Wurlitzer whirred into life, seconds later Led Zeppelin's *'Whole lotta love'* was bouncing off the walls.

'That's mine. Led Zeppelin are me favourite band. I sneaked it in when the gaffer wasn't looking. I'm the only one that knows it's there. I'll never forget, the first time I saw them. It was 1970 at an open-air concert in Bath. Jesus, Jimmy Page blew my mind away.' He gave her a knowing look. 'Those were the days of free love and I was fresh off the boat from Dublin. What more could a virile young Irishman want? Everywhere I went, the women were gagging for it.' He ran his hand across his balding pate. 'Mind you, I had a full head of hair then, so getting me end away was no problem.'

A mischievous grin creeping across his face, he winked at Roper and pointed at his crotch. 'Christ! I nearly wore it out.'

Open-mouthed, Roper stared at him in disbelief, ripped open the bag of pork scratchings and poured some into her mouth. The barman, his arms flailing at an imaginary guitar, made his way across the room to resume his post behind the bar.

'Her tits aren't real, by the way,' he yelled across the room.

Roper stared back, a blank look on her face.

'I'm talking about Dolly Parton, not the gaffer's missus. Jesus! The gaffer's missus is built like a fecking hippo, there's nothing false about those tits. She could feed a herd of elephants with those bloody things.'

One pack of cigarettes, four rounds of drink and four bags of pork scratchings later, the bar was shrouded in silence and resembled an opium den. Ethereal pillows of smoke drifted across the room and Led Zeppelin had finished their gig and gone back to the hotel with their groupies. Roper sat alone, stone-faced, staring into space, drumming her fingers on the side of an empty glass. She lit a cigarette then placed the burning matchstick onto the tabletop. Her eyes sparked into life, as she watched the flame eat into the polished surface. Suddenly, the door burst open and Harold dashed in, a cigarette dangling from the corner of his mouth. He was unaccompanied.

'What do *you* want?' she snarled.

Harold sat next to her.

'You said you wanted my help.'

'I did. But now I don't,' she said, tipping the last few morsels of pork scratchings into her mouth, straight from the bag.

'You wouldn't have asked for help if you didn't need it. For fuck's sake it was the first time in three years that you ever got in touch with me. It must have been important,' he said, getting to his feet. 'Do you want a drink?'

'Snake bite,' she said, without looking at him.

He returned with the drinks and sat down.

'Why, Harold?'

'Why, what?'

'Idi Amin. For fuck's sake! You're not a bad looking bloke. Christ! You were always on the pull. What the fuck do you see in him?'

Harold took a long swig from his glass.

'I thought that being out there, getting paid good wages for killing people was gonna be the ultimate high. It seemed like a step up from what I was doing for you in Belle Vale. I was fed up hammering the shite out of people who owed you money.' He paused, his eyes narrowed and a shadow fell across his face. 'The high didn't last long. Some of those people I killed were just babies, pregnant mothers and young kids.' He drained his glass. 'Then, there was the not knowing when you're gonna kop a bullet yourself.' He reached across the table and took a cigarette from her packet, his hands were trembling. 'Me and Bones got separated from the rest of our squad. We were holed up in a cave for eight days, hiding from UN soldiers. It was hell. I've never known fear like that.' He looked her in the eye, tears welling. 'Have you ever been lonely? I don't mean craving for someone to talk to, lonely or haven't got any mates, lonely. I'm talking about scared shitless, lonely. The kind of lonely, that won't let you sleep. The kind of lonely that leaves you scared to shut your eyes because when you open them somebody might be standing there with a gun pointed at your face. Well I have. Bones was there for me when I needed him. He put his life on the line to save my skin, more than once.' Harold lowered his eyes and gazed at the floor.

Roper shrugged off flashbacks of how she felt when the heavies had her suspended over a vat of acid. She needed Harold's help and wasn't prepared to let him know that she also had a moment of weakness. As always everything had to be on her terms. She leaned across the table, her face etched with contempt.

'You're fucking, pathetic! You're talking like a wimp! Get a grip on yourself!' She slapped his face. 'Just because Idi Amin saves your life doesn't give him the right to fuck you!' she screamed. 'You weren't a shirt-lifter before you went out to Africa. Christ! You were shagging anything in a skirt before that!' Roper jumped to her feet and strode to the bar, cursing under her breath. She returned with two large scotches and sat down. She started laughing.

'Some of those women you went with were real fucking ugly,' she said, throwing him a cigarette. 'That slag Sarah Hackett. She had a hair-lip didn't she? And a glass-eye! God, she was a real bowser! You must have been well pissed or really desperate to have got a hard on for that. There's something I've always wanted to ask you. Did her glass-eye pop out when she had an orgasm?'

They both burst into fits of uncontrollable laughter, unable to speak, out of breath, beads of sweat glistening on their brows. They sat, staring intently across the table at each other, their lips twitching as their brains searched for something to say. It was Roper who was first to speak.

'Get me another snake bite.' She banged the empty glass on the table. 'I want to tell you about this job.'

Grinning from ear to ear, Harold dashed to the bar and returned with the snake bite.

'Where's the job, then?' His eyes were sparkling excitedly, now that she'd welcomed him back to the fold.

'You like Toblerone, don't you, Harold?'

'Toblerone?' he said, a bemused look on his face. 'Well, yeah. I love it. I can't get enough of it.'

'Well that's where we're going.'

'I don't understand.'

'Where do they make Toblerone, Harold?'

'Haven't a clue, sis. Holland?'

'Switzerland, Harold. They make Toblerone in Switzerland.' She downed the snake bite in one. 'I think it's about time I dropped in on my old friend, Anton Munro.' She got to her feet and headed for the toilet. 'I'm especially looking forward to having a nice long chat with his posh girlfriend.'

'What about Bones?'

'Bring him. I've just had an idea. Idi Amin could be useful after all.'

'That's great!' he said, rubbing the palms of his hands together.

She stopped at the door and turned.

'There's one condition, Harold,' she said, a threatening look on her face. 'No hanky-panky with your pal on this trip. If you give me the slightest cause to suspect that you and him have been shirt-lifting, I'll slit your throats. And keep him out of my face!'

Harold started up the car. 'Where's our first stop, sis?'

'Belle Vale. I need to pick up my passport.'

The two hour journey passed mostly in silence. Roper climbed the stairs to her flat and banged on the door with her fist. The door opened slowly.

'Ash!' mumbled Jimbo, a startled look on his face. 'I didn't know you'd been let out.'

'Shut the door Jimbo, there's a draught,' yelled a soppy female voice from inside.

Roper pushed passed him. 'Of course you wouldn't know I'd been let out, you gangly twat? You never came to see me. Not once!'

Roper emptied the contents of three drawers onto the floor.

'Get your arse and the slag's arse out of here. You've got five minutes. Leave your key on the dresser,' she barked, rummaging through her belongings.

It took just four minutes for Jimbo and his young lady friend to vacate the premises.

Roper found the passport wrapped inside a plastic carrier bag, paused to take one last look at the flat, checked that everything was switched off and left.

'Are we gonna need some hardware for this job?' said Harold as she climbed into the car.

'No,' she said, flatly. 'It's not that kind of job.'

'What do you want us to do, Harry's sister?' said Bones

Roper banged her fist on the dashboard. 'Tell Idi Amin, to shut the fuck up and that he's not to talk to me unless I ask him to.'

Harold glanced over his shoulder at Bones and gave him a please do as she says look.

'Will this clapped-out deathtrap get us to Switzerland, Harold?'

'Stop worrying. If it breaks down I can always nick another one.'

'How did you find out where Munro and his missus were living?'

'I was in the slammer, Harold and every slammer has a least two bent screws who are only too ready to help a girl in need. They'll do anything for a few quid. But if you offer them a bag of cocaine, they'll walk on hot coals.'

The Cortina made it to Dover, without any problems, where they caught the early morning ferry to Calais. They drove through the night and just as the sun was rising, they arrived in Lugano. They parked the car outside a small fish restaurant. Harold and Roper took a short stroll to stretch their aching limbs while Bones relieved himself against the side of a baker's van. The trip had gone exactly as Roper had hoped it would and Harold and Bones had been the personification of subservience.

Roper pulled a slip of paper from her jacket pocket and studied it carefully. 'That's it over there, Harold. We take the road just past the garage.' She pointed to a small garage. There were half a dozen vehicles parked outside with for sale signs stuck on the windscreens. 'We follow that road for half a mile. Then we take the first lane on our right. We follow that for about a quarter of a mile and with any luck we should find ourselves outside a white, detached house, that's set back off the road.' She turned, looked at Harold and smiled. 'Let's pay Mr. Anton Munro a visit.'

Ten minutes later, they pulled up outside Munro's house.

'Listen up. Idi. You go in through the back,' she said, refusing to look at him. 'Harold, I want you to come with me. We're going in through the front.' She glanced at her wristwatch. 'They'll be asleep.' She removed a roll of gaffer tape from her bag and handed it to Harold. 'That's for Idi. I want him to take out Munro. He's to subdue him, but not kill him. I want these two alive.' She looked up at the house and smiled. 'Harold, tell Idi, that I've got a little reward in store for him, if he's a good boy.'

Bones made his way to the back of the house. Roper turned the handle on the front door and smiled. She couldn't believe her luck. The door opened with a click and they stepped inside. Harold dashed to the back door and opened it for Bones. They made their way upstairs, inching along the corridor, checking each room in turn. At the far end of the corridor, Roper placed her ear against a door. She raised her hand and gave them the thumbs up. The only sound to be heard as they entered the room was that of gentle breathing. They gathered around the bed, staring at the couple who were wrapped in each other's arms, fast asleep.

'Don't they look nice,' yelled Roper to her brother.

Munro and Charlotte sat bolt upright.

Before they could utter a word, Bones delivered a crunching blow to the side of Munro's jaw, rendering him unconscious before his head cracked against the headboard. Harold pounced on Charlotte and clamped a hand over her mouth while Bones dragged Munro's limp body across the room. Munro resembled a rag-doll as Bones propped him up in a chair and bound his arms and legs with gaffer tape. The Roper siblings were likewise engaged, lashing Charlotte's ankles and wrists to the bedposts leaving her spread-eagled across the bed.

After checking that the window blinds were secure Roper switched on the bedside light and lit a cigarette.

'Harold, get your arse downstairs and make some coffee,' she said, her eyes fixed on Charlotte.

She dragged a chair across the room and sat alongside the bed.

'Fancy seeing you here!' she chuckled, clouds of cigarette smoke pouring from her mouth and nose. She leaned into Charlotte's face. 'I bet you haven't missed me as much as I've missed you?'

Charlotte's eyes welled with tears.

'What's that you said? You haven't missed me at all! Well that's not very nice. That's no way to treat an old friend. I've certainly missed you, my little glamour puss. Every night, after lights-out, I'd lie in the darkness and all I could see was your pretty little face smiling at me. Like a vision from heaven it was. I'd lie there, thinking about all the fun we were going to have when I got out. Fuck me, girl. I've missed you so much it was painful.' Roper pulled a knife from inside her jacket and ran the blade down Charlotte's leg. 'I don't mean stubbing me toe on the corner of the bed painful. I'm talking about sneaky painful, the kind that gets inside your head when you're not looking and fucks around with your mind. It messes you up. Won't let you sleep. Fuck me, girl! I've never had a good night's sleep in over three years thanks to you!'

Roper's words went over Charlotte's head. Her eyes were fixed on Munro's lifeless form. She was far more concerned about him than she was for herself.

'Oi! Idi Amin! Fetch some cold water and wake him up!' barked Roper nodding at Munro. She turned and smiled at Charlotte. 'I'd hate him to miss the big surprise I've planned for you.'

Bones returned with a bucket of cold water and threw it over Munro. His head shot back and he opened his eyes.

'Rise and shine. It's rude to sleep when you've got house guests,' said Roper, grinding the butt of her cigarette into the carpet with her shoe.

Munro's eyes opened wide when he saw her. He tried frantically to wriggle free, causing the chair to rock back and forth. Bones clamped a hand on Munro's shoulder, holding him fast. Harold entered the room carrying a tray.

'Ah! Coffee,' said Roper, turning to Munro. 'I hope it's not that crap you serve in that manky restaurant.' She took a sip. Smacked her lips, rolled her eyes and smiled. 'Not bad. Not bad at all. It's better than the shit they served in prison,' she hissed, her face clouding over.

Roper drained the cup and lit a cigarette. 'Oh dear, here I am, smoking in your bedroom and I didn't ask for your permission. Being banged up gets you into bad ways, I'm afraid. What's that you're saying?' She leaned across to Munro. 'It's fine by you.' She dragged on the cigarette. 'No, I'm afraid I've overstepped the mark. You've both gone out of your way to make us welcome in your lovely house. I'll do the decent thing and put it out.' She ground the cigarette into Munro's upper thigh. Charlotte shook her head violently from side to side, tears flooding down her cheeks.

'So, my little brother. Do you want to know what I have in store for Idi Amin?' she said, her eyebrows dancing up and down like a ventriloquist's dummy.

'Well, yeah. Course I do,' he muttered, glancing nervously at Bones.

Roper walked over to the bed and lifted Charlotte's night slip with the blade of the knife. She pointed to Charlotte's vagina.

'That's what I want him to do.' She turned to Harold. 'Tell Idi Amin that in our country, we have a saying. If a job's worth doing, it's worth doing well. And I want this job, done well. Really, fucking well!'

Harold looked at Bones. 'You up for it, Bones?'

'No problem, Harry.' said Bones, taking off his jacket.

'Hang on a minute,' said Roper. 'I want Munro to have the best seat in the house. Move him over here.'

They lifted Munro, chair and all and placed it near the foot of the bed. Charlotte writhed about the bed like a woman possessed, blood oozing from her lacerated wrists and ankles.

'Idi Amin had better be up for this, Harold.' She held up her little finger and wiggled it in front of his face. 'Most men can't get a stiffy on when they've got an audience.'

Harold grinned affectionately at Bones. 'It's never stopped him before.'

Roper slapped him across the face. 'I warned you about that!' she screamed.

Bones walked to the foot of the bed, dropped his trousers around his ankles and climbed between Charlotte's legs.

Munro couldn't bear to watch. He closed his eyes and lowered his head.

'No you don't,' said Roper, wrenching his head back. She got Harold to pull Munro's eyelids back while she secured them with gaffer tape. When she'd finished, she patted the top of Munro's head.

'You're a selfish bastard, Munro. Not wanting to watch your wife's debut performance. This could be the big showbiz breakthrough she's been waiting for all her life.'

The bedroom door burst open and three men wearing sunglasses and Swiss refuse disposal uniforms, stepped into the room, their arms outstretched, each brandishing an automatic pistol with a silencer attached to the end of the barrel.

The assailants froze, open-mouthed. The dull, muted sound of three gunshots broke the silence and they lay dead. A horrified look of surprise, etched on their faces for eternity. Three more uniformed men entered the room and carried the bodies downstairs to a refuse disposal truck that was ticking-over in the driveway and tossed them into the back. Two of the gunmen set about untying Munro and Charlotte.

'Those animals will not trouble you again, Mr. Munro,' said the tall man, standing by the bedroom door with his arms folded across his chest. He was clearly the man in charge. 'It would benefit all of us if you said nothing about this to the police.' He pursed his lips and tilted his head to one side. 'Try and look on this unpleasant incident as nothing more than a bad dream. Put it behind you.'

Munro closed his eyes and nodded his head. He just wanted them out of his home. Charlotte wept uncontrollably, her head pressed hard against Munro's chest.

'Who are you? And how do you know my name?' said Munro.

'Who we are is of no importance, Mr. Munro. Concentrate on your lovely wife. She's very upset and needs you.' He turned as if to leave then stopped. 'I give you my word, Mr. Munro. You need fear no more and you will never lay eyes on me or my colleagues again'

The man turned and left the room.

Munro walked to the window to watch them leave, only to find the driveway was deserted. A large tow-truck, rumbling past the gateway, towing a clapped-out, white Ford Cortina was the only sign of life.

12

Munro never left Charlotte's side for nigh on a month and to justify his absence from the restaurant, he told the staff that she was suffering from a mysterious viral infection. Despite his absence the restaurant functioned smoothly and as soon as Charlotte appeared to be over the worst, he decided that a trip to Rome would do them both a power of good. Rome was a first for both of them and the Eternal City did more than exceed their high expectations. The first two weeks were spent sight-seeing and the third in simple relaxation.

One sunny afternoon they were sitting outside a bar in the Piazza Navona, doing nothing more than people watching, the waiter placed two glasses of wine on their table.

'I'm sorry. There's been a mistake, we did not ask for wine,' said Munro, with a friendly smile.

'Signore Magnani asked me to bring the wine, sir,' said the waiter, before scurrying away.

Charlotte called after him. 'Who is Signore Magnani?'

The waiter couldn't hear. He was otherwise engaged, catering to the excessive demands of an overly boisterous American tourist and his circus-fat family. They turned in their seats to see if they could locate the gentleman who had shown such generosity. Sitting alone in the shade of a parasol, a heavily tanned man sporting a magnificent grey moustache raised his glass and smiled. The wide brimmed straw hat, sunglasses, the stylish cut of his cream linen suit and canvass shoes suggested he was Italian… and wealthy.

Charlotte raised her glass and smiled at him. 'Do you recognize him, Munro?' she whispered, still smiling.

'Never laid eyes on him,' muttered Munro, as he raised his glass to say thank you.

Charlotte gave Munro's arm a prod. 'I think we should go over and speak with him.'

'You're right. Let's do that.' Munro, leapt to his feet. 'You never know, it could be fun.'

'Thank you, for the wine, Signore Magnani. It was very kind of you.'

Signore Magnani smiled at Munro, nodded his head and said nothing.

'Perhaps he doesn't speak English, Munro,' said Charlotte. 'Try speaking to him in French.'

'Parlez-vouz Francais, Monsieur Magnani?' said Munro.

Signore Magnani smiled, nodded his head from side to side this time but still maintained his silence.

Munro shrugged his shoulders. 'He doesn't speak French.'

Charlotte pointed at the stranger's empty glass. Signore Magnani declined with a shake of his head and a dismissive wave of his hand. They sat in silence for a time, grinning inanely, until Signore Magnani rose to his feet and walked into the bar. They presumed he'd gone for a pee.

'We can't just sit here smiling at each other all afternoon. When he comes back, we'll pay our respects and leave. Is that OK with you, Charlotte?'

Charlotte nodded somewhat reluctantly as if to say, what else can we do?

When Signore Magnani returned, Munro and Charlotte thanked him politely for his kindness. The fact that he didn't understand a single word seemed irrelevant under the circumstances but at least the thought was there.

'We must leave now, Signore Magnani. Thank you, so much. You've been most kind. I wish there was something we could do for you in return,' said Munro, waving goodbye. Charlotte slipped her arm around Munro's waist and they walked away.

'If you were to buy me some pie and mash from Ernie Bishop's Nosherie, that would go down a treat.'

Munro froze and a chill ran down his spine. He turned. Signore Magnani had removed his sunglasses and hat.

'Quigley! Is that you?' choked Munro, struggling to get the words out. 'It can't be!' Charlotte dug her nails into Munro's arm.

'You're dead! We were at your funeral for God's sake!'

'I know you were, and it meant a lot to me. You and Charlotte turning up at short notice like that, it gave me a warm glow, I can tell you,' said Quigley, smiling from ear to ear. 'Sit down the pair of you, for goodness sake. Let me get you a coffee.' Quigley looked at the stunned expression on their faces. 'No! Coffee's not what you need. I think you'll both need something stronger.' He beckoned the waiter. 'Marco, due grandi whisky di malto, senza ghiaccio o acqua e ...' He looked at Charlotte. 'What would you like to drink, Charlotte?'

She was staring at him with her mouth hanging open.

'Charlotte!' Munro nudged her with his elbow. 'Quigley, would like to buy you a drink!'

'Oh, ...a large brandy. Thank you,' she stammered.

The waiter repeated the order to Quigley before disappearing inside the bar. He returned moments later with the drinks.

'I owe you both an explanation. But before I do that I'd like to say how sorry I am to have misled you. It wasn't easy for me to do that, because I care about you. However, I think the things my family have done on your behalf, more than compensates for your noses being put out of joint.'

Charlotte and Munro nodded.

'What do you think of my new name?' said Quigley, beaming like a man who's just become a dad for the first time. 'During the fifties and sixties, there was this terrific Italian actress named, Anna Magnani. She won an Oscar for her role in a film called *The Rose Tattoo*. Burt Lancaster was the co-star. I thought to myself, Quigley, if you're going to have a new name, have one that's got a bit of class about it. So I chose hers.' Quigley turned his head to show off his profile. 'I got me a new nose, too. Makes me look very distinguished, wouldn't you say?'

Quigley looked at Munro who was staring at him blankly. 'You don't really give a monkey's about my new name and my new hooter, do you, Munro? All you want to know about is how I managed to pulled this off.' Quigley sipped his whisky. 'Ok. Fire away. What do you want to know?

'How did you manage to fake a brain tumour of all things?' said Munro.

Quigley laughed. 'That was the easy bit. My nephew's one of these bright lads. He's into technology and all that stuff. He works in the lab at County Hospital. It was him who found someone with the same blood group as me who died weeks earlier. He changed the samples and the scans to read as mine. The doctors were looking at a tumour that belonged to some poor bloke from Nottingham.'

'What about the weight loss and all the medication you were taking?'

'I starved myself. And I didn't swallow the medication they were giving me. Don't get me wrong, Munro. Being dumped in hospital by O'Farrell was all kosher. That was for real and he really did almost kill me. It was while I was in hospital that the idea for this little caper popped into my head.' Quigley tapped the side of his head.

'The doctor who pronounced you dead, don't tell me he was family, too.'

Quigley took a deep breath and shook his head slowly from side to side. 'No such luck! That was always going to be the tough part. I was going into uncharted territory there. It was the only part of the operation where everything could have gone down the toilet.' Quigley beckoned the waiter.

'Ti piacerebbe piu la stessa, Signore Magnani?' said the waiter.

'Si, Marco. Piu bevande per favore.' Quigley glanced at Charlotte, who was still in a state of shock. 'We could all use another drink. Some of us, I think, more than others.'

'If pronouncing you dead wasn't an inside job, how the heck did you manage it?' said Munro, somewhat impatiently.

'I believe you met my son-in-law, Kioshi, at my funeral?'

'Yes. Nice bloke,' said Munro.

'Did you meet his grandmother, Aeko?'

'I saw her, but I didn't get to meet her.'

'That doesn't really matter, as long as you know who I'm talking about. Aeko told me many years ago about a phial her grandfather had given to her. He told her to guard it with her life as it was the only remaining sample. Aeko's grandfather was a very enlightened man who spent his formative years training to be a Buddhist monk. The monastery he entered practiced a form of Buddhism called Jodo. After a time, he and a handful of younger monks broke away from the sect, to pursue their fascination with the afterlife and reincarnation. Their daily routine wasn't just about prayer and meditation. They became actively involved in exploring new areas of botanical science. Their aim was to develop a potion from herbs and opiates which would enable a man to *die*. Once *dead*, he could step over to the other side, have a look around, then spring back to life again. After years of experimenting on animals, primarily pigs and rats, they came up with an elixir that seemed to achieve their aim. They called it the Lazarus Kanji.'

Marco arrived with the drinks, placed them on the table and left.

'Aeko, told me the elixir is supposed to render you clinically dead for up to forty-eight hours. There's no pulse, no respiratory movement and no corneal reflex. The ingenious part is that it maintains a sufficient supply of oxygen in the bloodstream so that no brain damage occurs. And after forty-eight hours, Mother Nature kicks in and you rise from the dead... just like Lazarus.'

Charlotte and Munro sat speechless.

'However, there was a catch and a mighty big one at that. Aeko was absolutely certain that the elixir had never been tested on a man. That being the case, I would be putting my life on the line for what may have been nothing more than an old wives tale. As far as I was concerned, it was the *only* door marked open. I was prepared to chance my arm. I was tired of being caged-up and cut off from my family. I'd had enough of Kingswood.' Quigley smiled. 'Not that I didn't enjoy your company, Munro.' Quigley reached out and squeezed Munro's arm.

'By the time I checked in at the hospice, most of the psychological ground work had been done. The hospice staff knew that I'd refused to have chemotherapy and all that goes with it. As far as they were concerned, Cedric Quigley was waiting for the Grim Reaper to carry him away. So I was pretty confident they wouldn't check me out too stringently after I *died*. I pretended to swallow the morphine tablets, I spat them out when they'd left the room. And in order to maintain a regular weight loss, I was doing my anorexia thing after meals. Having an en-suite bathroom, came in really handy.' Quigley smiled. 'Once I'd persuaded the guards to stop searching my visitors as if they were criminals, the way was clear for Connie to smuggle in all the nutrients I needed, in a liquid form.' Quigley wiggled his eyebrows. 'Not forgetting the Lazarus Kanji, of course.' Quigley looked at Charlotte. 'It's funny, but when the time came to drink the elixir, I'd already convinced myself it was going to work. I had no fear whatsoever.' Quigley spread his arms out wide. 'You're looking at the man, who holds the world record for a leap of faith.'

'You could have died, Quigley!' said Munro.

'I did. You were at my funeral, Munro.' Quigley laughed. 'Yes, I know I could have died, but it was a risk I was desperately willing to take. Mind you, waking up in the county mortuary wasn't exactly a barrel of laughs.' Quigley pretended to shiver. 'To create the mortal remains of the late departed Cedric Quigley for my coffin, we were ably assisted by an old acquaintance of yours, Munro.' Quigley began laughing uncontrollably, unable to continue. When his amusement abated he reached for a napkin and dried his eyes.

'Connie read an article in the paper that our old chum O'Farrell had been killed by a hit and run driver.' Quigley chuckled. 'An eye witness said that he saw Mary Flanagan and Declan O'Farrell leave the pub at 11.30pm and that both of them were out of their heads on drink. They'd been in the pub since midday and Mary was struggling to stand up, let alone push him in the wheelchair. Mary tripped and propelled the wheelchair and the screaming O'Farrell into the path of a speeding BMW. By the time the ambulance arrived O'Farrell knew he wasn't going to make it and being a Catholic, he asked to be given the last rites. He told the priest that he wanted to be buried in St. Brendan's Cemetery. Apparently he had a plot there. Now my Connie is a lovely woman, with a heart of gold, but she does have a wicked sense of humour. She arranged for some of the boys to dig up O'Farrell's corpse. They filled his coffin with bits and pieces from an abattoir and kept him on ice until he was needed to replace me at the county mortuary.' Quigley began to chuckle once more.

'It's ironic that after a lifetime dedicated to making people's lives miserable, O'Farrell finally did something worthwhile. Connie sprinkled his ashes in her garden. She says it makes her giggle, every time she looks at the rose bushes.'

'You're family were *so* convincing at the funeral,' said Charlotte, shaking her head. Clearly upset at being conned.

'Don't take it personally, Charlotte and don't be too hard on my family. If this was going to work, we had to convince *everyone* and that included you *and* Munro. You have to remember, we make a living out of conning people. As far as we were concerned, this was just another caper, another sting.'

'How did you know we were in Rome?' said Munro.

'In much the same way I knew that Ashley Roper and her brother were driving to Switzerland to pay you a visit. Surely you haven't forgotten what Mr. Quigley used to say, Munro? *There's not a lot goes on that I don't know about.*' Quigley tapped the side of his nose and smiled.

'It was you who sent those men?' said Charlotte.

'I'm afraid so,' said Quigley, adjusting the cuffs of his shirt. He glanced at Munro. 'I often think of the time when you gave me the kiss of life.' Quigley was grinning from ear to ear. 'How I didn't burst out laughing when you were doing that to me, I'll never know?'

Munro leaned across and kissed Charlotte. 'What about you, Charlotte? What do you have to say about this scoundrel?'

Charlotte leapt from her chair, threw her arms around Quigley and hugged him. 'I'm just so happy for you. I'm so happy for Connie. I'm so happy for all your family, who love you so much.' She glanced over her shoulder at Munro. 'And I'm so happy for him. The man I love. And, I know how much he's missed you and how much he loves you.'

'Marco!' yelled Munro. 'Bring some more drinks, please!'

The sun had dropped behind the hills overlooking the piazza, when Quigley glanced at his wristwatch and got to his feet. 'It's time I left the lovebirds, alone.'

'Will we see you again?' said Munro.

'Who knows?' said Quigley, as he kissed Charlotte on the cheek. He turned to Munro. 'Ah yes. I knew there was something I forgot to mention. Henry Jessop. I heard all about that business.' He gave Munro a look that said I told you so. 'I never trusted that creep. He was too ready to be nice and too slippery by far.'

Munro seized him in a bear hug and slapped his back. 'We've so much to thank you for.' He held Quigley at arm's length. 'You were right all along.'

'Right about what, Munro?'

'What you said about living by your own laws and trusting your own judgment. We wouldn't be standing here now, in the heart of Rome, with our lives stretched out before us, if you hadn't done precisely that.'

Quigley squeezed Munro's arm, smiled warmly and walked away.

It was with a mixture of elation, pride and sadness that they watched him stroll across the Piazza Navona towards a waiting limousine. And each time he stopped to doff his hat politely and share a joke with a passing stranger, they smiled to themselves. Quigley had truly gone native. When he reached the limousine, a man wearing a black suit and sunglasses stepped out and opened the back door. Munro recognized him as the tall, refuse disposal man who had rescued them from Ashley Roper, that dreadful morning at their home in Lugano. The limousine pulled slowly away and Signore Magnani, nee Cedric Quigley, was gone. And possibly out of their lives, forever.